THE CLIQUE

# The Clique

## A Novel of the Sixties

### FERDINAND MOUNT

*faber and faber*

This edition first published in 2010
by Faber and Faber Ltd
Bloomsbury House, 74–77 Great Russell Street
London WC1B 3DA

A CIP record for this book is available from the British Library

ISBN 978–0–571–25974–8

# The Clique

Where is the world of *eight* years past? *'Twas there*—
I look for it—'tis gone, a globe of glass!
Crack'd, shiver'd, vanish'd, scarcely gazed on, ere
A silent change dissolves the glittering mass.
Statesmen, chiefs, orators, queens, patriots, kings,
And dandies, all are gone on the wind's wings.

Byron, Don Juan.

# I

The Last Great Englishman was on the way out. His vulgar splendour was dimmed beyond recall. His small fingers played with the sheet, curled themselves into soft pink nests. No longer could he clench his fist to signal that limitless pugnacity which had so gingered his countrymen. The large possibilities that sustain public men had fled out of the window, down the dripping garden into the wintry London air.

Only details got through to him now : the limping tick of the clock on the chest-of-drawers, the patch of light on the far wall, the crumbs caught in his bedclothes, the cramp in his right leg. His thoughts dribbled away from him. People hung about day and night to catch each word as it fell from his slack lips, but there was little to catch.

'I am a rock,' they thought they heard him mumble once, and they whisked the phrase to the waiting millions who were not disappointed. It was so robust, so defiant. Nobody but he could have said it.

But did he say it? The night nurse who had accompanied the august reporter of the phrase to the bedside thought that what the patient had really said was something she transmitted even to herself, for she was delicate of speech, as 'eff off.'

Did the patient himself know he was on the way out? Death was not exactly his line of country. He was a man for life, action, colour : the jingle of harness beneath a desert noon, the governor's plumes ruffled by the sirocco, tea with A.J.B. under the great oak at Taplow, plotting, bullying, teasing, a round with L.G. at Walton Heath, rootling in the yellow gorse for his ball while the old man talked of Chanak, dinner with the Pragger-Wagger at the Embassy Club, glazed shirts and glazed faces, charles*ton*, charles*ton*, no, not a dancing man, he had short politician's legs for stumping not stomping, the pain in that leg, and there was a new way of buckling your spurs with a little strap that went under, more like a bootlace, an impertinent attachment, he liked bounders, rascals, men from nowhere, men at war with boredom, dear Geordie, officers will wear swords, officers must always wear swords, the room was so dark, dark and heavy. All gone now, only strangers left. Unconscionable dark.

Outside, the syringe in the kidney basin winked at the Low cartoons and the signed photographs in silver-gilt frames. People tiptoed past his door, lengthening stride to avoid clattering on the stone gaps between the worn runner carpets. In the desert once he had sat on a carpet and watched plump Berber girls dance for a pasha who had sired forty-six sons and murdered fifteen of them by his own hand. Why did his leg hurt so much? There was nothing wrong with his leg, Wattie said. Bugger Wattie. A little strap like a bootlace. She looked so cool in the hat with the violets at the front. He watched the carriage all the way down the drive until it disappeared behind the laurels. Sword, sharp swords.

It was the end of an era all right. There was a feeling abroad that this must be it at last, which concealed a further feeling, not to be openly voiced naturally, that it was about time. An un-pleasantly jocular assessment of the ambience? That cannot be helped. Nations exhausted by their history lack the resources for public tragedy. Situation comedy is their only authentic genre. Such at least must be the excuse for starting this sour scamper at a deathbed. Besides, the Last Great Englishman was so old, had suffered so many strokes, heart attacks and assorted lesions, had worked so hard, been shot at, abused, rejected, imprisoned, fêted, bored, drunk, depressed, elated so often that he could be said without churlishness to have had not only his own innings but several other people's as well.

Even the crowd outside, dwindling now at half-past nine on a wet night, seemed to be waiting for the unnameable event. Their faces, glistening from the slanting, lowering rain, shone with expectation.

A slack line of policemen held them back from the doorstep which gleamed in the light of the old-fashioned carriage lamp beside the door. This lamp of extinct design seemed to come from a period film set, the Barrett section of Wimpole Street perhaps. Indeed the little crowd, parcelled together beneath the

10

barley-sugar light of the tall street lamps, looked like film extras under floodlights being soaked by the studio sprinkler.

Gunn Goater, heading for the Thirsty Seadog, saw the crowd from across the road. How still they stood, how unnervingly upright and attentive. Their white faces were in profile, eyes front, no whispering. Their attitude was devotional, inward. One old woman had a plastic rain-hat perched on her white curls. Hat and hair together formed the shape of a mitre. Gunn's gaze was so intensely focused on the little crowd that the group of individuals shambling in front of them at first registered only as intermittent blotches crossing his field of vision.

This sudden string of passers-by looked casual against the military stillness of the little crowd. They skirted the policemen in a manner that suggested they were anxious to avoid being enmeshed in the homage. They did not hang closely together. If they could be said to form a group at all, it was a broken-stepped kind of group that reminded Gunn of the desultory cortège which had followed the gun-carriage bearing the body of the murdered President a few years earlier.

First came a bustling, burly man, rather older than the others, bareheaded, his fair hair plastered over his forehead by the rain under a bandeau bearing a single bedraggled Indian brave's feather. He wore a huge belted spiv's overcoat with padded shoulders and jeans tucked into army spats and boots. Over one shoulder he had slung an army kit bag.

Behind him straggled two girls. The taller wore a long skirt and had an elaborately patterned shawl pulled over her head to keep off the rain. She carried a bundle of groceries and walked in a furtive, scuttling way like a betrayed mill-girl fleeing with her love-child to the anonymous sanctuary of the city. Beside her strolled a thin girl in tight silver jeans, a short afghan waistcoat and a broad-brimmed hat : *Act Two – In The Bandits' Cave*, from a minor opera.

At the back came a third girl, rather shorter, more plainly dressed in blue jeans, a donkey jacket with LAING in shiny letters on the back and a woollen hat. She was overshadowed by the exotic person prancing, sidling, gesticulating at her side. This figure, barely taller than the girl but apparently male, though from where Gunn stood he could not be sure, was wearing a a cloak with a large clasp, multi-coloured trousers in a harlequin

11

diamond-pattern and short pointed boots as worn by principal boys in pantomimes. On his head he had a rain-streaked topee of the high-crowned sort sported in the Zulu Wars. He had the zest of a warrior dancing to celebrate Rorke's Drift in the headgear of a fallen adversary.

Gunn crossed the road, reaching the far pavement just as this group was meandering past the tail of the little crowd. The chatter of the burly man at the head of the straggling column rippled back down the line to the dervish in the topee who responded with a leap and a languid whoop. As they sauntered on up the road, Gunn could still hear the burly man talking, volubly, varying his pitch from an affable low burble to a rapid, high tone. He sounded like a courier with an important message, whose head was being intermittently thrust under water by enemy agents.

The five of them turned a few heads in the little crowd. Some of the homage-payers, hitherto calm and motionless, stirred uneasily. Yet there was such an aimless diversity of eccentricity about the passers-by that the offence they gave was slight and fleeting. On a less solemn occasion they might even have aroused amusement instead of fear or anger. Their parody was too random to carry menace. They seemed less like enemies of society than old-time purveyors of street fun – organ-grinders, keepers of dancing bears, the legendary Human Salamander.

Gunn Goater looked at them as they passed with satisfaction, curiosity, even envy. Here unmistakably presented was the spirit of the age taken flesh and on the wing. Back in Lincolnshire they had of course heard of the Swinging Sixties – a decade already mythical though scarcely half-consumed. But this nonchalance, this freedom of foot was something else, unexpected, unnerving.

As the street lamps showered sheets of barley-sugar on the retreating backs of the group, their winding progress down the street seemed to his dazzled eyes to be directed by some hidden force outside themselves. They skipped round a no-entry sign as though directed by the throw of a dice. He liked the idea of hitching on to their caravan and making a sixth, but he preserved face to himself by imagining that the five of them would surely be rather ordinary persons beneath their fancy dress, concealing their insignificance like a man hiding a weak chin beneath a beard.

12

Gunn himself was soberly dressed for the night and the assignment : short showerproof car-coat with a ruche of nylon fur,
chain-store suit, matching shirt-and-tie set, dressed in fact like
an up-and-coming reporter, which he was, having come up to
London from Lincolnshire the day before, hot or at any rate
warmish from apprenticeship on the local paper. Three nights
earlier he had said goodbye to Josie, with whom he had been
walking out, on a strictly non-emotional basis, for the past fifteen
months. At least he had been strictly non-emotional. In any case,
he had to deal with London first.

This was his first assignment in the Street of Adventure (a
phrase now fallen into disuse no less than Baghdad-on-the-sub-
way or the Athens of the North, but handy enough in the present
context). He had been sent here to unearth and relieve Rory
Noone, a fellow-reporter of maturer years, who was among the
ringside team for the Last Great Englishman's final bout. It was
intimated to him that if Noone was not among those door-
stepping, he was not unlikely to be found in the Thirsty Seadog,
a public house of ancient origin whose wine had allegedly once
been bushed by the motto 'Blessed are the pure in heart for they
shall see God', the latter clause being corrupted by the mumbling
topers over the years into the Thirsty Seadog.

The weather and the nature of the task would have stung
protest from more experienced colleagues, but Gunn was still as
elated as the moment he had stepped out from the Eastern
Counties bus station and taken his first real look at London.

The view from the bus station was not quite the panorama
granted to the provincial heroes of Victorian novels; he could see
only a short rainswept stretch of the Pentonville Road, railings
preventing pedestrians from crossing the road, and a church,
boarded up.

Yet he had a sense of the capital; he experienced the ancient
thrill of arriving at the heart of things, in the place where society
was most concentrated and most dispersed, its members living
both alone and on top of each other. Moreover, he was a provincial Victorian hero in one respect at least; he had come to
London to get on. It was not so much this ambition that marked
him off from most of his contemporaries as the fact that he didn't
mind admitting it. He was on the make and took little trouble
to conceal the fact. An old-fashioned type, a throwback, almost.

He was a square young man on the short side. He had a bony nose and ears which had aroused comment in adolescence. Above all, he had very small eyes, no wider than gun-slits in a pill-box. He had been called Gunn from school onwards primarily because his name was Gunby, but the resemblance to an outmoded form of gun emplacement may also have had something to do with it.

Gunn's father was a Lincolnshire man, a teacher at a direct-grant grammar school who nursed a taste for Victorian poetry inside his usher's carapace. He had allowed this weakness to peep out like the soft glistening head of a snail just far enough to have his only son registered as Gunby (he did not hold with baptism) in the belief, happily shared by Tennyson scholars, that the following lines – his favourite quatrain – referred to Gunby Hall, near Skegness:

> And one, an English home—gray twilight pour'd on dewy
> pastures, dewy trees
> Softer than sleep—all things in order stored,
> A haunt of ancient peace.

Gunby's middle name was Hallam.

Despite this lyric voice whispering round his cradle, Gunn did not grow up to look poetic. Yet sheltering inside the pillbox, his imagination led its own life, a furtive refugee's existence always on the run from the stunning artillery of parents and teachers, the two armies combined in sinister alliance by the fact that Gunn went to the school where his father taught.

It was convenient for Gunn to seem a little duller than he was. He made up for this by a sort of sweetness, not smooth or charming – he had rough country edges – but the uncalculated, lingering kind.

'Like the ghost who disappears leaving behind a melodious twang,' said a sixth-form wit after Gunn had left the room (a remark later admiringly passed on to Gunn himself who did not quite know what to make of it). The fact that his temper was on the short side only enhanced Gunn's reputation for a certain crusty innocence. At school the popular pastime of goading him into a rage had been known as 'getting a goat'. It was a popular pastime which was not without affection for the victim.

At the moment, though, Gunn was not angry. He was merely in a hurry. The office had heard no word from Rory Noone since

14

opening time. At half-past seven they had sent another man out to search the neighbouring pubs. That man too had not returned. It was now nearly ten o'clock. The reporters gathered outside the front door had not seen Rory Noone at all. They complained of wet shoes.

A couple of men with big cameras on shoulder-straps were standing at the bar. Gunn asked them if they had seen Noone. They denied all knowledge of him, having only just arrived themselves, and suggested he ask a colleague at the far end of the bar who had been there for hours. This latter personage certainly seemed well entrenched. He answered Gunn's question by silently lifting the soda syphon off its mat and looking underneath it and then bending down, hands on knees, to peer under a small side-table. His face went deep purple. Finally he straightened up again, let the blood drain from his cheeks and said with slow precision :

'He's not here, old boy. Try the nearest nick. Or the casual ward.'

Gunn turned impatiently to ask the barman, a lugubrious man in shirtsleeves, who in strangled tones said that he had never heard of Mr Rory Noone. Gunn paused to get his breath back and ordered a whisky.

As the barman was pouring, a rangy girl in a black dress came through a door behind him and tapped him on the shoulder.

'Upstairs wants six more double Bells, a whisky mac, four lager-and-limes, and eight pints of special.'

'They'll have to pay for the last lot first.'

'Mr Noone says he'll settle up at closing time.'

'Like hell he will. You know quite well customers can't. . . .'

'Did you say Noone?' Gunn asked.

'Ah, Noone . . . Noone,' the barman spoke as though trying to recall the name from some unimaginably remote period of his life.

'Is he upstairs?'

'There's a private party on upstairs. Invitation only,' the barman said.

'I'm a friend of Mr Noone, and he had the kindness to invite me to his party,' said Gunn, raising the flap at the end of the bar and advancing, not without menace, towards the door behind the barman.

15

'Ah well, if you're a friend of his, that's all right then, isn't it? First floor, on your right at the top of the stairs.'

Gunn ran up the stairs two at a time. He tried the liverish brown door at the top. There was a great noise coming from inside : laughter and piano and heels clattering. The door was locked. He put his shoulder to it in gangster-film style. The door buckled but did not open. There was a bellow from the inside.

'Who's trying to knock the door down? This is a private party. It's not a public affair at all.'

'I'm looking for Rory Noone. I'm from the office.'

'Is there no peace?' A short fat man opened the door. He was in his shirt sleeves. His shirt was undone to the waist revealing a tract of wiry hair; his trouser zip was undone too. The sweat was dripping off him. And yet his appearance was far from gross; on the contrary, his conviviality had an elfin quality, like a Puck run to seed.

He flattened himself against the wall to let Gunn squeeze past. The room was low-ceilinged and seemed too small for the dozen or so people packing it. Like the stairs, its walls had once been covered with some embossed paper long since painted over in a brownish cream. The fireplace had been blocked up with hardboard. Over it there hung a framed and illuminated address, flanked by several dusty group photographs, suggesting that the room had at one time been the meeting-place for a club.

On the opposite wall there was a large coloured print of men in uniform getting off a train. Most of them were wounded; one in the foreground with a bloodsoaked bandage round his head was leaning on the arm of a nurse whose hair was nearly the same tint as the blood on the bandage. With some difficulty Gunn made out the caption underneath as 'Back from the Somme'.

In another era, an ambitious landlord must have opened the room up as an extra bar. The bar itself, a small mauve formica-topped structure curved at one end, was now jammed against the wall behind the cottage piano, one strip of formica lazily curling towards the flyblown ceiling. The room now seemed to be used for making music, for there was a percussion set and a tangle of music stands and sheet music stacked behind the door.

At that moment a tall man with a red face was playing honky-tonk on the piano with two smaller men leaning over his shoulders and trying to join in a song which neither of them

16

seemed to know very well. The tall man banged the keys with angry urgency as though trying to beat down the shouting and laughter. The smoky air was thick with noise.

The three or four women in the room were dressed to glitter. They held cigarettes at birdlike angles. One of them had her jet-black hair piled up in an old-fashioned beehive style. They wore bright lipstick except for the youngest one who had long straw-coloured hair and no make-up. She stood in the middle of the loud-voiced men quite expressionless, moving only to wipe her nose with the end of her sleeve. She wore a man's striped shirt. The shirt-tails almost concealed her short skirt.

'Gunn Goater.' Gunn introduced himself to the seedy Puck as sternly as a lawman flipping his badge.

'Where's your drink then, man? Come and get stuck in. We're having a bit of a shindy in my observation post.'

'Observation post?'

'Don't tell a single soul. It's my secret. Only an Irishman born in Birmingham would have had the vision for it. The rest of them, what do they see? Just another bar. But I've got an old bump of direction up here which tells me this isn't just a bar.' He tapped his dripping forehead.

'What is it then?'

'A *vantage point.* You tell me now, where would you say this public house was situated exactly?'

'In the mews at the back of the house, I can't remember the name of the street.'

'At the back. Exactly. And if you look out of a first-floor window on the rear side of this public house, what would you expect to see?' His voice, nasal, eerily midlandish, rose to a high note of interrogation.

'The back of the house, I suppose.'

'*Exactly.* Mark and observe.' Holding his trousers up with one hand and pointing prophetically with the other, he led Gunn to the window introducing him on the way to the other persons littered about the room. 'This is Ted, keep the music going, Ted, and Jimmy from the *Express,* and some Scots bugger who I didn't ask in either, and Carol-Anne and Inge from Lapland, now then, look. . . .'

Gunn looked out of the window, up the long thin strip of desolate garden. There was the house. Two or three of the

17

windows which broke the dark cliff of sooty brick were illuminated. On the first floor, Gunn could see a woman going upstairs
followed by two men. 'You see, young feller,' said Rory Noone
at his elbow, 'No curtains. Isn't that a break, a true godsend?
No need to share it with those ignorant hacks. Jimmy wouldn't
recognise the Last Trump even if they sent him a bloody hand-
out.'

His face was all expression and movement: eyebrows lifting
and dipping and knitting like rowing-boats on a high sea, his
plump little nose just managing to prevent his cheeks crashing
into each other, shiny as a couple of champion conkers, his tongue
ceasing its flapping only long enough to sweep the froth of stout
from his lips.

'Colour they want, colour they shall have then, a whole bloody
rainbow of it. The single light burning through the still watches
of the night, the lonely vigil, the brave figure at the window
looking out over the city he loved, the birds wheeling overhead,
what would they be? Starlings. That's right. The starlings he
used to love to feed beside the lily pond, now mourning their old
friend.'

'People don't usually feed starlings,' Gunn said. He watched his
breath on the pane blur the little scene in the lighted window of
the house across the garden.

'He loved all birds, all our dumb friends. No, loves, I should
say for even in his twilight hours, he called his faithful friend,
the – what was the bloody dog we saw waddling up the stairs
just now, Ted?' He turned to yell back into the din.

'Retriever, I think.'

'No, no. Retrievers are great big animals. This was a little dog,
the sort that yaps round your ankles.'

'Corgi was it?'

No, that's what they have at the Palace. No, more sporting
looking this was.'

'Spaniel?'

'Red Setter?'

'Amazing, isn't it? And this is supposed to be a nation of dog-
lovers. Where's Inge? Inge's a kennel-maid. What was it, Inge?'

'It was a Jack Russell terrier.'

'There you are, Gunn my friend. Takes a bloody Eskimo to
give you the answer. Isn't she lovely, though?'

18

The girl with the long straw-coloured hair sat on the table in the middle of the room, swinging her legs and shaking her hair out of her eyes, while Noone began to dance, very slowly, in a semicircle round her, watching his feet carefully, as though they might escape from him. Their movements seemed to bear no relation to the honky-tonk tune still being belted out from the other end of the room.

Gunn was more interested, more allured even, by Rory Noone himself than by the girl. For all his convivial bounce, Noone did not strike Gunn as unreservedly friendly. It was not that his bonhomie was false; it was more that his public personality appeared so weathered by constant exposure to strangers that it had ceased to express distinctions of mood. There was a kind of peremptory aggressiveness about everything he said which made it hard to tell whether he was joking or angry or indifferent. To Gunn's ear too, there was a plaintive, almost querulous note in Noone's West Midlands' accent which gave an impression not so much of underlying discontent as of a feeling that the words he was using had been forced upon him by circumstances beyond his control. As Noone danced, he began to take off his shirt.

'Drink up, lads, and slip into something looser.' He spoke in a serious, even reproachful tone, like a sports coach whose team's display so far lacked spirit.

Several of the men began, not without embarrassment, to remove jacket or tie. Then Noone himself let go of his trousers. They fell in wrinkled puddles round his ankles. He stepped out of them and stood in flapping shirt-tails, still broadcasting a stream of reportage.

'In the elegant luxury of his drawing-room, his family and oldest friends, watched over by priceless oil-paintings, gathered to eat a simple meal : soup, brownish sort of colour, say brown windsor, cutlets and cheese, well, say cheese, they drew the curtains after the cutlets, but you would not have a sweet, would you, with your loved one lying upstairs? It would turn to ashes in your mouth. And then the family retainers quietly drew the priceless curtains. No, we've already had priceless, just drew the curtains on another day . . . another day in the epic fight for life.' With slow, self-absorbed movements, Inge began to unbutton her shirt, no hint of the rollicking about her. There seemed an irremediable apathy in her fingers. The overhead light shone on

19

the pale flesh of her shoulders as she awkwardly pulled off the shirt. She stood for a moment with her hands behind her back tangled in the striped cotton. In the middle of the laughing, dark-clothed men, she looked like a romantic sacrifice, except for the surgical angularities of her white bra. Rory Noone, stilled an instant, stared at her with a kind of worried pride.

She tugged her hands out of the buttoned cuffs of the shirt and began to fold the garment, looking round for a place to put it. This neatness seemed to irk Noone. He snatched the shirt from her and threw it towards the jumble of musical equipment where it snagged on a music-stand like a scarecrow. With a trancelike deliberation, the kennel-maid drew down the small side-zips on her denim skirt.

There was a cheer, broken, rather nervous. Noone put his arms round her in a gesture which seemed unexpectedly considerate, even tender. Gunn began to feel uncomfortable. He began to wish he was out pounding the wet pavements. A puff of sweat floated past his nostrils. His own? Certainly his tight collar felt damp. Yet this was Life, this pungent carouse in the shadow of great events. He was there.

'Shouldn't we be filing some of this, Rory?'

'We, my friend? Talk not of we. I shall personally round these observations into jewelled prose and. . . .'

'But it's getting late and the editor. . . .'

'Don't speak to me about editors. Editors come and go but a good hard-news reporter goes on for ever. We are the life-blood. We are the poor sods who stand out in all weathers while they swan about in chauffeur-driven coffins. We. . . .'

At the third attempt, he managed to clamber on to the table where he was joined by the kennel-maid. The table was small and rickety and unsuited for such displays. Rory Noone put both his arms round the girl's waist, as much to stay upright as to demonstrate desire. They stood thus connected for a full minute, too precarious to carry out the coarse suggestions of the mob below. Even dancing on the table, presumably the original purpose of the ascent, seemed out of the question.

Yet what after all were two persons on a table to do but dance? The traditional duties of Rory Noone's situation appeared to outweigh thoughts of personal safety and undaunted by the violent wobbling of the terrain he began his semicircular shuffle. He revolved slowly enough, but his partner was not quick to respond, her eyes being fixed on the piano-player who was leading a chorus of 'My Old Man said follow the van'. Her failure to move concentrated their combined weight upon one corner of the table. They toppled in slow motion, clutching one another like lovers plunging to a watery grave.

The noise of the crash was brief but loud. As it died away, a fresh hammering at the door was heard above the clatter. From his station amid the beer-pools at Gunn's feet, Noone shouted :

'Go away.'

'Message from the office for you, Mr Noone.'

'Tell them my back's broken.'

'Said it was very. . . .'

'Oh all right, I'll take it up here.' He crawled on all fours to a telephone by the piano. As he waited for the call to be put through, crouched over the keyboard with his shirt-tails billowing, he looked like an illustration to some lesser known verse of Wee Willie Winkie.

'What? Stop that racket, Ted. It's a bad line.'

Gunn helped the kennel-maid to her feet and began wiping some of the beer off her with his handkerchief. He dabbed at her bare midriff with professional impersonality, like a doctor preparing a patient for an injection. Inge looked straight at him, blankly. For the first time Gunn felt a twitch of desire for her.

'Yes, that's right,' Noone said. 'I'm just ready to file now. Didn't you get my message about leaving the first edition to the front-door man? I don't care what the *Telegraph* says. Who's been to see him? She? Who's she?'

'Herself,' the voice on the telephone shouted.

'Whoself?' Noone shouted back.

'The bleeding monarch, of course. Paying her respects to her first citizen. She's still there. We can get her leaving, of course, but it'll only make the last edition.'

'I presume,' said Noone, 'that she went in through the front door in which case she's hardly my responsibility.'

'One front-door man was filing his story at the time and the other was looking for you. You were supposed to be covering.'

'I have enough to do without wet-nursing every reporter on the paper. I have one of your young men with me now, a Mr Goater. What's he supposed to be doing?'

21

'Looking for you.'

'Why is everyone looking for me? You seem to think I'm some kind of clockwork Dr Livingstone. I'm not lost. I'm merely pursuing my enquiries. To be sure, I'm flattered by your interest, but I can't believe that "where is Noone?" is really the big story of the night.'

During this conversation, Inge seemed to have come to herself, if the phrase could be used of so ambiguous a personality. She came up behind Noone, snatched the receiver out of his hand, replaced it firmly, and planted an equally firm kiss upon his neck.

'You have talked enough,' she said.

'Well now,' said Rory Noone. He stood in drooping perplexity for a moment or two muttering to himself. His hand strayed back towards the telephone, then moved more decisively to his glass on top of the piano. With his free hand, he grasped the kennel-maid round the waist. A decision of principle had been made.

'A discourteous fellow, that night-desk man,' he said. 'Not a man to talk with for pleasure. His manner is gross. And I find his obsession with the royal family distinctly warped. I am not myself a republican. Does that surprise you now?'

'I had not thought about it one way or another,' said Gunn Goater. Now the smell of the sweat was besieging his nostrils, seemed to be fogging his brain even.

'You're a hard man to read. But I will tell you honestly. I am not a republican. I accept the house of Battenberg. I have nothing against them. They may reign till the cows come home as far as I am concerned. But I am not going to stand out in the wet just for the pleasure of seeing the monarch slam the front door behind her. I am not prepared to drool. If pressed, I will describe the colour of the woman's dress but I will not say she looks radiant. I will not drool.' His voice rose from loud to louder, triumphantly soaring above the piano on the final 'drool'.

'You pulled out the stops just now,' said Gunn.

'That was a different thing. That was describing the last hours of a great man, a man of substance. That was not drooling.'

'Hadn't you better file your copy, anyway?'

'It would be a waste of breath. Mentally I have already shaken off the dust of this office.'

'You mean you're leaving?'

'I mean that they will let me go. I have been let go more often than any man alive. I can read the signs.'

'Will you be all right?'

'All right, my friend? I live for these moments of release. Life would be intolerable were it not for its sackings, as poor dear Oscar nearly said.'

'Well, somebody ought to file some copy.'

'So they should, Gunn, so they should. This is your moment of truth, your hour of destiny. File away, and help yourself to my storehouse. You are welcome to these poor jottings, the fruits of a lifetime's observation of . . . of life.'

Out of the pockets of his coat which had fallen behind a chair, Noone extracted, after a good deal of fumbling, a few crumpled sheets of paper torn from a notebook. He handed these to Gunn who thanked him.

'There is nothing to thank me for. We are brothers of the pen. I trust you will do the same for me when the occasion arises.' With these words, he sank into the armchair, dragging Inge with him.

Noone's retreat to the sidelines deprived the party of its inspiration; several of the company sloped off, mumbling goodbyes. Only two or three of the faithful continued to cluster round the piano whose virtuoso, sensing the general change of mood, shifted towards the slushier end of his repertoire. Gunn sat down by the window and peered out.

The curtains were drawn now on all the windows of the house, except for the tall window on the lower landing which was brilliantly lit by a huge chandelier. This window with its curved top was as sharp as a floodlit stage against the surrounding dark. From that distance it had also the miniature quality of a keyhole. Gunn felt like a clumsy boy peering into a doll's house. The chandelier and the two chairs on the landing seemed so delicate, so beautifully made, still but instinct with life, the air almost too thick for the fragile figures who breathed it. But there were no figures. He must get on with it and scribble something for the paper.

Just as he was turning to look at Rory's notes, a knot of figures came into view. They paused on the landing and resolved themselves into a man and a woman, both rather bent. The man pointed to one of the chairs and helped the woman to sit down.

23

He stood talking to her for a few seconds before stiffening to face away from her up the stairs. Another woman, followed by two men, came into view down these stairs. They looked like the three persons Gunn had seen going up the stairs when he first arrived at the Thirsty Seadog.

As they approached the seated woman rose and bowed, her bent head seeming to sink a little as she did so. The other woman held out her hand to raise her up. The two figures met and, it seemed, embraced. They held the scene for a long moment : the two women merged into a single dark image, the three men flanking them. Then the tableau broke up and the five figures vanished from view leaving the chandelier blazing down upon the two chairs.

The visit. The curtsey. The kiss. The two women. The on-lookers. And the old man in the bed upstairs with his soft pink nests of fingers. It was history. It was romance. But seen in the light of immediate necessity, it was a story. Gunn scribbled and kept on scribbling.

# 2

'First-class copy. Hit the right note exactly. And, of course, the royal kiss. . . . That was great. . . . We had it to ourselves, and you described it so vividly, almost as if you saw it happen. Who the hell's your contact, no, I won't ask, but I'm very pleased with you.'

The editor was a man of frigid aspect. In his voice there was the crackle of thin ice. Even his congratulations were edged with menace.

'We'll have to keep you on the story until the Crunch, but afterwards I hope we'll manage to find you one or two assignments which will stretch your mind – something with an economic or sociological background where you can use your qualifications. . . .'

He paused to move aside for a large, battered desk to be carried past them by two sweating men in aprons, part of the complex never-ending process of promotion, hiring and firing. Gunn was standing with the editor in the poorly-lit corridor which was the main office throughway, leading at the near end to the soft-carpeted apartments of the management and the lino deserts of the cuttings library and at the far end to the stairs down to the printing departments. All along one side stretched the main editorial floor; on the other, passages ran off to cubby-holes guarded by reeded glass on which, half torn off, could be read the names of executives long fired and departments long disbanded. The desk with the two sweating men in aprons underneath turned left up the passage leading to the lavatories before realising its mistake and reversing back down the corridor where it encountered a woman in a floral overall pushing a canteen trolley carrying several plates of congealed bacon and egg and chips.

'There's a lot of talent coming up on the staff just now. . . .

When I first arrived here the place was full of old men in braces. You won't see many of them on the floor now. We've even had to let old Noone go. First-class reporter of course, but his approach is a wee bit nineteen-forties-Sunday-Pic. Too downmarket for a modern sort of paper like ours. These days our readers are educated people, they're aware, socially concerned, questioning. . . .'

There was just room for the trolley to pass the desk using the full width of the corridor. The editor and Gunn backed out of the way through a half-open door into an office where several people were crowded round a desk looking at photographs. The editor smiled into the room. Nobody smiled back. The editor led Gunn back into the corridor in time to exchange a brisk greeting with a couple of large men in pin-stripe suits who passed on with purposeful tread.

'Advertising,' said the editor with a wave.

'The fact of the matter is that the old taboos are on the skids,' he continued. 'The old class divisions are being broken down. Personally I find all this intensely exciting. You get working-class guys and aristocrats making it together, even competing for the same job. I don't care what field you take, it's the same – photographers, actors, designers, even newspaper editors, ha.' It was more of a cough than a laugh.

The woman in the floral overall returned with an empty trolley. Gunn noticed she wore surgical stockings on her swollen legs.

'The whole place is exploding,' the editor said, making an exploding gesture with his hands. 'You've got to be flexible to stay with it. As a newspaper we have to be where the action is. There's a social revolution going on. And we need chaps like you to project it in depth. I've nothing personally against the old-stagers in dirty raincoats – best legmen in the business – but in the sixties there just has to be a more sophisticated approach. That's why we need men like you, men with balls *and* a university degree.'

Gunn sunned himself in this icy vizier's praise. The glow of being thought well of suffused him throughout the editorial conference which he was invited to sit in on as a mark of favour.

He was exhilarated by this new world. He liked the easy acceptance of ambition and lack of apologies. And he listened with innocent rapture to the jargon being flung about the con-

26

ference room, like a man who listens to a full orchestra for the first time.

'And the daughter?'

'We're keeping a close follow on the daughter. We've been doorstepping her home since Monday. But there's no story.'

'What do you mean?'

'She's clean. We've really taken her apart.'

'There must be a story.'

'She's just a respectable spinster who works for charity.'

'Spinsters make stories too, Jack. I want to stay really close to her. She could make fantastic quotes. And what are we doing about the other angles?'

'Well, we've finished updating the obit.'

'What about the son?'

'The son?'

'Come on Jack, you know about the son. This is supposed to be a people paper, for Christ's sake.'

'I know the tale of course, but does it stand up?'

'It's your job to make it stand up.'

'I thought he had just the one daughter,' said the only man who was not in shirtsleeves. 'I didn't know he had a son.'

'Illegitimate. Long before he was married. They hustled the girl off to Canada. So the story goes.'

'I thought it was Switzerland.'

'Anyway, somewhere. The mother used to get cheques. The lad would be about fifty now.'

'We've tried before, you know. We couldn't even get her name.'

'Well, try again. The death-bed bit may smoke him out. I think it's one for Keith.'

'Sorry, sir. Keith's in Rome. He's just telexed. Got a tip about the will.'

'*Rome*. Shit. Who said he could go?'

'Said he had to follow the trail while it was hot.'

'Well, get him back again, and send Noone to cover.'

'But I thought you just let Noone go?'

'I did but he's got to work his notice out.'

'He's already left the office.'

'Send Morgan then. No, not Morgan. How is Morgan?'

'Just out of intensive care.'

'That's good, very good. Well then, send Noel.'

'But it's Noel who's alongside the daughter. He's well dug in there.'

'Well, dig him out again. We don't want to waste too much time on the daughter. She's just a side-bar. The son is today's story.'

'You're too right.'

Long after the meeting had finished and Gunn Goater had stumbled out for a bite, he still felt the tingle of this talk.

'I told you, did I not?' said a voice at his left armpit. Gunn turned from inhaling the crisp air of the Thames to find Rory Noone, fresh as a daisy. 'They let me go,' he said.

'You look well on it,' Gunn said.

'It's a tonic. I told you that, too.' He took Gunn's arm.

'Where will you try, then?'

'The Lord will provide. The *Mirror* perhaps. It's a long time since I was last fired from the *Mirror*. The bastard in question has since been gathered. What a morning. A fine morning.' He lifted his face to the pearly sky, shutting his eyes tight like a man exposing his face to the full force of a shower.

Across the river the sun was just beginning to cheer the sullen concrete of the skyscrapers on the South Bank. The arches of the bridges hovered over the waters, their sparkle still muffled by mist.

'With the weather like this it is not a time to be thinking of such technicalities as jobs. It is a time for pouring libations.'

'I have these sandwiches,' said Gunn. 'I was going to eat them out here.'

'Go ahead,' Noone said. 'I will watch you. I like to watch a young feller making a meal of it.'

They sat down on a bench. Gunn took out from his overcoat pocket his round of luncheon-meat-and-sweet-pickle, his hard-boiled egg, his apple and his bar of chocolate. He tapped the egg on the arm of the bench (wrought-iron, painted green in the image of a sphinx to salute the proximity of Cleopatra's needle) and dipped it in the twist of salt provided by the sandwich bar.

Rory Noone stared upstream at the blackened obelisk sliced in two by the white arc of Waterloo Bridge. He patted the green sphinx at his side.

'I wonder why they brought that big stone prick all the way

back here and planted all these sphinxes round about it. Think of all the oxen and slaves, the sweating and suffering they must have needed to shift the thing.'

'Pulleys,' said Gunn, taking alternate bites from the hard-boiled egg and the sandwich.

'Pulleys, you say? You may be right. It's a fine morning but there's a nip in the air. When you've finished, we could repair to a hostelry.'

'It's an excellent thought,' Gunn said, catching a little of the grandiloquence.

'Is that fruit-and-nut you have there? I used to be a devil for the fruit-and-nut.'

'Have a bit,' said Gunn reluctantly.

'No, no, I never touch the stuff now. We could be getting along quite soon perhaps.' Noone was vigorously clasping and unclasping his hands to take his mind off the prospect of refreshment.

Gunn, suddenly annoyed at the interruption of his sober meal, slowed down the rate of intake. He took the chocolate a square at a time. Then he carefully polished the apple on the sleeve of his overcoat. Noone shaded his eyes against the sharpening light and fixed them on the black rigging of HMS *Discovery* anchored a few yards in front of them.

'A well-built ship. The steel plates on her bows are four feet thick. Think of it. Four feet thick. Nothing wrong with the ship.'

'Do you mean there was something wrong with the man, then?'

'I would never say a word against the poor man. Perhaps he was just unlucky with the weather.'

' "Had we lived, I should have had a tale to tell of the hardihood, endurance and courage of my companions which would have stirred the heart of every Englishman." At least he wrote well'.

'Great copy, I give you that. Fantastic copy. But it's always *had* we lived, isn't it? It's always failure you glorify. If he'd have got back all right, you'd have given him a knighthood and forgotten him entirely. He might well be still creaking around in a wheelchair in Eastbourne.'

Gunn finished his apple and threw it in the river.

'How much notice did they give you?' he said brutally.

'No technicalities now. It is time to deal with our thirst.' He took Gunn by the arm and led him across the street, discoursing on the various means by which Captain Scott could have prevented his Last Voyage from being his last voyage.

'They should have eaten the huskies,' Noone said. 'They ate the ponies, why didn't they eat the huskies?'

'Nobody left to carry the stores, I suppose.'

'Listen, by that stage there were no stores.'

'Perhaps they did eat the dogs, but didn't like to say so.'

'In that case the bones would have been found. No, they were too bloody refined to eat the dogs. They lacked the will to survive.' Rory Noone stepped off the traffic island into the path of a van. The driver braked, swore and then accelerated as Noone waved at him.

On the far pavement, a group of dossers were queueing for soup and rolls. The queue was long, stretching back down a path which led between dusty shrubs strewn with cigarette packets and sweet papers. The heavy overcoats and the shuffling movements of the waiting dossers were so unlike the light coats and high step of the other passers-by on that fine morning that they seemed to have strayed in from somewhere quite else, extras perhaps from a Russian epic, their frost-bitten feet wrapped in layers of torn rag, or survivors from HMS *Discovery* herself, trooping ashore from the terrible winter to discover the shrubs in the London parks already blossoming sweetpapers and Woodbines.

The mobile canteen was pale green to the waistline, then cream above, like the walls of a hospital room. As Gunn looked, he became aware of something familiar about the woman behind the canteen, something about the set of her shoulders, then the slight droop of the neck as she shook her head, as though her long face was convulsed with laughter.

Margaret Wood was a few years older than him. Their birthdays fell on the same day. They had shared birthday parties, both Gunn's parents and hers being economical by disposition and necessity. Schoolmaster's son and parson's daughter had their coupons pooled, and out of egg powder, margarine and other wartime substances a joint birthday cake emerged.

The shared party was all their parents' doing. The arrangement began at an age when Gunn still despised girls and by the time that he was prepared to associate with them on anything like equal terms, she was too old for him. Almost but not quite without meaning to, she made him feel as if he was being mocked, belittled. They had never really been friends, but they had been so much part of the same landscape that to see her neck and shoulders made him tremble.

'I've just seen an old friend,' Gunn said. 'You must come and meet her, you really must.' He did not know why he was so emphatic.

'If I must, I must.'

They walked over to the mobile canteen. Already Gunn was wishing he had not saddled himself with the burden of explaining Noone.

'I would not be missing this for the world,' Rory said. 'A soup-kitchen saint, the Mother Theresa of the Embankment.'

She was unpacking some plastic cups from the shelf underneath the steaming vat of tomato soup. There was no pretence of recognition being slow to dawn. The moment she straightened up she knew him, beamed and held out her hand.

'Gunn. What are you doing? Oh, I know, you *are* a journalist. Your father said you were going to be but I didn't believe him.'

'And here's another. This is Rory Noone. Margaret Wood.'

'Inskip,' she said. 'I'm married. To Dick. You haven't met Dick, have you?' A tall, thin man in an anorak stopped fiddling with the tea-urn and turned round to give them both a smile and a brisk handshake, before turning back to deal with the next client. He had a cigarette hanging out of the corner of his mouth and irregular teeth. His skin was very dry and flaky. He did not look well.

'Would you like a cup of tea, Mr Noone?'

'Well, it's very kind of you but we were just off in pursuit of something a little stronger. You couldn't slip away and join us for a wet?'

'No. No, I'm afraid not.'

'Your husband couldn't mind the shop for a minute or two?'

'I'm sorry, but it's slow with just one helper. And they really are hungry. It may be their only square meal for forty-eight hours.'

'A little drop would warm you up.'

'That's enough, Rory,' said Gunn.

31

'It's a pity. I would like to have come,' Margaret said. She did not sound as if she meant it.

'Another time, no doubt. I must not disturb you any longer,' said Noone, taking his leave with an unexpected bow.

'Yes, I hope so. Gunn, you must come and see us. In the telephone book – Rev. Richard Inskip.'

'Vicar's daughter marries vicar. Very nice.'

'Unfrocked, I'm afraid,' said Margaret.

'You mean it?'

'Oh, Margaret, don't muddle the poor man,' said Inskip, without apparent annoyance. 'I've given up parish work, that's all. You see before you a Social Worker Grade Two, seconded from Tower Hamlets Borough Council to DBNO.'

'DBNO?'

'Down But Not Out. Our outfit. Look, I'll explain another time, your friend's half-way to the pub by now.'

Goodbyes said, Gunn bustled down the street after Rory Noone, who was already a twinkle in the middle distance.

Outside the pub was a news-stand. A tiny man, face hidden under flat cap, sat behind the placard. He was so small and seated so near the ground that the placard looked like a sandwich-board on him. Below the headline of bold black type on the bill Gunn read the single word scrawled in a hectic hand, as though in haste or panic, SINKING.

Sinking now. Down into the soft-sprung dark. Down under the bedclothes, safe from the dragons flickering in the nursery fire and swooping across the far wall. She never came up to say goodnight now, not properly. She just put her head round the door with her fingers pressed to her lips. She didn't even blow the kiss. Then the door closed and there was nothing, only the smell of gardenia she said it was. What a silly name for a flower, garden-y – no, gardeenia, she said. Comfortable dark.

Gunn pushed open the door into the warm smoky cave. Between the tossing heads he caught sight of Rory at the far end of the long bar raising a hand to attract the barman. Gunn began to push through a knot of pin-striped lawyers passing drinks back to two girls in flocculent afghan coats. When the lawyers turned round, he was caught in the middle of their circle. As he searched for a decent way through, he was suddenly overcome by . . . the smoke, the night before, the drink, the excitement? He broke through the cordon and forced his way to the gents. Puking, he blessed the white cool of the porcelain and praised the maker's mark in blackletter type round the bowl – *Fowler Ware – The Shakespeare*. He began, though, to wonder whether he really had the stomach for the job.

# 3

'Do you officiate still?'

'Officiate?' Dick Inskip blinked at the word. He spent a lot of time with his spectacles off, as if he had deliberately chosen to make himself look vulnerable, his strong features being softened by the white skin around his eyes and the red rub-marks on his nose.

'Take services,' Gunn said.

'Yes, I do help out sometimes. It's not that I . . . feel above all that. I don't want to pretend to be doing something better, it's just that for me, for us. . . .' The amplifications and corrections followed upon each other with no sense of haste.

'Yes, we thought that this really would be *work*. The other seemed more like pleasure.' Margaret was brisker, more definite than her husband. She spoke with less spontaneity, as if she had threshed out her thoughts before she committed them to speech. 'Of course, we didn't know exactly what it would be like. But we wanted to *do* something, instead of just being a vicar and a vicar's wife.' Margaret spoke always of 'we', Dick mostly of 'I'.

'A vicar's very much a being person,' said Dick. 'He's just expected to be there. It's not so much what he does as the way that he does it that people notice.'

'Here we are judged by what we do.' Margaret poured more instant coffee into Gunn's mug. The blue-and-white crockery was almost the only touch of colour. The room had a vast purity. It was a large attic bedsitter. On one side, the pitched roof ran down to the floor interrupted by a single dormer window. On the other, a door led through to the bathroom and the kitchenette, both carved out of the landing. There was a double bed, two upright armchairs, a low plain deal table and a small pitch-pine bookcase. Only the top two of the four shelves were filled. The

34

top shelf contained devotional books : several well-worn bibles, two prayer books, a commentary on St John's gospel in a bright orange cover and some other theological volumes. The second shelf held paperbacks; as far as Gunn could see, they mostly seemed to be concerned with sociology and social work. On the lower two shelves were a couple of ornamental gourds.

'Afraid I don't get much time for reading these days', Dick said when he saw Gunn looking at the shelves. He laughed ruefully as if referring to some licentious pastime of his youth.

'We're always on call. Always somebody knocking at the door, day and night,' Margaret said.

'Well, not always, Mag.'

'Remember last night. It was after midnight when Dusty got in, and it was at least three before Tosh. . . .'

'Yes, yes,' Dick seemed abstracted. 'Tell me, what do they think of us in Fleet Street?'

'Of. . . .'

'Of Down But Not Out. Is our . . . image right?' He brought out the jargon with a blend of pain and pride.

'I've not been there long enough to. . . .'

'You think we should publicise ourselves more?'

'No, I only meant I don't know.'

'Oh, I see.'

'You could do an article about us perhaps – or would that be too much for your readers?' Margaret said.

'Not in the least. It's just the kind of thing they want to read about.'

'Are you sure? Some of our customers aren't very pretty.'

'The uglier the better,' Gunn said. 'Lice, d.t.'s, the lot. The thicker you lay it on the more the reader will think "there but for the grace of God go I." '

'We don't want to impute any moral blame,' Dick said. 'Their plight is an indictment of society as a whole, if it is anything.'

'It's not a question of blame,' Gunn said. 'People just like having a look into the abyss, that's all.'

'You seem to be very hard-bitten already,' Margaret said.

'You asked me.'

'I don't see anything wrong in what Gunn says,' Dick interposed. 'There's no use in being sentimental. If people are moved

35

to charity by looking into the abyss as you call it, then let them look. We could do with the cash.'

Margaret turned fully towards her husband every time he began to speak. Dick seemed unworried by such unwavering attention. Perhaps he was used to it, or perhaps he failed to notice it.

Gunn liked being with them, though. The blank walls and bare floor of their room were restful. The pure air made him conscious of the smell of stale tobacco that hung around his coat. The disinfectant from the floors below where the dossers slept, the urine from those corners of the staircase which the disinfectant had failed to reach . . . this room, so bare and clean, was yet alive with odours. The smells seemed to reverberate in the quiet.

'Nice and quiet here,' he said, listening to each word fall on to the scrubbed floorboards. His voice sounded loud and overbearing.

'Not too quiet, you don't think?' said Dick. 'It doesn't seem too much out of the world to you, a bit of an . . . ivory tower?'

'How can you say that, Dick, when you think of downstairs?' Margaret said.

'They seem very quiet tonight, too,' said Gunn.

'Oh, we're almost empty tonight,' Dick said. 'Sometimes they have a right old barney. Even up here, you can't hear yourself talk for the racket. But I don't mean that.'

'What do you mean then?' Margaret asked sharply.

'What did *you* mean, Mag?' Dick said mildly but with the air of someone determined to get an answer.

'It's obvious what I meant,' said Margaret. 'No ivory tower would accept the very people whom society has labelled inadequate and rejected.' Gunn liked the look of her when she was arguing. She became heated so quickly; her voice, usually flat and not easy to listen to, took fire.

Dick thought for a moment, not speaking until he was ready. 'I'm not quite sure exactly what an ivory tower is. It may not be the right phrase. But what I mean is that here we are, Margaret and I, living in a kind of enclosed community, at least that's not how the dossers see themselves or may not be, but it's how we see them. And by living with them, no, living in the same house as they do, we are in a way cutting ourselves off from everyone else but them, accepting their world as the norm. If

36

we don't, we would be slumming. I suppose we are slumming too but pretending all the time that we aren't. So we comfort ourselves by saying that what matters is our work, that's what gives us our certainty, not our intentions or the state of our soul or anything like that. And we're certain that this is the right work for us to do, not because it's good in itself, even if it is or could be, but because nobody else will do it. So we are living with people nobody else will live with, doing work nobody else will do, not sharing in any of the general concerns of our time. Isn't that being cut off?'

'I don't see anything wrong with it at all.'

'I didn't say there was anything wrong with it, at least that was not what I meant to imply,' Dick said.

'Couldn't you have said the same of the early Christians?' Gunn asked. 'Wouldn't they have been very cut off from the fate of the empire, down in their catacombs?'

'Yes, and wouldn't they have been right to cut themselves off?' Margaret added.

'Perhaps they would,' Dick said. 'But they would also have been right to ask themselves whether they were right.'

'Can you go on asking, asking, the whole time? Isn't there a moment when you have to make up your mind and fix on an answer?'

'Yes, I expect there is,' Dick smiled into the polo neck of his jersey, as if he had been talking to himself throughout.

They moved on to supper, a fry-up cooked by Margaret. She kept the fried eggs from running into each other with controlled ferocity, using her whole arm to chop down with the spatula. Gunn finished the sausages and ate three slices of bread and butter. Purity seemed to work up an appetite.

'Normally we eat downstairs with the customers,' Dick said, 'but seeing how you and Margaret had not seen each other for so long, we decided to have a snack up here for once.'

'I'd very much like to see downstairs if that's possible.'

'Good, good.'

'Lil's there tonight. Dick's youngest sister. You'll like Lil.'

'Ah,' said Gunn.

'Yes, you will,' Margaret spoke as if he had contradicted her, then, realising that he had not, slipped into a smile.

Even as they started down the stairs, things began to warm

37

up : a grumbling low noise of conversation, the shriek of a radio being tuned, a shout, not particularly loud or angry.

'Splendid, just after closing time,' Dick said, looking at his watch. 'There'll be a few of the lads coming in now.'

The room, much taller and longer than the room they had just left, contained a dozen dirty divan beds disposed along the walls. On two or three of these beds there were men huddled under brown blankets, apparently not asleep for they stirred constantly, some violently. In the corner there was a radio on a table playing two programmes at once. A tall, gaunt man was bent over the set, gently thumping it at intervals. One of the men sitting on the beds got up and came over to shake hands with Dick.

'Evening Reverend.'

'They just won't call him Dick,' Margaret whispered.

'Evening Tosh. How's it going then?'

'Terrible day, terrible.' Tosh started on the story of his day. It was jampacked with misfortune. He had been given a scarf by a friend quite unexpectedly, a fine scarf, silk according to some, nylon but not far off it according to others; he had not gone but a few steps down the road when it had vanished, melted like butter off his neck. Dick might think he had dropped it, that was certainly a possibility, but he and a friend had looked over every inch of the pavement and there wasn't a sign. Dick might think some villain had picked it up, it was an excusable thought, the same thought had occurred to him and to his friend, perhaps somebody had made off with it, he was not going to rule out the possibility, but his friend had sharp eyes and had spun round like a top (Tosh spun slowly through a quarter-circle, tense hands slicing the air), but no scarf. And the scarf was only the start of it. There was the bottle of wine, a good bottle of wine, smashed by an invisible hand. And the old woman outside the pub, ignorant old bag. He was coming out of the place entirely normal, happened to lose his footing, they'd put a little step there quite without warning, anyone who was cut didn't stand a chance, rude old bag she was.

Tosh's conversation had the same unhurried flow as Dick's; he doubled back, corrected himself, narrowed down the desired area of meaning without any semblance of haste or hesitancy. Dick himself encouraged Tosh by asking for more precise descriptions of the scarf, the old woman, the fatal step outside the pub, suggesting recourse to the police, the off-licence, the landlord, putting forward a variety of theses : that Tosh had left the scarf at home, that bad luck always came in threes, that the old woman was more startled than hostile, that Tosh in fact had had a jar or two more than he realised. These comments, varying between the sympathetic and the reproving, were all delivered in exactly the same tone of voice, quite unlike the low, rather mumbling way he had been speaking upstairs. Talking with Tosh, his voice had a bloom of pleasure on it, like a girl at her first party surrounded by admirers.

Gunn was introduced to Tosh, who filled him in on the history of the scarf. Dick circled the room to greet the other men sitting on the beds. Most of them were pleased to see him, some unmistakably fond of him, but one or two, either wrapped in their own concerns or actively resentful of the visiting party, failed to return his greeting. Even more delighted, if that were possible, by this challenge, Dick laid a firm hand upon their shoulders as he talked to them, like a bishop confirming a line of converts.

As he passed down the line, he handed out cigarettes from a packet battered by constantly being fished out of his pocket and thrust back in again. Now and then a dosser would stare quizzically at the bent cigarette offered to him before accepting it with a word of thanks. Dick himself sucked continuously but gingerly, with little appearance of pleasure. For him the habit seemed less like a weakness of the flesh than an act of communion, a calculated show of solidarity.

At the end of the room a broken-down old man was staring down between his legs, scarcely moving. Dick paused before him and, evidently deciding that the shoulder treatment would be too much, squatted down in front of the old man and patted his knees. From a distance, the two of them appeared to be playing some variant of pat-a-cake. Gunn could just hear the old man saying to himself in a soft monotone : 'Fuck it, fuck it, fuck it.'

Margaret meanwhile tidied the room. She dragged blankets from under the beds and folded them with an impatient flip. Dick was still talking to the old man when she suggested that they should go further downstairs to see how Lil was getting on.

On the ground floor, the atmosphere was livelier. There was

a long table with beer bottles, a lot of smoke and two groups of men sitting on mattresses playing cards.

'This is our social room,' Dick said. 'The council discourage cards and booze, so we allow both within limits – no gambling, no wine and no meths of course. I can't say the rules are always kept, but it helps to make the place more of a home.'

'The bloody tea-urn's seized up again.' The girl behind the table spoke in a nasal drawl in which a faint resemblance to her brother's voice could be detected. Dick acknowledged both her presence and her complaint with a gesture of familiarity bordering on irritation. Without introducing Gunn, he strode up to the machine which was peacefully hissing and slapped it hard with the flat of his hand. A chugging noise indicated success. He then strode back again, interrupting Gunn's greeting to his sister :

'There. Any other queries, Lily?'

'Some of them are quite cheeky, aren't they?'

'This isn't South Kensington, you know. You have to be broadminded.'

'I didn't say I didn't like it. I just said they were *cheeky*.'

'I'm sure there's plenty for you to do without getting fussed about that kind of thing.' The flow of Dick's good humour was definitely stanched.

Lil, on the other hand, looked increasingly cheerful. The soft tailing away of her voice did not seem to mean any of the usual things such as hesitancy or lack of confidence. She brushed the hair off her round face with a vague hand, missing a few strands with the first sweep.

'I'll take over now if you like, love,' Margaret said.

'I'm OK, thanks.'

'You've been on since seven.'

'I'm enjoying it,' Lil said.

'There'll be some of the more awkward ones coming in soon.'

'I don't mind.'

'You may not mind, but they might. It helps if they see a face they know.'

'Razors and broken bottles, do you mean?'

'Of course not.' Margaret's annoyance suggested that she had indeed meant to hint delicately at something of the sort and that Lil had spoiled her tactic by putting it into words.

'Razors and broken bottles? It's foolish to talk like that, Lily,

40

very foolish,' Dick said. 'It's just the kind of scare story we're trying to stamp on.'

'Margaret said there might be *trouble* later on,' Lil said.

'Nonsense, with respect. There's more violence in so-called respectable society than you'd see in a month here. Margaret, you ought. . . .'

'I just thought Lil might be tired and. . . .'

'Tired, we're all tired. I'm tired myself.' Dick spoke with restraint. It was an act of some condescension to class their petty fatigue with his exhaustion.

He turned to greet two more dossers who had just arrived. They, like the majority, responded to his interest in them. They enjoyed his company, felt no embarrassment, perhaps because Dick's warmth was strangely impersonal. He talked to everyone in much the same way. On balance, this seemed a restful quality. The other person did not have to worry whether Dick liked him or not, whether he was making a good impression. To prefer one individual to another did not appear to enter Dick's head; he either did not notice the difference between persons or did not care about it. This seemed to suit the dossers. His indifference protected their dignity.

While Gunn was watching Dick, there came the sound of a squabble from the passage and in tottered a tiny man in a beret, slamming the door behind him. 'He's go' a bo'le, a bo'le, a bo'le.' The tiny man made a wild bottle-shaped gesture and subsided to the floor.

A pause. A growl from the passage. Another pause. Dick moved forward toward the door, evidently trying to look as little like a riot squad as possible. In this he succeeded nobly, giving the impression more of an anxious host going to the aid of a guest stuck in lavatory or lift.

Before he reached the door, it was flung open and there stood a giant of a man : black-bearded, mountainous, his huge, mouldering coat shining wet in the light of the passage. One hand carried an enormous object tied up with string, somewhere between a suit case and a sandbag. The other hand was thrown forward at about chest level holding something which glittered as he tried to get a firmer grip on it.

'Ah, Dusty, how goes it? Come in and dry off,' Dick said.

The huge figure said nothing.

41

'He'll chib ye if ye dinna watch oot,' said the tiny man in the beret. 'He's a heid-banger, tha'n, a fart in a trance.' The huge figure stood there. Then he began to chant solemnly in an unexpectedly high voice, like a child reciting a lesson :

> Ah want ma hole,
> Ah want ma hole,
> Ah want ma hole-idays,
> Tae see the cunt,
> Tae see the cunt,
> Tae see the cunt–ery,
> Fu' cu–
> Fu' cu–
> Fu' curiosity.

He fell silent again. 'Ah lairnt tha' at school,' he said after a long pause.

'I haven't heard that one for a long time,' Dick said.

' 's a Glesga sang.'

'Is it? I didn't know that. They sing it down here too, in the schools.'

Dusty advanced, stretching out the hand holding the broken bottle.

'Ah foond it. In the passage.'

'There's a dustbin over there. Behind the tea-urn.'

Dusty shambled over to the bin and dropped the broken bottle in it. As he passed, the bare light caught his firm, red-brown cheek ; beneath the layers of greasy cloth and hair, he was quite young, little older than Gunn. He joined the queue for a cup of tea. Close up, he looked smaller too.

Dick showed little sign of triumph. He began talking to Gunn again about the possibility of more publicity – and hence perhaps more cash for Down But Not Out. He did not even seem particularly excited by the incident; he showed none of that elation which had spurted from him when he first started talking to the dossers.

Gunn could not decide whether this sang-froid was assumed or whether it had never occurred to Dick that the broken bottle might be intended for offensive purposes and, if the latter, whether Dick had been right. Perhaps Dusty had just tripped over the bottle and picked it up in a confused state, which might have

42

boiled into fury if the wrong remark had been made. The fact remained that Dick's response, whether arising from insensibility or cunning, had worked.

He had also prevented Lil and Margaret from pursuing their struggle for the tea-urn, forced them to a compromise by which Margaret would take over when she had finished tidying up. The sealing of this agreement was cut short by a bellow from the bench where Dusty was sitting nursing his tea-cup.

'Aw, ah a'maist forgoat. He's deid.'

'Who is?'

'The auld bugger.'

The Crunch had come. It was in these tenebrous circumstances that destiny had decreed that Gunn Goater should learn of the death of the Last Great Englishman.

'I think,' said Dick, 'that we should pause for a moment to mediate on what this event means personally to each of us.'

'A sort of two minutes silence?' Gunn asked.

'I wasn't thinking of any kind of structured response, Gunby,' Dick said. 'In fact it is better if we clear our heads of irrelevant mumbo-jumbo and try to search out some personally meaningful aspect in this event. What does it say to you, to me, to Tosh and Dusty here? Has it in fact any significance for the under-lying socio-economic structure?'

Cycling on an autumn morning not long after the end of the war, Gunn and his father had come upon an empty bus parked in the road. Beside it, almost filling the country lane, stood two dozen men in dark clothes, entirely motionless, standing stiff to attention but irregularly spilled all over the road as though frozen by a supernatural force. Gunn's father, disliking fuss, especially fuss tinged with patriotism or religion, shouted to him 'Two minutes silence, keep going, pay no attention.' But as they rode nearer, a large man with the British Legion badge on his jacket made as if to block their path. Gunn's father, not willing to cause a scene, that too counting as fuss to be avoided, stopped and swung his leg off his bicycle. He made a furtive slow-down motion with his hand to his son like a tracker warning his companion of Indians ahead. Gunn stood stationary astride his lady's bike, feet on the ground, looking at the old man's beard and the red berries in the hedge beside the road. The silence was made deeper still by the country sounds: the dripping from the trees,

43

the little birds moving about in the hedge. Gunn liked that sort of deliberate silence.

Silence now. All silence. The plotting over. The House risen. No more parades, no hoofs flinging puffs of sand, no more swords. He could hear the carriage clatter over the new cattle grid at the gate beyond the laurels. Her hand, soft pink hand like his, would fly up to hold on the hat with the violets at the front. There would be a little frown on her face, a little wrinkle on her white forehead. He knew that frown.

Dusty explained how the news had reached him. 'Ah was in the Kings Head when this bloke wi' a trannie. . . .'

Two dossers linked arms and began to dance a slow pavane down the middle of the room. A middle-aged man seated on a mattress began to cry, rocking backwards and forwards as if on a rowing-machine.

'. . . "He's deid," he says. "Cobblers", ah says. "Listen for yirsel", he says.'

Somewhere at the back of the room, a hoarse voice embarked on the national anthem, stumbled, hesitated, started again and then stopped.

'. . . they even interrupted that feller to give the news.'

'What feller?'

'Mon wi' a wee band, Italian.'

'Semprini?'

'It wasnae Semprini. Semprini plays the piano.'

'Mantovani then.'

'Aye, Mantovani it was. In the middle of "Fingal's Cave", they stopped him.'

Gunn went upstairs with the three Inskips to listen to the radio, but in the meantime the tall, gaunt man had lost his temper and thumped the set so hard that it was now silent as the grave into which the Last Great Englishman was soon to be laid.

# 4

Chooo! The steam train blew its proud, mournful blast as it slowly chuffed up from the sheds. Steam had been phased out of normal service years before. But this particular engine had been hearsing and rehearsing for the putative corpse too long to be replaced. The brass rods were bright; the boiler's green sheen, the heavy embossed metal of the nameplate, the gleam of the great wheels – all reflected the high noon of the railway age. Even the driver and the fireman seemed to shine with metallic zest; they had managed to hang on to the old uniforms : black cloth, silver buttons, big watches with leather straps.

The driver and fireman were not alone. All over England middle-aged men were dressing up. Ceremonial men not otherwise much noticed in these times had their uniforms brushed and sneaked a glance in the mirror. Pursuivants, commissioners of police, stationmasters, Elder Brothers of Trinity House and Lord-Lieutenants gathered in robing-rooms with unusual smiles on their faces.

Gunn Goater was waiting down by the river. Lacking the seniority to cover any major part of the ceremony such as the service or the entrainment, he had been detailed to report in graphic and where possible poignant detail the reactions of ordinary Londoners. 'Grab 'em by the nuts if you can,' the news editor had told him. So far Gunn had interviewed half-a-dozen Brazilians, a party of French schoolteachers, a Maltese pimp, a Nigerian nun and several Eastern Europeans. There remained, however, one native-born section of the community which patronised this bend of the river, even on a public holiday, and Gunn accordingly took up his position in the middle of the dossers.

Morale here was not high. The mobile canteen was late. The unusual crowd of foreign tourists aggravated the dossers' vague resentment that the funeral was in some obscure way aimed at them. Not that they could as a body have been said to be against the Last Great Englishman; if anything, he was viewed with a certain caustic approval; but the whole business of his obsequies appeared to them to be an imposition breaking into the normal run of things. Critical comment was hence directed at the organisers of the occasion rather than at its protagonist.

'What they want to bring him up the river for?'

'Bad luck it is to take a dead man upstream.'

'A number eleven bus would do him just as well.'

'Or a number fifteen.'

'Depends where he wants to finish.'

'Number fifteen would be better.'

A ripe girl with an olive skin came up to Gunn. He put his notebook away smartly, like a voyeur caught standing on a chair at a window.

'Please, what is this?'

'It's a state funeral. They are burying the Last Great Englishman,' Gunn unfolded the portentous phrase without misgiving.

'A funeral? In there?' She pointed to the grey waters of the river. Gunn began to explain but she turned to her companion, a dark man dressed in assorted crinkly leathers from head to toe and began to talk to him in a foreign language. The man reacted angrily as if personally insulted.

'He says it is not clean to give a dead man into the river.'

'No, we do not give him to the river. He just floats up it.'

She passed the message on to the leather man. He reacted even more angrily.

'My friend says it is stupid. Dead men cannot go upon the water.'

Gunn prepared to have another try. Then he saw the funeral barge riding upon the water : the coffin draped with the national flag and ratings at each corner like four dark-blue stanchions and the sullen warehouses beyond. And his heart lifted like a weary gull.

As the coffin went by, the dossers consented to a ragged cheer, not less than half sincere but still overlaid with enough mockery to keep their self-respect. The tourists twittered, not wishing perhaps to give offence but giving it nonetheless, in the usual manner of persons observing the mysteries of an alien culture.

46

The funeral barge passed on upstream with the police launches bouncing in its wake.

The cortège was undoubtedly a challenge to the dossers' cherished detachment from conventional society; and their cheer was a concession which had left them uneasy. The unease was dissipated by the arrival of the mobile canteen. When Lil jumped down from the driver's cabin, she was greeted by a cheer far louder than the cortège had got.

'You here, are you?' she said, as he watched her ladling out the tomato soup.

'Yes.'

'Are you writing about Down But Not Out? Will you write about me?'

'No, I'm writing about the funeral. Getting people's reactions.'

'Oh, the *funeral.*' Her voice had the trick of falling midway between irony and innocent surprise so that he could not tell whether she thought the funeral a piece of meaningless mummery or whether it interested her, even touched her.

'Is this a good place to be?' she asked.

'It doesn't seem to be very good. Most of the people I've talked to so far have been foreigners.'

'Our boys here aren't foreign,' Lil said.

'No, but they don't seem to be very excited by the occasion.'

'Well, can't you put that in? Isn't that part of what people think? Or don't they count as people?'

'Not if they go on saying it's a lot of bullshit.'

'Well, isn't it – an old man dying?'

'Better to dole out soup?'

'Mm. In fact, I'm only doling today because Margaret's ill. I'm really *unemployed.*' The dying fall began to irritate him.

'Do you have to talk in that way?'

'What way?'

'I'm really *unemployed.*'

'We all talk like that.'

'We?'

'Everyone at school.'

'You aren't still at school?'

'Don't be stupid, but we still keep together. We're a group, like in Mary McCarthy, only we were called the Clique. It's funny,

47

but I've kept all the friends I made at school but none of the ones I made at university. Of course, they were mostly men.'

'You went to university?'

'Yes, didn't like it much. Had a bad BD. *Break Down.*'

'You're still talking like that.'

'I thought you wouldn't know about breakdowns.'

'I wouldn't have known you had had one. You look . . . strong.'

'Very misleading appearances are in that way,' she said, grinning through the tomato steam. The cold had reddened the cheeks and the tip of her nose. The little knitted hat jammed down over ears made her look like a determined small boy. There was a long mangy strip of fur wound round her neck. She was wearing a worn mauve velvet dress which reached down to her calves. The nap of the cloth had rubbed away at the seams, and the dress was too small for her. Both the fur and the dress had a certain faded pretension and could once have been sported by a pre-war soup-kitchen lady but had now come downhill to the level of the oddments worn by the few women dossers.

'That's a funny dress,' he said.

'I got it at the market. Seven-and-six, including the fur. Isn't it lovely? I call it the landlady's best friend.'

Without warning, Gunn experienced a moment of elation, a feeling that he had been hollowed out and filled with cold light. He was translucent and weightless. His skin caressed the air like balloon silk. His solidity had been taken from him. He shimmered in the morning light; his shoes, though seemingly filled with lead like an astronaut's, only just tethered him to the ground.

The wraiths of tomato steam billowed through the golden haze. The ladle rose out of the steam and swooped in a tight arc up and over and down into the paper cup. There was a miracle in the way the scoop of soup was gathered by the horns of a crescent moon and charioted across the sky into the little cup; each dosser shambling by, muttered thanks as he accepted his viaticum. He noticed with mild interest that she was talking, had indeed not stopped talking since he had taken off for his olympian perch.

'In fact, the three of us still live together.'

'The three of what?'

'The three real Clique people. The closest of us. Clara, Poppy and me. It's Clara's house. It's funny how close we still are.'

'After so long, you mean?'

48

'I suppose it is a long time. No, I mean considering how different we all are. You must come to our house. Come back with me and see it when I've finished, won't you?'

She had certainly not put herself out to make her household attractive; they sounded a cloying threesome. But he wanted to see more of her. He also wanted to see how she lived, how girls lived together.

First though, Gunn had to earn his bread. Emboldened both by his flight into the haze and by his scoop of the royal kiss, he dashed off his report there and then. Sitting on the parapet of the embankment, he described the haze on the river and the bare plane trees and the funeral barge riding on the waters. Then he panned in on the army of the defeated along his section of the route. Out of the column of derelicts, he plucked in the approved manner two or three individuals. Taking care to get their names right and not forgetting to insert their ages, he appended to each some emblematic phrase, such as 'fought in two world wars' and 'out of work for fifteen years' or 'self-confessed alcoholic' or even, though this on shakier testimony, 'former public-schoolboy'.

From each dosser thus ticketed, he reported some comment on the proceedings, all uniformly surly in tone ranging from 'blooming waste of public money' to 'what did the old blighter ever do for us?' Gunn wrapped up this symposium of disaffection with a brief peroration of his own : 'Yes, there was bitterness on the Embankment yesterday. Far from the trumpets and the captains and kings, some of Britain's less privileged mourners also had memories they could not forget.'

By the time he had finished telephoning this rebarbative piece through to the paper, Lil was ready for him. Dick had come to relieve her.

'I'm taking him to see my pad.'

'Good, good. Where are the bread rolls?' Dick asked severely.

'On the driving seat.'

'Thank you.' There was an infinity of tolerance in his voice.

'You said I could go when you came.'

'Of course I did, my dear. That's the whole point of the relief system. You buzz off.' Dick's forbearance was boundless.

The two of them set off together at a fair pace. Lil took his arm.

'Dick's been having a hard time recently,' she said.

49

'And handing one out?'

'No, he is basically very kind. He's having trouble with the council grant, and stuffy neighbours, oh, and everything.'

The streets leading away from the processional route were still crowded with people. Glassy-eyed spectators wandered without aim, displaced in mind and body by what they had seen, spilling out of alley ways, drifting through the traffic in anarchic swathes, suddenly turning to squint at a street-name to regain their bearings and being run into by those who were still plunging on; then separated from one another by people coming the other way, gesturing and calling until they were reunited; a tide of strangers released upon the empty city by the raising of some distant floodgate, quite unlike the purposeful streams of weekday people.

Out of the sun now, between high buildings, Gunn and Lil walked in a grey light. The brilliance of the day was already gone. Echoes of the spectacle still rang along the blank pavements.

'The catafalque was so. . . .'

'It was never a catafalque . . . a catafalque is a. . . .'

'. . . he looked so frail, be his own funeral next.'

'Was that one of his sisters. . . .'

'A sister-in-law. The music must have been. . . .'

Gunn stopped at a telephone kiosk and went inside to ring his office. Lil waited outside, blowing steam on to the glass panel. She pressed her lips up against the glass, leaving behind a squashy cupid's bow. Gunn pretended to rub it out with his sleeve from inside. Behind her, an elderly man had already began to form a queue. He was stamping his feet to keep warm.

'Do you want any more colour words?' Gunn asked the news editor.

'No, that'll do us nicely. We'll have to take out the stuff about the tramps, though. Too morbid.'

'But the tramps are the whole point of the piece.' Outside, Lil had taken off her glove and was carefully writing with her finger on the glass. She wrote UP MOSELY in capitals.

'Sorry, old boy,' the news editor said. 'On a day like this who wants to know what a lot of old tramps think? It's a historic day, this. Those tourists you talked to would be more what we're after.'

'Would a Maltese pimp do instead?'

'How'd you know he was a pimp?'

'He said he was. He also said he was a great admirer of the

50

deceased.' The elderly man was peering over Lil's shoulder, trying to make out what she had written on the glass.

'That's not bad. Malta G.C. The defiant ones, the man and the island. Why not file an add., but leave out about him being a pimp, there's a good lad.' Lil was starting on a swastika. Gunn ended the conversation and quickly left the kiosk.

'You can't even spell Mosley,' he said.

'It would make it even more convincing, getting it wrong,' she said.

'Fascists don't look like you.'

'Don't they?'

'No, they're much tidier, more organised-looking,' Gunn said. 'Try Lenin next time.'

'I suppose you're very interested in *politics*,' she said.

'No more than in other things.'

'That's a good way to be, I should think.' She had a way of starting off on a provocative tack and then dissolving into vague appeasement. These changes of directions, like her brother's, were managed without fluster, as smoothly as a disc-jockey changing records.

'What are you *against*?' she said.

'Oh, I suppose corruption . . . secrecy – all the things we put in the papers.'

'What's wrong with secrecy? I like secrecy.'

'Not your sort of secrets,' he said.

'You don't know what my sort of secrets are.'

'I can guess.'

'Can you?'

'Imagine the sort of thing, I mean, not guess exactly. For God's sake,' he said. They sat down on a bench next to the kiosk while he scribbled a few more evocative words on his notepad.

'You must be rather *clever*.' She said it not without irony but without rancour, or so he thought, as he got up to telephone his addendum.

In front of them, twenty or thirty people stood blocking the pavement in a rough semicircle. They were all staring into the window of a television rental shop. Six television sets were arrayed in an answering semicircle, each showing a coffin draped with the national flag being carried by bare-headed guardsmen, very slowly and gingerly, down a long flight of steps. The procession

51

had passed that way not much more than an hour ago, so most of the persons watching the shop window must have seen the event itself.

'Lot of fucking sheep,' said Gunn loudly.

'You've got quite a *temper*, haven't you? Why shouldn't they watch if they want to? Do you mind them *reading* all about it in your newspaper?' She spoke of his temper with interest rather than dismay. She might have been commenting on the texture of his hair.

'I just get annoyed when people are so passive.'

'Not much else they can be at a funeral, is there? Anyway, what's wrong with being passive?'

'Passive . . . secretive . . . you make yourself sound like a sphinx.'

'Oh, well.' She paused before murmuring, 'I didn't say I was anything in particular.'

But something in particular was precisely what she was. In her company, he had a sense of perilous good fortune. She was a testing windfall.

They strode on under a pigeon-breasted sky towards the heights of Brondesbury Park where the Clique hung out. He was three or four inches taller, but their strides matched. On the lower slopes of St John's Wood, he heard himself puffing and began trying to breathe more quietly. Lil's breath still came evenly.

# 5

'Ring the bell,' she said.

'You haven't got a key?'

'You must ring the bell.'

He tugged the wrought-iron stem hanging from the roof of the tiled porch. The other side of the door a laggard peal of electric chimes broke into a tune he could not recognise.

' "We'll keep a welcome in the valleys". Specially made for the 1947 Eisteddfod. Note the dragon-and-leek motif on the bell-pull,' she recited in a sing-song voice as she unlocked the door. 'Mind the exhibits in the hall.'

He stumbled into a dark passage banging his hip on a solid projecting object. He took a few more strides then ran into something flimsy and rippling which went chush-shush against his face. Clawing at this, he stubbed his hand on an unyielding crag. He stood still and waited.

Eventually he heard a click and a light came on. The light was a fan-shaped wall-lamp in biscuit-and-umber bakelite. He looked around him. The passage was so crowded that even with the light on it was hard to navigate without injury. The flimsy barrier was revealed as a curtain of coloured beads arranged in a pattern to represent an oriental building, not quite the Taj Mahal, not quite the Temple of Heaven either, just generally oriental. The rugged object which had drawn blood from his palm was a hat-rack made out of stags' antlers; on the points hung an assortment of berets. 'Women's Land Army, Boys' Brigade, WVS and either the Blackshirts or the Blueshirts, we're not sure which,' Lil said.

'All these things yours?' asked Gunn, edging round a huge chest-of-drawers with round knobs painted in the colours of the Royal Air Force target emblem. On top of the chest was painted the RAF crest below which was inscribed on a wind-tossed scroll *Per Ardua Ad Astra.*

'No, this is all Antic's stuff. He collects things.'

'Who's Antic?'

'Antic Hay. He's called Anthony really. He's married to Clara.'

'Does he like living with the Clique?'

'It's his house. He could throw us out if he wanted to. Come upstairs and see him, if you like.' The stairs were lined with old carpet sweepers with wooden dust-boxes stamped with the royal coat of arms. 'Ewbanks,' she said reverently. A pair of electric-purple chrome tail-fins tied to the banisters formed a triumphal arch at the top of the stairs. 'Cadillac fifty-three.'

A large man with a mop of fair hair bustled down to meet them. He was dressed in a grubby calf-length robe of Moorish aspect. Despite this, he somehow recalled the schoolmasters who had infested Gunn's youth. Perhaps it was the baggy grey flannels and scuffed Hush Puppies which peeped out from under the robe. He appeared to be in his late thirties.

'Been to the funeral, have you? You must come and see my special Memorial Exhibition.'

He led them through a crowded cavern containing objects so striking and garish that even the first dazzled glance could not help taking some of them in : a pottery ashtray in the likeness of Mahatma Gandhi's head, a chamber-pot shaped like a cow, a dartboard with a naked girl curled round the bullseye, a candelabrum held up by a brawny youth clad only in lederhosen, a huge china carrot embossed with the words 'Dig for Victory'. But even this bric-à-brac receded into insignificance beside the corner devoted to the Memorial Exhibition.

In this Brondesbury nook was crammed every object that the human mind had ever conceived of stamping with the likeness of the Last Great Englishman. He glared down from toby jugs, table mats, ashtrays, firescreens; there was a jack-in-the-box in his image lolling in the extended position, a rubber doll, a water pistol which squirted water from the great man's crotch, a folder of sheet music entitled, below a cartoon of his head, 'He's the stuff to give the troops.' There was one of those little glass globes which, if shaken, enveloped his sturdy figure in a snow-storm. Hanging from the ceiling was a toy barrage balloon bearing his face stretched almost beyond recognition. There was a tattered puppet which made him resemble one of the seven dwarfs. And dominating the whole collection was a large cardboard mock-up of the White Cliffs of Dover upon the edge of which was planted a working model of the Last Great Englishman, which revolved in the manner of a lighthouse, illuminating with its feeble beam still more souvenirs of the immortal deceased : soap-dishes, plaster bulldogs endowed with his features, a hot-water bottle, a complete picnic set, a plastic sphinx in which the original enigmatic head had been replaced by the image of English certitude.

'Breathtaking,' said Gunn.

'There are one or two gaps. I could have done with more time,' said Antic Hay. 'There were some nice plastic fans made in Hong Kong. And I couldn't get hold of any of the condoms.'

'Condoms?'

'They did them in Port Said after D-Day. Limited issue and obviously perishable. You can imagine what they looked like from that barrage balloon on the ceiling. On a smaller scale, of course.'

'Someone must have been pulling your leg.' Gradually recovering from the Memorial Exhibition, Gunn took in the two girls sitting cross-legged on the floor near the fire. They were drinking coffee from a brass cobra, another fragment of the detritus of empire. The pot stood on a tray stamped with the by now unbearably familiar features. The two girls sat hunched in shawls like poor women in photographs of the Great Depression. They were reading tattered back numbers of the *Radio Times*. As soon as they spoke, Gunn recognised the Clique voice : low, nasal, sliding easily from the casual to the emphatic.

'Hallo. I'm Clara. This is Poppy.'

'Hallo,' said Poppy. She was darker and thinner. They both had long jaws and long noses. Their hallos had a resonance which took his mind off the alleged gaps in the Memorial Exhibition; they stirred in him memories of lost opportunities for adventure, like a bare arm seen at dusk in a gap between the bedroom curtains. The two of them looked at him without seeming to blink. He looked away at Lil, who was taking off her knitted hat.

'The Clique?' he asked with an uneasy gesture, linking the three girls.

'Yes.'

'Then there are the castanets,' said Antic Hay. 'They were very popular with the British tourists in the fifties. They had his head on one clapper and a Carmen-figure with a rose between her teeth on the other. They're supposed to be quite common.'

'Antic, this is a really nice number,' said Clara, holding up her copy of the *Radio Times*. 'It's got an interview with Anne Ziegler and Webster Booth.'

'Tell me who was in 'Workers' Playtime' that week and I'll date it for you.'

'Ruby Murray . . . Flotsam and Jetsam . . . Winnie Atwell.'

'1951 . . . 1952. Early 1952. March?'

'Warm, quite warm.'

The quiz continued as Antic Hay showed Gunn round, the girls raiding a tall pile of old *Radio Timeses* for fresh questions.

'Nervo and Knox . . . Semprini . . . Ten-ton-Tessie?'

'1955. No, later.'

'Where did you get all these back numbers?' Gunn asked.

'I kept them,' said Antic Hay. 'I've got a complete run from my tenth birthday. Before that, we didn't have a radio.'

'Al Read . . . David Hughes . . . Elsie and Doris Waters.'

'Can't do that one. You know Gert and Daisy are Jack Warner's sisters, of course.'

'Do you . . . sell all this?'

'No, my living is selling books. This is my avocation.'

'I suppose you could turn it into a museum eventually.'

'A museum of *kitsch*? I could, but it would destroy the point. It would turn everything into *art*.'

'Would that be so terrible?'

'Oh, I think there's enough art as it is, don't you?'

'The Man of a Thousand Voices . . . Charlie Kunz . . . Gilly Potter?' came the voice from the far end of the room.

These nostalgic amusements made Gunn uneasy. The mixture of the familiar and the bizarre threw him off balance. How well he knew the *Radio Times* of that period – the small print, the clotted lay-out, the advertisements for greenhouses and correspondence courses on the back. Lying on his front on the hearthrug he would flip through its pages in search of items about the programmes he particularly liked : 'Norman and Henry Bones – the boy detectives', 'Dick Barton – Special Agent', 'Round Britain Quiz'.

56

Some of the objects here on show in inverted commas had been part of his childhood too. The handle of the Ewbank carpet sweeper used to fall out of the cupboard whenever he went to get his coat; giant tail-fins whisked through the village en route from the American air base; and the tall radio was like enough to the machine they had had at home with its dark-brown trellis covering the loudspeaker, through which as a small boy he fancied that, on a good day, not only sound but faint pictures might be transmitted. Yet though he could call these things to mind, the objects as here exhibited meant nothing to him. They were selected with such cold irony, juxtaposed so brutally.

Antic Hay paused on his guided tour. He looked at the three girls browsing through the *Radio Timeses*. They were chuckling. Antic did not seemed pleased. He tugged irritably at his robe to hitch up the trousers under it. Despite his unnerving superiority, he had a fidgety woebegone sort of unease that Gunn found endearing.

'Don't spill the coffee on that tray.'

'Oh, *Antic*,' said the thinnest of the three girls.

'It's a nice tray, Poppy.'

The girl shook her hair out of her eyes and smiled, humouring him. Her cheeks were flushed, like Lil's.

'You look like the three witches in *Macbeth*.'

'Shut up, Anthony,' said the third girl, Clara.

'Yes, like the three witches.' The comparison pleased him. 'The three witches,' he said again. He was delighted to have got them labelled.

'Shut up.'

'This is a house full of women. A very strange thing. Women dominate this house. I am just a kind of commissionaire or security guard, a nothing. Luckily I happen to like the company of women, as it happens. Do you?'

'Yes, I do.'

'Do you really? I'm sure you like them for screwing and so on, but do you like them to talk to?'

'I do,' said Gunn firmly.

'That is interesting. It's quite rare, you know. Most Englishmen don't. We are oddballs in that way, you and I.'

'The only reason any of us ever talks to him is because he owns the house,' Poppy said.

'Hmm-mm.' It was hard to tell whether Antic's hum was meant to pacify or encourage the girls.

'I haven't talked to him for pleasure for years,' said Clara.

'Clara wants to become one of those wives who haven't spoken a single word to their husbands since VE-day.'

Clara modified her blank gaze. She might have been amused and not willing to show it, or irritated and not willing to show it either.

'I have always attracted silent women, the kind of women who are supposed to be difficult. Clara isn't difficult at all really, just doesn't like talking to men. It's a Clique thing, you know, preferring to talk to women because women are real people while men are just . . . not brute exactly but a more primitive form of life.'

'You don't know anything about it,' Clara said. 'You don't know anything about anything.'

'Well then, come and talk to us.'

'I've got to give the Piddingtons their tea.'

'You haven't met the Piddingtons?' Antic asked Gunn politely.

'No. Who are they?'

'Our two kids. Known as the Piddingtons after the celebrated mind-reading couple of stage, screen and radio in the days of our youth.'

In the misty middle distances of his memory, Gunn could just descry the Piddingtons : a man and his daughter, no, his wife, who practised the usual tricks of telepathy, guessing cards from an adjoining room, describing a picture drawn by a member of the audience, divining the contents of a sealed envelope – but who had somehow managed to climb into a prominence unusual for such performers. For a period the papers were full of them; scientists and public men rushed to pronounce whether the Piddingtons were psychic or fraudulent. Then just as suddenly they had sunk from view again, Gunn could not remember whether because they had died or split up or because of a scandal or just because they had come to the end of the time allotted them on the public stage. They lived on as legends only in Antic Hay's Museum of the Twentieth Century.

'This is Elfin. This is Xanthe.' Two little girls, aged somewhere between five and eight, wearing sack-coloured sacks with holes cut for head and arms, came in and nodded at Gunn. They stood

58

side by side and looked at him without expression. They cowed the company into silence.

'Buzz off kids and get some tea,' Antic Hay said eventually.

'Come on, Piddingtons. There's *baked beans.*'

'We want to see the man,' said the smaller of the two girls.

'Well, there he is,' said Antic Hay, waving at Gunn as at a second-rate exhibit of dubious authenticity. 'Now you've seen him.'

'We want to see him properly.'

'Go on, Piddles, go down and have your tea.'

'No, we have to look at him all over, so we shall know him *next time.*'

'If you don't hurry up, there won't be a next time.'

'Why not? Isn't he going to come and live with us, upstairs, in Lil's room?'

'Oh, Elfin.'

'You said he was Lil's friend.'

'Friends don't always live in the same house. You don't live with Quentin Finsberg.'

'Quentin Finsberg isn't my friend.'

'Well, he was.'

'He was till you said he couldn't come and live with me.'

'Go *on,* Piddingtons,' Antic Hay's voice twisted into a scream.

'Don't shout at us.'

'Don't tell me not to shout at you.'

'Why are you wearing those sacks?' Gunn asked by way of diversion.

'They probably aren't sacks at all, they probably come from some pricey infants' boutique,' Antic said.

'They are sacks. We cut them out ourselves. We're ancient Britons.'

'Keep right on to the end of the woad.'

'That's not funny,' said the smaller of the two children.

'You see what it's like. A house full of women.' Antic Hay creakily lowered himself on to a floor cushion and sat clasping his hands round his knees looking broody.

'Thank you for coming,' Xanthe said to Gunn.

'It was nothing.'

'There's no party today. I had my party last week.'

'I'm sorry I missed it.'

59

'I did not ask you.'

'That's all right.'

He watched the women round the coffee table. One of them, Poppy, had scrumpled some loose sheets of paper into a ball and they were batting it idly to and fro with the palms of their hands. Elfin stared at them with flinty contempt. Xanthe listed the parties she had been to recently and expressed regret that she had not met Gunn at any of them.

'I believe in play,' said Antic with a spurt of energy. 'Real play, I mean, like batting that paper ball about, not fascist organised games. In this house we all play.'

'Including the children?'

'Oh, not them. They've been brainwashed. They're rat-race freaks already. They are obsessed by sexual and social competition, go into a decline if they don't come top of their class – the whole bit. Where did we go wrong? It's too late for them, but there's still hope for us.'

'Stop talking. Stop talking. STOP TALKING.' Elfin's voice cut through her father's soft burble. He stopped talking.

'I want to talk,' Elfin said.

'There's baked beans, Piddles. And doughnuts,' pleaded Clara.

'The doughnuts are for tomorrow,' Elfin said.

'You can have them now.'

'You said they were for tomorrow.'

'Well, now I'm saying you can have them now.'

'The important thing is to rediscover our sense of play,' said Antic. 'It is *Homo ludens* not *Homo faber* who has raised man above the slime. If we want to learn how to love, we must first learn how to play.'

Poppy batted the paper ball at him. Antic took a great swing at it with a full shoulder-turn and sent it cartwheeling through the Memorial Exhibition. It hopped over the White Cliffs of Dover and disappeared behind. Antic stood on tiptoe and carefully stretched for it but could not reach it without standing on a chair. When he emerged clutching the forlorn object, the girls had turned away in a huddle of talk. Antic tossed the paper ball from one hand to another with awkward nonchalance as he resumed his theme : 'We have to go back to school, which of course as you recall originally only meant leisure. We have to relearn the arts of idleness, appreciate the value of the futile. One

60

of the most heroic passages in all literature is when Bertie Wooster spends a whole afternoon in his club throwing cards into a hat with some of the better element. If only – Christ, is that the time, I've got to go and see a man about some books. You'll stay for supper, stay the night, the weekend. . . .'

'I'm hard to shift once I'm dug in.'

Antic Hay cranked himself to his feet and threw the paper ball at the waste-paper basket; it fell short by several feet. On his way towards the door he met Lil returning with the cigarettes she had been looking for. He put his arm round her and kissed her on the cheek. She did not go so far as to turn away from him, but nor did she enter fully into the embrace, so that their encounter looked artificial, as though it was really a cover for the transfer of narcotics or the insertion of a knife in the ribs. Antic went out, followed by Clara and the Piddingtons.

From the doorway he turned round to tell Poppy to put the *Radio Timeses* back where she found them. Clara, beyond him on the landing, jerked her head, impatient with the fuss about a few old magazines. Lil and Poppy, hunkered down amid the piles of dog-eared newsprint, grinned up at him.

They were caught now in a moment of stillness, each ironically surveying the others. Gunn, standing a little apart from the strung-out group, remembered for the first time where he had seen them all before. This was the same broken-stepped group that he had seen scampering along in the rain past the little crowd outside the Last Great Englishman's house on his first night out in London. The brave's feather, bandit's sombrero and high-crowned topee, the dashing cloak and the spiv's overcoat had flitted across that scene of sober reverence with a stagey brio. Even here, backstage, the Clique did not look quite natural. Yet the four of them still had an unsettling air of mastery about them. The fifth, the one in the topee, was lacking.

After Antic had gone, a vast lassitude settled over the room. Gunn looked at the girls, trying to think of something to say. They looked back at him, sternly, as though daring him to commit the vulgarity of speech. He tried out a few openings in his mind but rejected them all as too obvious, the kind of remarks that had given conversation a bad name.

He glared at the sheet music of 'He's the Stuff to Give the Troops'. The black notes began to blur and knock against each

61

other on their staves. Eventually Poppy relented and, taking care to keep sideways on to him and continuing to stare vacantly straight ahead, said they had an old 78 of the song and Gunn said he would like to hear it.

The man singing on the record had a high, mannered voice in the fashion of the period. The record was scratched, which increased its feeling of remoteness.

> He's the stuff to give the troops,
> For he's the only chap
> To put us on the map;
> Just watch that foolish Hun
> Like a rabbit on the run;
> So pilots, loop your loops,
> He's the stuff to give the troops.

The singer's delivery – exaggerated, epicene, saucy – suggested that, when performed live, the ballad might have been accompanied by a sequence of obscene gestures. As the record came to an end, Gunn noticed that the beam on the lighthouse had given out, though the bulbous features continued to revolve.

# 6

'I didn't ask you to stay,' Lil said.

'No, your friend Antic asked me. Do you mind?'

'No. I just wanted to get it straight that it wasn't me who asked you.'

'I've got it straight,' Gunn said.

'Antic wants to turn the house into a crash pad, full of hippies and junkies and *crazy* people. But you're the only one here right now, except for Happy.'

'Happy?'

'You don't know about Happy? I thought everyone knew about Happy. He's *famous*.'

'One of the seven dwarfs?'

'Partly.'

'He either is or he isn't.'

'No, I mean he is a Snow White freak. But that isn't why he's called Happy. He lives with Poppy. In the basement. He's horrible really.'

'Happy and Poppy?'

'Yes.'

'Jesus. Why's he called Happy?'

'Short for Happening Man. Now do you know about him?'

'No,' Gunn said.

'It's really wonderful, not to know about the Happening Man. I like that.'

Gunn lay on the broken sofa in her white attic. The walls were all bare. It was as pure an attic as her brother Dick's, but different. Her little bookcase was filled with American novels; on top of it were propped three old sepia postcards of languorous naked women. Hanging askew from a nail on the wall was a stringed instrument which looked like a long-stalked onion sliced in half. It twanged slightly when he trod on a loose floorboard. Gunn

63

wondered whether it was a mandolin. The room was cold. She lay on her bed with the patchwork quilt around her like a hare crouched in its form.

'Can I stay here?' he asked.

'You said Antic already asked you.'

'No, here. In this room.'

'You can sleep on that sofa if you want, as long as you don't tell Antic. He wants the house to be filled with *couples*.'

'I don't want to sleep on the sofa.'

'That's sad,' Lil said. 'You have to if you want to stay in here. I'll give you a kiss, though.' She got up off the bed, shuffled over to the sofa, still clutching the quilt round her shoulders, and kissed him slowly. She crawled back on to her bed and looked across at him with a smile.

'It's a very uncomfortable sofa,' he said. 'The spring's digging into my back.'

'I know it does.'

'Aren't you rather a . . . tease?' Gunn asked.

'I don't like that way of talking.'

'Your other friends don't talk like that?'

'No, they all do, until they know about me.'

'What about you?'

'My *past*.'

'Well, tell me your past, then,' Gunn said.

'Not now, I'm too tired. It's a tiring subject.'

He let it go.

'Did you like Poppy?' she asked.

'She seemed all right, but I hardly saw her. There were the two girls together, it was hard to tell them apart properly.'

'Everyone loves Poppy. She's so . . . *sharp*.'

'And what about Clara then?'

'Oh, Clara's a different person totally. I like her because she's so genuine.'

'Yes,' Gunn said.

'I wonder what they thought of you, Poppy and Clara. They're always right about people.'

'Like children and dogs, they always know?'

'Poppy's more instinctive. She'd just kill you if she took against you, but Clara. . . .'

64

'Clara?'

'Clara weighs things up, carefully. She's so fair,' Lil said.

'If Poppy has such a fine instinct, how has she landed up with this man who's so horrible?'

'She knows he's horrible. You can't not.'

'But she likes living with him all the same?'

'Being right about people doesn't mean you choose the right person. It doesn't mean you want to choose the right person. You ought to know that.' She rolled over on to her back in a lazy victory roll.

This was not, to be sure, the way he had imagined the evening turning out, and yet there was something appropriate about it, all the same.

He lay on the sofa staring at the ceiling; to his surprise he found himself at his ease. Lil began to get ready for bed. She shut a half-open drawer, set her boots straight and folded back her bed clothes to a precise angle. Then she started to undress in the far corner of the room. She undressed quickly, like a boy in a changing room. He set his mind to breaking down the peculiar fragrance of the sofa upon which he was lying. Dust and old sweat certainly, but something else too, some intended scent of flowers, too faint to be named. She went next door. He heard the flush of a lavatory and the brushing of teeth. She came back.

'I'm coming to terms with this separate arrangement,' he announced.

'Are you? That's nice.'

'You don't think it's unmanly – to tolerate it?'

'You *are* old-fashioned.'

He had meant to be old-fashioned, to strike a period pose. He did not really feel his acceptance, temporary or otherwise, to be unmanly. It was, if anything, not so much feeble as . . . he couldn't quite think what. Matter-of-fact, a bit flat. Yet to sleep in the same room as her was a soothing thing. No harm could come to him. He was all right. He lay quiet.

'Light out?'

'If you like.'

She raised her arm to pull the string that put out the overhead light. The flap of her sleeve fell away; for an instant the arm was bare. He was moved by the sight of it, so thin and bony

65

at the wrist, then the slight swelling towards the elbow, and the echoing curve which vanished into the torn sleeve of the old shirt she wore to bed.

It was not dark in the room even after she had switched off. There was a skylight. He could still see the curve of her cheek against the sheet, and the untidy black shadow of her hair. The gentle tide of his desire stirred little physical symptom, no more than a rustle in the bracken, but it carried with it all the flotsam of old romance. Girls in garrets had golden hearts. Women with pasts were the only virgins.

Inside the room, silence. Outside, rain, the siren of a far-off ambulance. An owl hooting. More silence, more rain gravelling on the attic roof. A fox barking or what sounded like a fox barking. Brondesbury was a haven for wild life. Perhaps the fox had come over from Hampstead Heath; he had read there were foxes in Hampstead. Had she heard the fox? If she had not been brought up in the country, she might not know what a fox sounded like. Gunn thought of the big red animal baying at the city sky, its flanks trembling beneath the hair matted by rain; surely she would like that thought.

'Did you hear the fox?'

'Wha. . . ?'

'The fox.'

'What fox?'

'The fox barking at the bottom of the garden.'

'Is there a fox in the garden? How wonderful.' She was awake now. 'We must go and give it something to eat.'

'It will be gone by the time you get the back door open.'

'A saucer of milk or something.'

'A chicken would be better,' said Gunn.

'There's a frozen chicken in the fridge. Clara got it at Sainsbury's. We could de-freeze it.'

'Foxes normally eat them with feathers on.'

'A starving fox wouldn't be fussy.'

'How do you know it's starving?' Gunn asked.

'Why would it bark if it wasn't starving?'

'Oh, they do,' he said vaguely.

'It could live on the chicken for weeks,' Lil said.

'Perhaps it isn't a fox, after all. It could have been a car backfiring.'

'Not possibly. You know what a fox's bark sounds like.'

She got out of the bed, tugging the quilt round her, and bustled out of the room. He followed her. By the time he got down to the kitchen, she had the chicken out of the fridge. She stood still under the kitchen light holding the pale polythene-wrapped bundle in front of her with stiff arms. She looked like a doll holding a toy chicken from a doll's house.

'What's the quickest way to de-freeze it?'

'Put that thing back in the fridge.'

'I'll put it in a saucepan with some water.' She took it out of the wrapper and put it in the pan.

'Put it back. It's not your chicken,' Gunn said.

'If everyone thought like that, Oxfam would never have got started.'

'Oxfam feeds starving children, you're taking chicken out of their mouths.' They sat down and waited for the water to boil.

'Ooh, I say, midnight feast in the dorm, how scrumptious,' said Antic Hay in a stage Billy Bunter voice. He bumped against the doorpost slightly as he came in. 'What are you chaps having then?' He peered into the saucepan. 'I say, *chicken.*'

'It's your chicken,' Gunn said.

'We're de-freezing it. For the fox. We heard a fox bark.'

'A fox. Good, good.' Antic prowled round the kitchen until he found a half-empty two-litre bottle of wine. The label was stained. It had a picture of a swallow on it.

'Swallow, swallow,' he said, and took a long gulp, stretching his head so far back that he seemed almost to be balancing the big bottle on his lips. He passed the bottle round, then peered into the saucepan again.

'It's a lot to eat for the time of night,' he said after a pause.

'It's for the fox,' Lil said.

'For the fox. So you said. Shouldn't you give it to the fox raw? They don't like cooked food. At least to the best of my knowledge and belief, they don't like cooked food.'

'Raw, but not frozen,' Lil said.

'That's it. Raw but not frozen. Quite right.'

'I think that'll do,' Lil said, prodding the chicken. She took it out of the saucepan.

Antic looked at it closely and prodded it twice with his little finger. 'Just right,' he said. 'Raw but not frozen.'

67

Lil carried it out of the back door. They stood irresolute in the dripping night.

'Where do you think we should put it?' Antic said.

'By the back door. Foxes are scavengers. They always come to back doors,' said Lil.

'But we might frighten it away. Wouldn't be better out there somewhere?' Antic Hay squinted in the direction of what looked like the rubbish dump. 'He could eat it there without being disturbed.'

'I don't think that's such a good place,' Lil said.

'It's his chicken,' Gunn said.

'It *is* my chicken. I have certain rights in the matter.' He took the chicken from her and strode towards the far end of the garden where he deposited the pale blob. He stood in front of it with bowed head for a moment, like a dignitary laying a wreath, before returning to the back door.

'There,' he said. 'We have fed the hungry. Now we can all have a drink.'

They went inside and had a drink. Antic Hay swung himself up on to the draining-board and perched there with crossed calves.

'It's a devastating thought,' he said, 'how many people would you say heard the fox? Hundreds, probably thousands. Possibly the entire population of Brondesbury. Yet not one of them, not one, lifted a finger. For all they cared, the fox could have crawled off to its earth and died of exposure and malnutrition.'

'We can't be sure the fox will find the chicken,' Gunn said.

'That fox could find that chicken if it was a mile away and buried under six foot of concrete. Their sense of smell is unbelievable, quite unbelievable. You wouldn't believe it.'

'Oh, he'll find the chicken all right,' Lil said.

'Of course he will. But will there always be a chicken there waiting for him? That's the point. Will the neighbours feed him when we're away? It's all very well for them to worry about the starving Vietnamese, quite right to worry about them, of course, but what about our responsibilities to the world of living things in our own back yard . . . the foxes and rabbits, the blackbirds, the voles, the bumble bees? We have a lot to learn from the Buddhists in that department, no doubt about it.'

'What department?'

'Not taking life, that's what department,' Antic Hay said, burrowing in the fridge and coming up with a short length of salami sausage. 'It's a matter of education,' he continued. 'We should start a kind of wildlife community project here . . . get the neighbours to knock down their garden walls, involve the kids, have a pets' corner, it would become a feature of the urban landscape. There would be photographs in *The Times* : the first swallows arriving at the Brondesbury sanctuary, the Brondesbury vixen playing with her cubs. School outings would come to see me feeding the grass snakes through a pipette . . . the snake man of Brondesbury.' He took alternate bites from the salami and from a French loaf as he talked.

'But you hate animals,' Lil said.

'I hate books too but it doesn't stop me selling them.'

There was a hammering at the back door. Antic strode to open it. Outside stood a medium-sized, wet policeman. He looked rather pleased with himself.

'Mr Hay?'

'Yes, this is he,' said Antic. He had thrown his chest out and his left foot forward. He spoke with resonance, as if pleading guilty to the storming of the Bastille.

'This man says he knows you.'

The policeman moved into the room to allow them to see the man behind him. The man was a little smaller than the policeman. He was wearing a cloak and a rain-stained military topee; their outline corresponded so closely to that of the policeman's cape and helmet that he looked like the policeman's shadow.

'He says he lives in your house,' the policeman said.

'It's me, Happy. Remember? Please say you remember little Happy,' the man in the cloak said in a movie-rat's whine. He had a sallow face and bright black inquisitorial eyes, set close in to his beaky nose, more like a raven than a hawk.

'I have never seen this man in my life before,' said Antic with continued resonance.

'When I caught him in your garden, he was carrying this.' The policeman drew a sodden object from under his cape.

'I can identify this chicken, officer,' Antic said proudly.

'You can?' Having pulled off his moment, the policeman was letting his trained observer's eye roam round the kitchen. It rested on the bottle with the swallow on the label.

'This chicken was stolen from these very premises not half an hour ago,' Antic said.

'It was fantastic,' said the man in the cloak. 'I was just leaping from garden to garden being a kind of a strange person in the night. You know, look outa your window as you draw the curtains and wow! There's Batman riding the storm : Freak-out, thrombose, write to the *Psychic News*. And as I come over the last fence and swoop down on to your garbage dump, what do I see? A chicken. A tasty, oven-ready chicken. No feathers. Weird.'

'I hope you didn't smash up the fence, Happy. I've just had it repaired.'

'Listen man, the Happening Man doesn't smash, he swoops, swoooooop. . . .' He described an elegant landing with spread palms.

'Why were you leaping over fences, Happy?' Lil asked.

'Forgot my key, baby . . . was gonna come in de back way. Then I thought, let's make tonight Dracula Night and bring a little terror into your lives.'

The policeman put his notebook away. He no longer looked pleased with himself.

'Is this your chicken?' he asked Antic.

'It is. I'd know it anywhere.'

'And you do in fact know this man?'

'I cannot deny it.'

'I see.' The policeman gazed at the Happening Man. 'He is a friend of yours?'

'I wouldn't put it so strongly myself. But he lives under my roof.'

'You know it is a serious offence to waste the time of the police.'

'I plead guilty. Can I make amends?' Antic waved the bottle with the swallow on it.

The policeman looked carefully at the bottle as if he wanted to imprint its aspect on his mind. 'No, thank you,' he said. He looked at the Happening Man. 'I suppose I could do you for trespass,' he said.

'Remember what de Lord say, de Lord say forgive us our trespasses.'

'But then we haven't had any complaints yet. So I reckon I'll let you off this time.'

'Constable, you are a *good* man. De Lord will reward you.'

70

'So I reckon I'll leave you good people to get some sleep.' He accented "good people" with the most delicate stress imaginable.

'He'll go far in the force, that lad,' Gunn said after the policeman had left.

'Outasight,' said the Happening Man. 'No feathers.'

# 7

'Cornflakes . . . do you like cornflakes?' Antic darted about the kitchen distributing milk and sugar, butter and toast with earnest nimbleness. His two children watched him with impassive faces.

'Pour the flakes in first, Hay.'

'You know I like the flakes in first.'

'Sorry, Piddingtons, only got three pairs of hands.'

'I told you I like the flakes in first.'

'You look very fat, Hay.'

'They always call me Hay at breakfast. I keep on hoping that one day they'll address me as pater.'

'We call him Hay because he looks like a haystack.'

As he passed the back of Lil's chair, Antic bent and deposited a butterfly kiss on the back of her neck. She swatted it away.

'She's so lovely,' he said, looking across the table at Gunn in the manner of one old connoisseur selling a fine figurine to another.

'You've spilt cornflakes in my hair,' she said, shaking her head angrily.

'Stop bugging her,' Clara said.

'You must stay here Gunn. You fit in here very well,' Antic Hay said.

'It's kind of you, but I'm really looking for a place of my own.'

'No, you must stay here.'

'Nobody ever seems to ask me whether I want another person living in the house,' Clara said.

'Nobody asked me whether I wanted to live here,' Gunn said.

'Don't you? Everyone always wants to *live with* Lil.' Poppy gave the words the Clique treatment, low, nasal and thrilling. It was the first of the morning and it scalded Gunn like a hot shower. She was wearing an oilskin over her pyjamas. She looked

72

sleepy. The pyjamas had large Mickey Mouses all over them.

'Who left this frozen chicken out?' Clara said. 'You know they go bad if you leave them out, in fact this one has already gone . . . Oh no, it's covered with *mud*. Mud, why mud?' Her voice faded into a musing softness.

'It's something to do with Happy, dear. I saw him playing with it last night.'

'How do you play with a frozen chicken?'

'Happy is teaching us to play with everything . . . plastic macs, cornflakes, everything, even frozen chickens. We shall become as little children.'

'Stop *talking*, Hay.'

'Take us to school now, please, Hay. It's late.'

'Roight then, me old beauties. It be toime for your school larnin be it? Come along of old Antic then.'

'Hm,' said Elfin.

'Would you like to come too, Gunn? It's on your way to what I believe they call The Street. And I've got to go on down to the book-barrows in Farringdon Street.'

'All right.'

'Now then me old beauties, show a leg there, 'cos Maister Goater the famous scribbler from Lunnun is a-comin' too.'

'Come on, Hay.'

Gunn kissed Lil in a husbandly way and hurried down the front steps after Antic Hay, who had put on a cap of the sort sported by Hamburg sea-captains at the turn of the century.

Elfin and Xanthe ran down the broad pavement. At the street corners, they stopped and practised high kicks. The sun turned the young leaves on the privet hedges to a bright yellow.

'What's the Happening Man's real name?'

'Jim Brown, Jack Brown, can't remember which. I gave the wrong one once to some official ringing up and Happy was furious. Or perhaps I said the right one and gave him away.'

'He doesn't like being pinned down?'

'He disapproves of anything stereotyped and regular. He never has meals with the rest of us.'

'Yes, I didn't see any sign of him this morning.'

'Night of passion, I expect. Wait for me, Piddingtons,' he shouted down the street as the children disappeared round the corner. He broke into a heavy trot as they skipped across the road.

On the other side a large educational building loomed behind high walls. The walls were topped with broken glass.

'Well, here we are, Piddles. I won't come in because we don't want to keep Mr Goater waiting.'

'You have to come in because we're so late.'

'Surely you can cross the playground without. . . .'

'You have to come in.'

They went in through an ironwork door in the wall. The gaps between the bars of the door were covered with wire netting. He opened it with extreme caution as if it might be electrified. Just inside the door, an ample woman with a red scarf round her neck jumped at him and wrapped herself round him. He recoiled a pace or two.

'Tess, my dear, you were lying in wait for me.'

'As always, love.' She let go and stood back and looked at him with sparkling eyes. Overcome by the encounter, Antic waved a hand in Gunn's direction and muttered. 'Gunn . . . Tess,' before backing towards the door keeping a watchful eye to forestall any renewed attack. The children ran off, laughing.

'Hellish old bag. She's always there. Poppy teaches here, you know. Part-time.'

'She teach your children?'

'No, thank God.'

'I didn't know she was a teacher.'

'You wouldn't, to look at her. But we all seem to be members of the clerisy.'

'The clerisy?'

'The learned clerks, the intelligentsia. Teachers, preachers, scribes. The word crowd.'

'What do you class Happy as then?' Gunn asked.

'A mendicant friar, a pardoner – one of the half-educated wandering conmen who used to work the roads in Chaucer's day.'

'And yourself?'

'Oh, an antiquarian, a dabbler in our yesterdays.'

The sun glistened on street signs and tarmac, caught the drops shivering on the leaves. It was one of the first mornings after winter which reveal the toll winter has taken; the light poked into

74

neglected corners of grime and decay, exposed tired eyes and flaky skin. Antic Hay himself did not look exactly well, but there was something about him which suited the weather, a zestful front edged with melancholy.

'Lil's a damaged person, you know. Her parents more or less threw her out. She's been through a lot. That's why she's so . . . like she is.'

'Like what?' Gunn asked.

'Well, free.'

'In her affections?'

'I shouldn't have said that, but perhaps it's as well that I did. Now that you know, it may be easier for you to build your relationship upon an honest foundation.'

'Who said I wanted to build anything?'

'I hope you will treat her kindly. Do you mind if I just pop in here to pick up a parcel?'

They went into a second-hand bookshop, newly painted, with gleaming tooled volumes in the window. A thin girl in an old-fashioned tweed skirt was serving behind the counter. She handed him the parcel and said :

'Next time, please send somebody else to collect it.'

'I came in on purpose, Viva, because I didn't want there to be any hard feelings.'

'Well, there are. So don't come in.'

When they got outside, Gunn said :

'I won't ask.'

'Don't worry, I don't mind talking about it. She's a dear girl but the whole scene was a disaster. Don't you think she was a knock-out, though?'

'Yes and no,' said Gunn.

'You probably didn't see her properly. Would you like to go back and look at her again? There's a gap between the shelves where you can see her without being seen. I used to stop and look at her for five minutes every day on my way in.'

'I think we'd better be getting on. It's nearly half-past ten.'

'You're a serious man, you know. I like that.'

'What do you mean?'

'You have character.'

'You're not exactly nondescript yourself.'

'Hollow, I promise you, quite hollow.' Antic tapped his chest, cocking his head on one side to listen for the echo of his emptiness. 'I am a hollow man. We are all hollow men – except you.'

'Bullshit,' said Gunn.

'We are the stuffed men, leaning together, headpieces filled with straw. *Alas!*' He bellowed the 'Alas' so that three girls walking past them turned their heads and giggled.

As they approached a large pub, a small, round man came out through the swing doors, was nearly pinned between them indeed, as he turned to shout something back into the pitch-dark bar : Rory Noone.

'Ha,' he said, 'Gunn Goater, the young lion of Fleet Street. How are you keeping, young man?'

'Fit. You look blooming yourself. This is my new friend, Antic Hay. I've been staying with him.'

'Arctic, a cold name for a warm feller. I like the look of you, Arctic.' He surveyed Antic, shading his eyes from the glare of the morning with both hands. 'So you got fixed up with a place then,' he said to Gunn. 'I'm hoping for a place myself. You need a place to pull the birds.'

'Would you like to come and stay too?' Antic said eagerly.

'Ah well, I don't know about that,' Rory Noone said, taken aback by the invitation. 'I should have to make enquiries. Very kind of you, though. Are you a reporter too?'

'We are all reporters nowadays,' said Antic delphically.

'Because I prefer the company of reporters. I am at ease with them, do you understand? Arctic Hay – would that be your by-line?' He made the eye-shade with his hands again.

'Antic, in fact. A–N–T–I–C.'

'That what they call you, is it, Antic? An unusual name. And where's your place?'

'Brondesbury Park.'

'Ah, that's a bit far out for me.'

'Only just beyond Paddington,' Antic said.

'Because I don't like to be too far out these days. I like to be handy for the office.'

'Where is your office?' Antic asked.

'I am between offices. Temporarily, I am a colleague of Gunn here. But I am holding myself in readiness for a new appointment. At this very moment in fact I am on the starting blocks. Just an early wet to get the taste of breakfast out of my mouth,

76

and – off we go.' He did a little sprint along the pavement, coming to a halt with knees thrown high like a professional runner in a false start.

'You really must come and stay in my house,' Antic said. 'It's quite big and there's plenty of room.'

'Well now, Gunn, you know my tastes. You know the sort of man I am. Do you think the place would suit me?'

'No, I do not,' Gunn said.

'And why do you think that? I am not a fussy man. I am content with little.'

'Because there is not plenty of room.'

'But the gentleman says there is. He says it is a big house. Surely there would be a corner where old Noone could curl up and –'

'The house is already full.'

'Full of whom?' asked Rory Noone.

'Antic's family – and a couple of girls.'

'*Girls*. I'll just collect my bag from down the road and I'll be with you in a jiffy.'

'Great,' said Antic Hay.

'Christ,' said Gunn.

He did not like to think of Noone barrelling up the uncarpeted stairs into the chaste white attic, disturbing its stillness with his chatter and his smoke. It was not a place for him. Lil, he fancied, already thought little enough of journalism and little of The Street; Noone would confirm her suspicions.

'I'll give you the address,' said Antic.

Rory Noone took out a pencil and a reporter's notepad. Antic dictated the address in a loud voice. It looked like an impromptu press conference. Men hurrying towards their City offices stared back for a moment, trying to identify in Antic some celebrity tracked down by an energetic reporter.

'Now we have a problem here,' Rory Noone said. 'My luggage.'

'Your luggage. . . .' Antic hitched his trousers to the theoretical waist-level. Gunn noticed he seemed to do this when any idea caught his fancy; it was an automatic girding of loins.

'I left it in a hostelry near Liverpool Street. Saves paying those bandits in the left luggage office. But that was an unfortunate thing, you know. There was this girl, Inge – you met Inge, didn't you Gunby? Beautiful girl. I was on to a good thing with her, she had a nice place up Finsbury Park way, so I packed myself up and eloped. Twenty-fours house later I'm back out on the street. An argument about the late Major Vidkun Quisling was the start of the trouble, her happening to be Norwegian, though I'm not saying sexual incompat-i-bility didn't have something to do with it.'

'I thought Laplanders were Finns.'

'That's what I thought. But she turns out to be a frigging Norwegian Lapp. Anyway, here I am, one of London's homeless. You'll have to excuse my deshabilly, kind sir.' He gave Antic a mock cringing salute.

'But we must collect your luggage. We must get it immediately.'

'There's no cause to fret. This evening will be time enough.' Gratified by the anxiety in Antic's voice, Rory rocked back on his heels and cocked a leisured eye at the sky. The sun caught the stubble on his chin, umber dusted with grey. He ground his heel into the pavement and wiggled it to and fro, squinting down at it as if its ability to wiggle had suddenly caught his attention. Rory's indifference to the fate of his luggage spurred Antic on to further flights of urgency.

'We must rescue your friend's luggage, Gunn,' he said.

'Can't he rescue his own? I have work to do.'

'Of course he can,' said Rory affably. 'We must not detain our young friend here. He has a fine future ahead of him. I can hump my own bags.'

'No, no, we could share a taxi, or, better still. . . .'

Gunn took a curt leave of them and strode off in search of his future. As he turned the corner, he looked back to see them still in amicable conference : Rory spreading out his arms, presumably to indicate the size of a suitcase; Antic pointing down the street, perhaps indicating a possible route.

Even when they were out of sight, the question of Rory's luggage continued to prey upon Gunn. He had visions of huge shapeless bundles secured with ropes belonging to the same category of luggage as that which the giant Dusty had brought into Down But Not Out; of old pyjamas protruding through torn zips; of bottles and clanking tin mugs tied on with string. His own suitcases, now deposited at the modest hotel where he had spent his first nights in London, were battered enough, but it was a respectable sort of batteredness. As he picked them up during his lunch-hour, Gunn looked round the hotel lobby nervously. He would not have put it past the two of them to have worked out some complex plan by which Rory's luggage was parked here, leaving Gunn responsible for taking it on to Brondesbury. He did not relish the task of having to claim the malodorous bales from a disdainful porter while other customers quizzed him, mentally resolving never again to patronise a hotel which accepted such broken-down custom. Even when he was not put to this test, the vision of the clanking packages punctuated his afternoon and his journey back to Brondesbury.

As Gunn carried his own suitcases up the stairs, Rory Noone appeared on the attic landing. He seemed well established.

'This is a fine house,' he said, 'and the room service is first-class.'

Gunn peered into the little back room next to the water tanks. Lil was making up a bed.

'Have you seen Rory's suitcases?' she said.

'No,' he said, fearful that they had gone astray and that he would be condemned to spend the rest of the night hunting for them in desolate parcel depots and brewers' yards guarded by Alsatians.

'They're unbelievable.'

He peered glumly round the door. There were two of them, matching suitcases, the two most splendid suitcases Gunn had ever seen. They were made of some infinitely soft chestnut-coloured leather that appeared to breathe and tremble like the flanks of a live animal, like the Brondesbury fox perhaps. The gleaming metal handles were connected with a wealth of flaps and tassels to twin parallel strips of deep-pile leopard-skin running across the middle of each side.

'Wow,' Gunn said.

'At least they keep my shirts dry,' said Rory. He began to shave. 'There was a feller I did a story about made suitcases. He took a fancy to me and I did what I could to help him out.' He waved his razor in a manner suggesting limitless perversions of the truth.

Gunn looked at Lil to see how she was taking this stale breath of corruption blowing through her attic.

'You mean you changed the story to get him out of trouble?' she asked.

'Ah-ha-harr.' The noise Rory made seemed to imply that the matter was far more complicated and that when she was older she would understand the amusing naiveté of her question.

'But wasn't that wrong?'

Rory put the razor down with theatrical emphasis and turned to face her.

'Listen, my dear, when you've held down a fifteen-year-old kid on a table in a Glasgow backstreet and watched an old bag, three-quarters cut, scrabbling about inside her with a rusty knitting needle and had to empty the mess yourself in an outdoor shithouse, then you can start talking to me about right and wrong, and not until then. . . .'

'This man, the one who makes suitcases, had got this girl pregnant and told her to have an *abortion*?'

'No, love. That was another time.'

'I don't see what you mean.'

'Well. if you don't see what I mean it's not much good me going on telling you then, is it?' They were delighted with each other and exchanged reflected grins in the shaving mirror.

Gunn might have foreseen that she would like the seediness of Rory Noone but he had not imagined that she would find his corruptibility so alluring. Then he recalled the sensuous murmur in which she had talked of the possibility of *trouble* in Down But Not Out the night he met her. If there was any word Rory spelled, it was trouble.

Noone produced a quarter-bottle of whisky and passed it to Lil who took a swig. She looked at him with daughterly fondness.

Rory himself was doing his best to annihilate the twenty-five years that separated them. He shadow-boxed with a cushion, holding it out with one hand to deal it a haymaker with the other; then he clasped the cushion to his chest and rumba'd slowly round the room with one arm at the stiff horizontal, whipcracking his head from eyes-right to eyes-left like a Latin-American dancer.

'It's snug up here, very snug,' said Rory Noone.

'It was quite snug enough before,' said Gunn.

'You're going to lose your temper. I can always tell when a man is going to lose his temper.'

'You are quite right.'

80

'I can always tell. You're the type that goes pale . . . there, just below the cheekbone.' He dabbed lightly at the spot. Gunn seized his hand and wrenched it away. Rory completed the pirouette thus forcibly begun, coming back to his starting position to face the blast of Gunn's anger.

'You're in the way here,' Gunn said. 'Do you know what that means? You are an obstacle, a hindrance, a nuisance, a pain in the arse. Do I begin to convey anything to you?'

'Jesus, but you're a mouldy parrot,' Rory said. He sat down on the bed beside Lil and offered her a cigarette with aristocratic nonchalance.

'Have you ever in your life paused even if only for a moment to reflect that you might conceivably just conceivably have butted in where you aren't wanted?'

'He has a way with words, does Gunby, you have to give him that. But of course he's a young man with a future.' Rory Noone turned towards Lil and pointed at Gunn with his whole arm, as though pointing at a distant landmark.

'Oh Gunn,' Lil said, smiling.

'If you'd had as much of his Irish bullshit as I have, you wouldn't smile like that. You'd be running for your life. You'll never get rid of him, I'll tell you that.'

'I don't want to get rid of him.'

'That's the girl,' said Noone, passing her the bottle.

'Well, I want to get rid of him because he's a greasy parasite, an idle sponging. . . .' Noone had stopped looking nonchalant. Some other emotion – misery or rage – seemed to be taking hold of him. Gunn's fluent choler fled. A sweet, lazy shame stole over him. He grinned at Rory and put out a hand for the whisky bottle.

Rory pursed his lips and said : 'You're bloody daft. You know that? D–A–F–T.'

Gunn began to look on the two of them with a certain charity. Lil was an orphan in an attic. Rory was another, though of an earlier vintage. Beyond the din of the bedroom farce, there were sadder tunes to be heard. He sat down on Lil's other side. She smelled of soap. Rory had now stretched himself out on the sofa, expanding the story of the fifteen-year-old Glasgow girl and the knitting needles, having apparently quite forgotten Gunn's bombardment.

'Sing us a Glasgow song, Rory,' she said.

'A Glasgow song? I can't remember any.'

'You must know that one Gunn and I heard the other night. You know.... "Ah want ma hole...."'

'Oh yes, I know, it's not exactly a song, more of a chant really. It's a bit too rude for me.'

'I don't believe you. Go on.'

'All right. I can't refuse a lady. I can't even refuse you.'

She bridled as if he had tossed her a compliment. He took up the scabrous chant with an air of cheerful resignation. On his lips, it had none of the solemnity with which Dusty the dosser had endowed it. Rory made it a jaunty thing, more like a jig.

'You're quite a freak, really. I like your bad temper,' Lil said, as Gunn refilled her tooth-mug.

'You're quite a freak yourself.'

'This erotic conversation is too much for me,' said Rory Noone. 'It is time for poor old Noone to go to his lonely bed.'

'Goodnight, poor old Noone.' She kissed him and he shambled off.

'No, I really do quite like the look of you,' she said to Gunn.

'Well then, you could show it.'

She tried.

'I'm sorry. I can't make it yet.'

'Yet?'

'Not for about the last six months.'

'What happened?'

'Oh, a man. It wasn't his fault exactly. But after it was over, I just couldn't any more.'

'Not at all?'

'Well, if I was held down by a whole gang, obviously I could, otherwise not. I don't know why. It's more like a physical thing, muscular.'

'Our muscles seem to be working against each other,' Gunn said gloomily.

'I'm sorry. And you have such a nice muscle too. I'm rather fond of it already.'

'We'll just live in hope then, me and my muscle.'

'Take a seat, please, the doctor will be with you in a moment,' she said, drowsily groping in the dark.

There was a knock at the door.

'It's me, Noone.'

'What do you want, Noone?'

'Those water tanks make a terrible noise. I can't get to sleep at all and I have a testing schedule tomorrow.'

'Get the hell out of here, Noone.'

'Put cotton wool in your ears, Noone.'

'I've tried putting my fingers in my ears but the whole bed vibrates with the racket.'

'You've got bad vibrations, Noone,' Lil said.

'I was wondering if maybe I could shake down in here?'

'In here?'

'On this sofa. I'd be as quiet as a pianissimo.'

Without waiting for approval, he crawled on to the sofa and flopped down like a tired turtle. Gunn thought of trying to rescue his trousers from underneath the recumbent Noone but could not be bothered. Just as he was getting a good hold on sleep, he was dragged away again by Rory's angry grunts. 'Blast these springs . . . like a bed of bloody nails.'

'Blast Noone,' mumbled Lil, nearly asleep.

'What's that, my darling? I'm coming, my love.'

Barely rising above a simian crouch, Noone made his way across to the bed and, after a few false starts, burrowed his way into the bedclothes.

'For Christ's sake. . . .'

'Ah, shut up, Goater. You'll be able to tell your grandchildren you slept three in a bed, shock them rigid. You'll be the Charlie Dilke of the twentieth century. Jesus but it's snug in here.' Gunn could feel Rory enfolding Lil in an unseemly embrace.

'I'm so glad you and Gunn are friends,' she said.

'Mmm?'

'Before you turned up, I thought Gunn was . . . stuffy.'

'Oh, he's not a bad lad. And now for pity's sake, woman, let me get some sleep,' said Rory Noone, with the righteousness of a householder disturbed by revellers.

# 8

The Last Great Englishman was in his grave. The daffodils that sprouted in the graveyard had come and gone. Yet still the air was filled with ancestral vapours. 'I smell the putrescence of the late bourgeois age,' Antic Hay pronounced at breakfast. 'I should know, I am in the putrescence business myself.'

The shops were still full of souvenirs of the life and dying of the Last Great Englishman, and Antic kept his collection up to date. This cost him money, as he often remarked, but the collection was beginning to bring him a certain return. He rented out items for television documentaries; he himself was photographed for a Sunday newspaper in the midst of the Memorial Exhibition.

The Clique seemed to like newspapers and magazines. Most of the rooms at Brondesbury contained a pile of back numbers of the *Daily Mirror*, *Woman's Own* or the *Illustrated London News*, which they read with as much care as the issue of the day. At first Gunn thought his work would give him some interesting things to tell them. He passed on inside stories which he had heard at the office. But somehow each fresh revelation of crime and politics seemed stale and even tedious when he told it to them. The Clique had other interests.

Gunn, pointing at the politician being grilled on the screen: 'You know, they paid him a quarter of a million dollars to throw them the Boeing contract.'

Happy: 'That's a cruel thing to say, Gunn. He looks so innocent, like Mickey Rooney in an Andy Hardy picture – all clean and ugly and freckly. When he comes on, you think he's going to say "let's do the show right here".'

Clara: 'And where do you think he gets those strange, lumpy cardigans, like a west-country vet?'

Antic: 'Look at that sofa they're sitting on. Pure 1930's Maples. Terrific.'

Poppy : 'Do you think he still goes with his wife?'

Gunn : 'Well, I don't – '

Happy crawled across to the screen and glared into the eyes of the politician's wife. He seemed to be climbing over the arm on her sofa and on to her broad lap. 'Nooo, she looks neglected.'

They were not unkind to Gunn. It was just that their cool drawl made him feel so slow. Every time he tried to catch up, the Clique were waiting for him round the next corner. He was as clumsy as a snow-clogged army harassed by Cossacks. Happy in particular seemed so fly, so vigilant, so ahead of things. His raven's profile twitched, instantly sensing implications, nuances. His bright black eyes missed nothing.

He watched television with the alert, steady stare of a man in charge of an instrument panel. Behind him the rest of the Clique sat in a solemn row. Happy would squat at their feet in a lotus position, looking like a small boy in a family photograph except that his right arm was massaging the inside of Poppy's thigh. The Clique talked in low murmurs throughout the news programmes but hushed during the serials.

They were obsessed with a serial called 'Waiting-room'. It was set in a Harley Street house which contained the consulting rooms of, reading from the top floor to the bottom, a psychiatrist, a general practitioner, a paediatrician, a brain surgeon and, in the basement, a dentist with a comic moustache. They all shared a waiting-room.

'Apparently the Prime Minister. . . .' Gunn would start.

'Dr Tynan's got a new receptionist,' Happy said casually, as if he was breaking a silence.

'Not the one with the red hair?'

'Not the one with the red hair. A mousey one. She looks like she's going to have a breakdown.'

'I read an interview with the one with red hair. She lives quite near here.'

'You know the Prime Minister has this hate against dogs, well. . . .'

'I think Dr Fisher's a fag deep down,' Happy said.

'Mr Fisher,' Clara said. 'You don't call surgeons Dr.'

'I think he's going to be struck off the register.'

'You don't get struck off for being a fag.'

'It seems there was a dog at this. . . .'

'Mr Fisher's lovely. He's got such a kind mouth.'

'It's a slobbery mouth,' Happy said.

'Slobbery but kind. Do you know if Mr Fisher's a fag, Gunn? He doesn't look like a fag.'

'Who plays him?'

'I don't want to know who plays him. I don't want to know the names of the actors.'

'Do you mind if I switch over to the news now?' Gunn said.

'Do you want to?' Clara said. 'I mean it's not *our* news, is it?'

'News is a non-event. News is olds,' Happy said. 'The real news is what doesn't get into the news. God is dead. News is dead. Only kitsch lives. This is reeshauffay time. . . .'

'I don't see why he can't watch the news,' Lil said.

'It doesn't matter,' Gunn said.

'I mean, if he really wants to.'

'I don't really want to.'

Happy's contempt made Gunn both indignant and ashamed. He could not deny it – there was something old-fashioned about newspapers. He liked Rory's company but Rory was shopworn too. His imitation of the old sweat with a soft centre had been given too often.

Rory was ill at ease with the Clique. He and Gunn sneaked out for a drink when they had a chance.

'You have to get out for a breath now and then,' Rory said. 'I can't stand that hen-coop much longer. They'll drown in their own chicken-shit if they don't take care. They're irrelevant that's what they are. And I'll tell you another thing, they're not half as bloody clever as they think. Load of ignorant parasites.'

'Didn't know you were a social critic, Rory.'

'No, young man, I'm more what you might call a social historian.'

'Historian?'

'I like to do a bit of digging around my patch, nose round the nooks and by-ways to bring the place alive. For example, down there, second on the right past the church, that's where they arrested the Kilburn Poisoner.' Gunn peered at the jumble of red roofs beyond the bright green of the plane trees, half expecting a cornered killer to appear from behind a chimneystack and creep along the tiles, his white face staring down over the gutter at the hubbub below. 'And there,' said Rory with another broad sweep of his arm at the shop-fronts blazing in the sun, 'is the laundry I patronised when I lived in these parts. They ate my shirts for breakfast. Now here is an interesting pub, the Cranworth Arms, this is where Lenin and his lads used to drink, before my time of course. But the upstairs was a flophouse in my young days and I had my first woman in London there, sophisticated Spanish type, came on like a tank, I was terrified. It wasn't much of a pub though, too full of bloody republicans. But there's plenty of social history in there.'

Gunn stared up at the pub's dirty brick façade with its ornate frieze of encaustic tile. Over the dusty door there was a new sign painted to look like planks crudely nailed together. The sign said Ponderosa Saloon.

'I suppose if a barman stayed there long enough, he could have served both you and Lenin.'

'No chance, Gunby. Barmen don't live that long.'

'What do you think Lenin drank?'

'Gin and water, I expect. Or a port-and-lemon. One of those old bag's drinks.'

As they walked along, Gunn's mind still played on the image of the neat, bald man with the pointed beard trying to attract the barmaid's attention and make her understand his broken English through the din of the crowded Ponderosa Saloon.

'I'll show you this city, Gunby, I'll show you its crummy old heart beating, I'll show you how the ordinary bloody people live, the people they don't tell you about in school, the people who live and shit and screw and maybe love a little. . . . There now, not many people are aware of the fact but that's where Pavlova taught rich kids how to dance.'

The sky-blue LCC plaque shone on the stucco wall like a work of art. Every house ought to be plastered with plaques. Gunby Hallam Goater lived here. Here screwed Rory Noone. An inhabited city. Russians dancing and spouting. Poisoners poisoning. Barmen dying. Read all about it in the Noone news.

It was Rory who showed him round the office. At the back of the tinny partitions, underneath successive coats of cream and pale-green paint, behind the ramparts of back numbers and flaking, dark-green cabinets, the more grandiose materials in

87

which the founder had built were still to be seen : pilasters of marble, recessed and moulded panelling of some rare wood, Nigerian perhaps, which still retained its strange ginger colour and whorled grain, window frames of bronze metal opened and closed by elaborate handles, all in that same founder's mixture of Babylonian, Egyptian and Roman styles.

Over the years these Assyrian halls had been converted into a cut-price rabbit-warren, just as sheep may graze and shepherds squat in ruined halls where once a capricious emir chopped off the hands or heads of their ancestors. The office where Gunn's desk was now situated had a closer resemblance to the hovels of such squatters. It was called The Shed, after the popular stand at Stamford Bridge football ground. The sloping ceiling which roofed one corner of it was made necessary by the stairs to the canteen above. The clatter of feet going up and down formed a continuous background noise which made telephoning difficult. Older residents claimed to be able to distinguish descending steps by the weight of their despair, even, in moments of fantasy, to be able to pick out customers who had chosen the canteen's most notoriously stodgy dishes – the treacle pudding and custard, the shepherd's pie.

Here had drifted all the unassimilables on the paper, refugees from the continuous rearrangements of desks and jobs. The Shed was both a last staging-post for the decayed and an unpleasant initiation for the up-and-coming. Although by no means large, it accommodated an elastic membership. During the redecoration of other offices, as many as a dozen desks might crowd into its dim recesses. In slacker times only an occasional face peered out from behind the wall of filing-cabinets and rows of Hansard.

It was Rory too who introduced Gunn to the denizens of this neck of the backwoods : a tiny man with rimless spectacles who was, Rory said, a legendary war correspondent, the 'Last Man Out Of Dien Bien Phu'; the paper's astrologer, a prosperous burgher who at any lull in the talk said, 'You know, I must be one of the last men in London to drink pink gins'; and an elderly man with fine manners who was said to be the last reporter to join the old *Chronicle* before it folded. At first Gunn thought that this quality of last-ness must be peculiar to Rory's circle. But then he began noticing that everyone was doing it. His father wrote to him, complaining about the traffic and claiming to be nearly the last man in Lincolnshire to ride a bicycle. The man at the next desk claimed to be the last man he knew who wore sock-suspenders.

The Last Man Out Of Dien Bien Phu was now loosely attached to the features department. He rendered down best-sellers for serialisation and composed his own series on famous trials and little known war exploits. The beautifully mannered refugee from the *Chronicle* now dealt with the obituaries. The astrologer called in once a week to collect his huge mail. His services had recently been seduced from a Sunday newspaper for an undisclosed sum.

They all led lives of exquisite regularity, each clocking in at the pub opposite according to his own unvarying schedule. The Last Man Out Of Dien Bien Phu went over the way for his 'elevenses' at eleven o'clock on the dot. At half past eleven he was joined by the obituarist who took his first scotch of the day. A little later Rory would make his entrance. He flung open the double doors of the saloon and stood there challengingly, the light from the street flowing round his stubby outline. Then he would stride up to the small group at the bar and without greeting, join in the conversation as though he had only turned his back on it for a second.

'He's a sour bugger, that one.'

'Our lord and master was displeased?'

'Cut the piece to bloody ribbons and then said it needed a few anecdotes. *Anecdotes.*'

'You know why?'

'Why what?'

'Why the old man was not his usual sunny self this morning. Keith cabled. From Zagreb.'

'I thought he was in Dar-es-Salaam.'

'Mombasa in fact. He was, but he isn't, but that's where they sent his notice to, which apparently hasn't caught up with him, as he is currently offering Unbelievable Exclusive Soonest if only they'll send him a few thousand dollars exes.'

'What's he on then?'

'Same old story.'

'Not the son?'

'Mm.'

'Whose son?'

'Oh wake up.'

'But that's all cobblers, isn't it?'

'That is what our lord and master is beginning to suspect.'

'Keithie is something else. They never seem to catch up with him. I don't know how he keeps it up.'

'I don't know how any of us keeps it up.'

'We don't, is the answer.'

'It's so long since that I've forgotten which way up it goes.'

'Didn't you read the instructions on the bloody packet then?'

'Ah but that was the special offer.'

They drank their way over the hump of the morning, eventually trickling back to their desks to fend off calls from angry superiors and flustered press officers, thence to be carried back across the street in the great lunchtime surge. The ebb and flow of these tides appealed to Gunn as did the thought of their brackish eddies washing up on distant shores: Keith flitting from Mombasa to Zagreb and on again, one step ahead of the messages of recall or dismissal, always managing to surface again with promises of irresistible scoops.

Yet even Keith's footwork seemed to belong to a pre-war age. The only fresh thing about him was his whereabouts.

It was all stale. Happy was right. News was olds. Keith too was working over trodden tracks. They all lived in a used-up world. Even their emotions had had their day.

'Love,' Antic Hay said, 'is the last of the bourgeois illusions. Love is for the chop. In the new era we shall return to the hygienic common sense of the ancients. There will be pair-bonding, blessed by the state for the purpose of procreation. The rest of the time, we shall take our sex as and when we need it.'

'Stale buns,' interjected Happy in a schoolgirl voice.

'You, or for that matter, I,' Antic continued, 'will see a girl in the street. We fancy each other. Zowee! Into the government comfort station on the corner. Afterwards, we shake hands and go our respective ways. No more fuss than drinking a glass of water when one is thirsty, in the words of the divine Alexandra.'

'She another of your old slags?' Clara asked.

'Alexandra Kollontai was the pioneer of free love, my dear. Lenin couldn't stand her, said he didn't fancy drinking from a glass touched by so many lips. Lenin was pure bourgeois when it came to sex.'

90

'You need some middle-west type to play Lenin,' said Happy. 'Henry Fonda would make a great Lenin.'

'Leaving aside the obvious external physical criteria,' Antic continued, 'what reason is there to prefer one person rather than another for the purposes of sexual congress?'

'Or maybe Glenn Ford. No, Glenn's too much the crooked lawyer from the East. Glenn would do for Trotsky maybe. Hank Fonda would be just great for Lenin.'

'You don't know what you're talking about,' Clara said.

'You think perhaps that I am neglecting the woman's point of view,' Antic said.

'You don't know what you're talking about.'

'The truth is that the emotional differences between the sexes are the most superficial product of early conditioning. Among the old Bolsheviks, for example, there were no distinctions of any sort between the sexes, no allowances had to be made.'

'You are not an old Bolshevik.'

'All I am saying is that beyond the secondary sexual differences. . . .'

'Here come Elfin and Xanthe.'

'Elfin and Xanthe must learn the truth some time and the sooner they learn it the better their chances of growing up into healthy human beings – '

'Like yourself.'

'Like me, if you wish.'

Unlike Poppy and Clara, Lil seemed to enjoy listening to Antic. She did not laugh at him, although she didn't appear to agree with him either, judging by the few remarks which she threw out. It was more the erratic flow of his words which she seemed to like. She gazed at him with the vacant absorption of a small boy watching ripples in a stream.

'Well, he's not sweet exactly, but you know. . . .' Lil tried to explain.

'He's more sort of. . .' Poppy said.

'Kind?'

'No, not really kind.'

'Perhaps Antic *is* sweet.'

'No, he isn't sweet. He's pathetic,' Clara said.

'Pathetic, ye–es.'

'It's not irresistible, his pathos. But it's sort of *intriguing.*'

91

Antic's company meant more than that to them, though. His timewasting was a kind of assurance that there was time to spare. Gunn watched Lil watching Antic and felt that all would go well. Suddenly perhaps she would jump to her feet and take Gunn's hand and lead him upstairs and they would make love till noon the next day. It would all happen in the most matter-of-fact way you could imagine, like drinking a glass of water. It had not happened so far.

In fact, things seemed to be moving in the other direction. They lived on the same floor. But that was now all. There had been a week of the same imperfect communing in bed together. Then Rory moved out. 'I have had an interesting offer,' he said and would say no more. When Lil came back tired from Down But Not Out late that night, she found that Gunn had moved his things out of her room. Gunn, tucked up in bed in what had been Rory's room, heard her run back down the stairs and call his name several times on a rising note. He lay quiet with some satisfaction. She opened the door and came into the room where he lay.

'What are you doing in here?'

'It seemed like a good idea.'

'You're playing at being hurt.'

'What?'

'You heard what I said.'

'No I didn't. Because I've got cotton wool in my ears. For the water pipes.'

'Oh. It's quieter in my room,' she said.

'I find it quieter in here. I can think better.'

'What do you want to think for at this time of night?'

'Because I do.'

Yet they still saw each other every day, made plans together, got on better at this distance, it seemed. Only occasionally did they in a teasing way return to the dangerous ground.

'Do you think two people really need to know each other to. . . .'

'Or can get to know each other? Is there such a thing as love, is that what you mean?' They were having lunch at I Scacchi di Beluzzo, a cheap haunt of his, named after a chess game legendary in the annals of Italian chivalry, in which a prince had played against a duke for his daughter's hand, or something of the sort. The waiters, dressed in grubby chessmen's uniform, were a jovial, unshaven crew given to bellowing Italian pop tunes while shovelling the *tagliatelle* on to the plate.

'No, I mean should there be such a thing as love?'

'*Permesso, dottore.* Ees hot and lovely, like the lady.'

'*Grazie.* Why not?' He said.

'Isn't love bound to be selfish, even when it's honest, if it ever is?'

'*Fagiolini, professore.* They are a *canzone d'amore.*' The Red Bishop blew a kiss at the beans.

'I thought it was supposed to be unselfish,' Gunn said.

'Of course it's selfish. You concentrate on one person, forget everyone else, your parents and friends, oh, everyone.'

'Do you think anyone else lives like us?' He asked abruptly.

'Blocked, you mean?'

'Call it that, if you like. I don't like it.'

'Which – the phrase or the thing?'

'Both,' he said.

'I don't know. Are you complaining then?'

'Yes.'

'I suppose you don't think it's *normal,*' Lil said scornfully.

'It isn't. Statistically.'

'Natural, then. You don't think it's natural.'

'Well, we can't go on like this for ever.'

'Ees everything all right, *dottore*? You like the *Ossobuco*?'

'Who said we were going to go on for ever?' She enquired.

'Isn't that what – aren't you supposed to feel like that? Isn't it the test, whether you think of being together permanently?'

'What's so great about permanence? Why does something being permanent make it beautiful? Anyway, that's not why you mind. You just think you look *silly.*'

'Is that what I think?'

'I mean, you don't have to worry,' Lil said earnestly. 'Nobody's looking.'

'But it is a bit strange. In the Sixties. H. M. Bateman cartoon : The Man Who Wasn't Permitted To in the Permissive Age.'

'Who's H. M. Bateman?'

'He drew pictures of people making exhibitions of themselves. Only cartoons my father ever laughed at.'

93

'Oh *exhibitions*. You can always have other girls, you know. I'm not stopping you. Do you have other girls?'

'No. I don't want other girls.'

'It might be bad for you, not having them? "Day after Day there are Girls at the Office",' she sang.

'You can't have everything.'

'You can't have everyone.' She laughed at her own joke. Her lower lip trembled with pleasure as she laughed.

Even now, teasing him with deliberately crass words, she could not estrange him. He could find in himself none of the apartness or the inability to feel that was attributed to his generation. He rose to her as a fish leaps.

Yet there remained this unconsummated business, this intimacy unachieved. Gunn did not like to use even in his mind the rougher language of his colleagues, not only because there remained in him an unacknowledged core of gentility, a still inviolate chivalry but also because that sort of talk did not fit the case. He could not think in terms of not having had her; it was so manifestly she who would not have him.

As the soft evening came on, they linked arms and set off for Happy's Happening. The Clique had been talking about this artistic event for weeks, but as Gunn climbed the steps of the Brondesbury Institute he felt irritable and low-spirited.

They almost all came : Rory Noone with noisy reluctance, the Hay family, Elfin and Xanthe rubbing their eyes with sleep rather than wonder, Tosh and a few of the more inquisitive dossers invited by Lil. Of the people Gunn had met since he came to London, only Dick and Margaret had refused, telling Lil that after careful thought they had decided they did not entirely go along with the concept.

The rugged terraces of the Institute were well peopled. The spectators had arranged themselves in separate clear-cut groups. Near the front sat a well-dressed crowd, all shirt-ruffles and velvet, described by Happy in a gangster mutter as 'my backers'. The backers were careful to keep their voices down. Only an occasional effete vowel strayed up to entertain the rougher element behind them. Antic Hay had disposed his party towards the middle of the steeply tiered benches; 'for we are persons of the middle station', he intoned in the rather deeper voice he assumed

94

on public occasions. Clara unpacked sandwiches and flasks of swallow wine from a large flower basket of Greek aspect. 'We wanted to give the Happening something of the flavour of a *fête champêtre*,' Antic explained. Gunn thought they looked more like picnickers forced indoors by the rain.

A couple rose from the velvet-and-ruffles crowd and began to climb the tiers towards them. They both capered from one bench to the next with an assumption of child-like innocence. Their faces were vaguely familiar to Gunn from the newspapers, their names more so from Antic's conversation. They were in their way minor celebrities.

Johnny 'Brick' Wall was tall and bald. He had no back to his head and a long flat face like an Easter Island god. He also had a high, flat voice in which he doled out argot. He traded on his alleged criminal connections. If you wanted a bouncer or were harassed by hoods demanding protection money, Brick was the man to go to, or so it was said by people who did not in fact require such services. His principal employment was as business manager of his companion's boutique, 'Smash Hit', where he spent a lot of the day lounging around and accosting the customers with such abrupt greetings as 'Come to my drum', 'Let's split' and 'Like, we could make it together'.

Minty, the boutiquière, was short and stubby with deep red frizzy hair which looked like a wig. She was a good-natured energetic banker's daughter, Brick's type. They both seemed to have a glow of fame about them. Unwillingly, Gunn was awed.

Brick and Minty talked in slow glum phrases about the movements of people he had never heard of.

'He went to the Coast.'

'Did he now?' said Antic brightly.

'Yeah.'

'When's he coming back then?'

'I wanted to see him in New York. But he just flew out.'

'Ah,' said Antic.

'Deedee split.'

'Like, it didn't work out,' Minty put in.

'You surprise me,' Antic said.

Gunn began to wonder just how well Antic knew the persons under discussion.

'Deedee flew out too.'

'To the Coast?'

'No, to Mexico.'

'Acapulco?'

'Nah, Acapulco was last year.'

'Tijuana,' Minty said, making the word sound like a sneeze, 'The grass is fantastic.'

'Is it indeed? That's great,' Antic said. His initial pleasure at being recognised by these glittering personages was giving way to unease.

'Dave's in Marrakesh.'

'I don't think I know Dave.'

'He's in Marrakesh.'

'He used to be with Smudge.'

'What happened to Smudge?'

Brick smiled and flipped his wrist in a gesture which could have meant either that he didn't know or didn't care or that Smudge had vanished, perished or even triumphed in the way that Smudge might have been expected to. As they sat down for the start of the show, Gunn made a mental note to ask Antic about Smudge.

The stage stretched the whole width of the cold hall. One corner was taken up with a grand piano, evidently pushed there because it was too large to move off the platform. In the opposite corner reared the White Cliffs of Dover, lent to Happy by Antic with a flurry of instructions and warnings to take extreme care. Its chalky ramparts and bulbously anthropomorphic lighthouse had dominated Antic's sitting room; in this open space, they seemed small and insignificant, the monstrous bulldog features reduced to feeble pastiche. Otherwise, the floor was bare. From the rafters hung half a dozen thick ropes, each reaching down to about a yard above ground level.

'Looks like a bleeding assault course,' Rory Noone said.

The cheerless scene was relieved by a hammock strung diagonally at a height of six feet in front of the White Cliffs of Dover. As they arrived, Poppy in a black bikini was climbing up the nearest rope and clambering into the hammock.

She was always good at climbing ropes, said Clara with that breathy reverence she reserved for all reminiscences of the Clique at school, of Poppy in particular. She was the first to be kissed,

Clara said. She had climbed over the school wall and run down a long lane to meet the boy. None of the others had dared as much for love.

Poppy settled herself firmly in the hammock, holding the sides with her hands. She began lazily to rock from side to side. The audience straightened into attention. Gunn thought of the skinny schoolgirl hoisting herself over the wall and running down the lane.

Happy came in through a side-door and strolled across the stage, scratching his chest. He was dressed as usual in tee-shirt and jeans. Poppy beckoned him over to the hammock and leaned over the edge, haranguing him. He looked up at her, grinning at her beneath his dark glasses. He went out.

There was a hush. Then Happy came back in again carrying a blanket which he threw up to Poppy. She wrapped it round her. He exited to scattered applause.

'Excellent,' said Antic Hay. 'The spontaneity of the ordinary. You see a girl in a hammock. The girl feels cold. She asks for a rug. He fetches one. A perfectly banal event given intense significance by the conventions of the stage – far deeper significance in fact than the dreary chatter written by so-called playwrights.'

'It's bloody cold in here,' Clara said. 'You told me not to put Elfin and Xanthe in their anoraks.'

'It'll warm up soon, love,' Lil said.

There was an intermission of some ten minutes. One of the well-dressed gang began a slow handclap but was shushed by the others.

With a sudden burst of activity, the show began. The lights went down. A projector at the back of the hall threw whirling patterns of light on to the back wall of the stage. The hall was filled with the squeaks, jangles and squawks of concrete music, sounds which were unexpectedly cheerful and soothing. A spotlight, after several near misses, homed in on Poppy rolling violently to and fro in her hammock. She had thrown away the rug.

'Seasick,' said Rory Noone.

'Don't spoil it,' said Lil, leaning forward.

Three more girls, also in bikinis, one rather fatter than the others, trotted in and began climbing the ropes. When they had

97

got a little way off the ground, they nervously jumped to the next rope and swung to and fro.

'I find this all rather too stagey,' Antic said.

'I see plenty Jane, but where Tarzan?' Rory said.

Happy re-entered, wearing a cardboard mitre but otherwise unchanged. He was carrying a spray gun and a pot of paint. His walk had a carefully untheatrical shamble to it. He stood grinning at the audience for a bit. Then he turned towards the nearest girl and began spraying her with the paint, which turned out to be green. He started at her midriff and went down to her feet, then went all the way back up to her neck. As she was still spinning on the rope during the operation, the paint went in a spiral round her body. She looked like a stick of green seaside rock.

Two of Happy's henchmen shambled in, similarly equipped. They grinned at the audience and pointed at their paint pots before starting on the other girls who, like the first one, remained expressionless. Poppy too was spattered with the green paint. One of the henchmen aimed his spray gun up at her with the care of a gardener spraying the top of a climbing rose.

At this moment the White Cliffs were switched on. The lighthouse revolved satisfactorily, but its puny beam could not compete with the spotlight on Poppy or with the projector throwing its garish kaleidoscope.

'Happy never told me about the paint,' Antic grumbled. 'He'd better keep it off the White Cliffs or. . . .'

More henchmen came in and handed pots of paint and spray guns to the people in the front row who were reluctant to take them, until one of the henchmen gave them a burst from his own spray gun. There was a squeal, and resistance to joining in crumbled. The men took their spray guns and scrambled up on to the stage, firing wildly. The women grimly accepted the fortunes of war and, on the instructions of the henchmen, began dancing limply in the clear space in front of the stage. Happy wandered down amongst them with a fixed grin on his face.

'He must be high,' said Antic.

'Are you joking? He's been walking on the ceiling since Tuesday. Shows how much you notice in your own house,' Clara said.

Happy climbed back on to the stage and pulled a lectern out

98

from beside the piano. He carefully placed it in the middle of the paint-spattered chorus swinging doggedly on the ropes. He then stood behind it and recited Rupert Brooke's *If I should die* in a soulful manner.

'It's all a bit too Edith Sitwelly for me,' said Antic. 'I had hoped for something rather more Brechtian in tone.' Having enjoyed the early low-key passages, he seemed irritated by the relative brio of the present scene.

'I think it's nice. In a way,' Clara said. 'Only the next thing is Happy will go *too far*.'

Happy moved on to *Three Blind Mice*. He delivered this in blues style larded with raucous terminal-junkie shouts. Then he unzipped his fly and urinated first to his right, then to his left, and finally straight ahead, falling well short of the front row, but sprinkling with golden drops the ruffles and velvet of the press-ganged dancers.

'Oh, not that again,' said Clara.

'Seen one, seen 'em all,' Rory Noone said. 'What's he going to do for an encore?'

'Let us hope there will be no encore,' Antic said.

But Happy knew his audience. The applause from the dossers in the back rows shook even the impassive girls twirling on the ropes. The dancers, on the other hand, stood for a moment in startled silence. Then a young man in a dark suit already hatched with green paint rushed the stage, wrenching at his fly, and charged up close to Happy. When he stepped back again, Happy's tee-shirt was drenched and his face was bedewed as far up as his black spectacles.

'We have become as little children again. Throwing paint, seeing who can piss the furthest, doing what comes naturalee,' Antic said.

Happy remained quite still, grinning at the bellows of rage swirling round him. The man in the dark suit, having shot his load, stood a few paces from him at the edge of the stage. He seemed unable to decide what to do next. One of the girls who had been dancing below tugged at his trouser leg. He put a hand down to ward her off, then recognised her as an ally, took her hand and jumped down, like an infantry-man regaining his trench after a tough patrol in no-man's-land. Gunn and the others began to clamber down over the benches towards the stage, dodging

99

round some of the more timid girls in ruffled shirts who were fleeing towards the heights. The audience had dissolved into a panic-stricken rabble.

'It's like the Odessa Steps,' Antic shouted in Gunn's ear.

'Like what?'

'The Odessa Steps.'

'Oh.'

Happy went on grinning. His zip was still open. He reached down into it and began very slowly pumping.

There was a great crash. A scream. A series of lesser crashes and lesser screams. Gunn suddenly got wind of the fresh urine.

Happy stopped pumping. In any case he had lost the attention of his audience. Gunn turned his eyes to see the hammock empty and swinging wild. Down below, kicking legs in black tights protruded over the top edge of the White Cliffs which had suffered a severe landslip. The lighthouse in the likeness of the Last Great Englishman had completely disappeared.

Poppy hoisted herself out of the wreckage. The green paint all over her was now mixed with blood and plaster from the White Cliffs. She felt her hip and her knee with some solicitude. She was trembling too but not, it seemed, with fear, for she found no difficulty in standing up and shouting 'I told you never to do that again.'

'C'mon baby. You should have stayed in that lil'ole hammock,' said Happy, 'and leave your Big Daddy to ennertain the folks.'

'I was coming down to stop you. It's phoney and it's disgusting.'

'It's the one I was born with, babe. Can that be bad?'

'Oh no. There must be a hundred pounds worth of damage there,' yelled Antic who had jumped up on the stage to inspect the wreck. 'I won't blame you, Poppy. You were provoked. But you're a stupid, callous bastard, Happy. I was crazy to lend it to you. I knew you didn't appreciate its value. I knew you had no understanding. Look at it, look, look – ' He broke down, keening over his treasure, stroking the fractured cliff-top in helpless grief. It took him several minutes to recover the composure needed to bend over and tug out the battered lighthouse from behind the cliffs. He held it to his chest like a baby.

'That's the end, I promise you. That is the end. It really is. The end. The end,' Poppy cried, battering her fists on Happy's sodden chest.

'Get out of my house you shit. Get out, get out, get out,' Antic yelled, tenderly dusting the hulk of glass and metal and plaster.

'Waal folks, I reckon we'll take a break there,' Happy said.

# 9

'You can't be serious.' Gunn said.

'Of course not,' said Happy. 'Nobody can be serious now – unless you're helping Bengalis to grow rice. But if you mean, do I mean what I say? Yes, I do mean, it baby. I really, really do.'

'It's a very nasty idea.'

'Nasty? Nooo. . . I don't think *nasty*. The rest, the spiritual bit, is all harmony, I know that. But to be deprived totally, well that's *bad*. And Poppy is, you know, passionate. So – why don't we swap, like in the Sunday papers?' He lay back on the unmade divan bed. The grin faded as he looked at the ceiling. From this angle his profile seemed ascetic, almost noble until another wave of mirth broke over it. 'And think of Antic. The comings and goings, especially the comings. Chicks on the stairs. The ceiling, the floor . . . every little bump, you know, and he thinks they're at it again . . . then the ceiling again, now they must be. . . . Whoo, it'll be torture, man.'

'Sounds nastier every minute.'

'Well, you must take us basement folk as you find us. Down here we don't aim high like you attic people. We just give the beast in us a big hello.'

'Anyway, what makes you think Lil would even. . . .'

'Hey, you do *want* Poppy, don't you? I've seen you looking at her like *hungry*.'

'I look at a lot of girls.'

'Don't we all, baby.' Happy managed to squeeze a noxious complicity out of him. Gunn could not remember quite how he had come to admit his problems with Lil in the first place. He had come down to the basement only because one of the children told him when he arrived home that Happy wanted to talk to him. Happy started off by describing the repercussions of last week's

Happening – the £10 fine imposed on him for insulting behaviour, the bill from the local council for the damage to the hall, the withdrawal of his backers. From this harmless beginning Gunn somehow found himself tangled in an intrusive, alien conversation. Yet he could not bring himself to break off. Every time he thought he had been disgusted beyond enduring, Happy would change direction completely, make him laugh, romance him with an anecdote.

'I expect that was what bugged you about the Happening – Poppy being sprayed with paint. That *beautiful* body . . . all . . . defiled.'

'She hasn't got a beautiful body, particularly,' Gunn said.

Happy giggled, holding his hand over his mouth as if to repress a cough. Gunn wondered how high Happy was. His eyes looked normal, but his voice had more indolence than usual.

A knock at the door.

'Come in. That will be my brother. No relation.' He chuckled more loudly.

A young black man entered. He wore spectacles and a dark suit of old-fashioned cut. He was not very tall and slightly built. His appearance was attractive in a markedly self-effacing mode.

'Come in, Nigger. This is Nigger Brown. Gunn Goater. This is the man who's trying to take my girl away from me.'

Gunn looked at the young man to see whether he minded being called Nigger. It seemed not. He more or less ignored Happy and shook hands with Gunn, smiling. He had a charming smile.

'Nice meeting you, Gunn,' he said.

'We met first at a writers' workshop. In Berlin,' Happy said. 'We shared the same name, though worlds and skins apart. Him from shantytown, Kingston, by way of Bedford-Stuyvesant, New York City. Me? Well . . . ,' he spread his hands in impish mystification. 'I wanted a name for him, a name to wrap up the whole amazing connection. It came to me one afternoon as I was moseying down the Ku-'damm. It had to be . . . Nigger Brown. Just had to be.'

'Why did it have to be? The name seems plain rude to me.'

'How do you think it seems to him then?' Happy crowed. 'To him, Nigger Brown is all the suffering of his people, all the lynching and segregated lunch counters and Sidney Poitier movies. But

103

to us what is Nigger Brown? The colour of schoolgirls' stockings. Wow.'

'You can call me Jim, if you find it embarrassing,' the young man said. 'But most people do call me Nigger.'

'What are you doing over here?' Gunn asked.

'Over here? That's perfect. Beautiful.' Happy bounced up and down on the divan with pleasure. 'Niggers ought to know their place. They ought not to come *over here* bothering white folks without a licence.'

'I'm studying mostly,' said Nigger Brown, twitching an arm with books under it. Gunn peered to look at them. Nigger held them out so he would see : *The Wretched of the Earth* by Frantz Fanon and *How to Make Your First Million in Property* by somebody indecipherable.

'Hey, would you believe it, Nigger. This cat wants to trade in his own model and take my Poppy flower in part exchange ! What do you think of that?'

'Mm . . . well.' Nigger looked amused, expectant.

'Don't try that on. It's your idea, and you know it, Happy. It's typical and stupid and disgusting. Only you could. . . .'

'Okay, okay. Perhaps I did think of it first. But, you know. . . .' He pulled his knees up to his chin and gave a pixie grin from between his hands.

'What do the chicks think? Have either of you asked what. . . .'

'Don't try and involve me in this,' Gunn said sharply to Nigger.

'They're nice girls,' said Nigger. He looked for a place to put his books down in the crowded basement. With the back of his hand he carefully wiped some cigarette ash off a low table into his other hand and shook it into a tin dustbin. He placed the books in the swept area. 'They have class,' he murmured. '*I* don't know, it's a weird kind of scene.'

'Well, we'll have to see about it,' said Happy, adopting the teasing manner of a parent dangling a treat before a child.

'Look, this is nothing to do with me – or Lil,' Gunn said. 'Whatever you may have cooked up down here, I – '

'Don't go on about it, please, man. Would you just do me that favour? It's a mood thing, no use rationalising.'

Gunn protested further but heard himself being verbose and stiff. Why could he not make himself sound convincing? Nigger's amused expectancy began to wear thin; he began to fidget; he sneaked a couple of looks into the top book on the pile; all these protestations were too much. Gunn dropped the subject; the conversation had left grease marks all over him. At the same time, he was not exactly angry, or at most he felt angry that he was not angry. It was unreasonable somehow to expect the other two to see how repulsive the notion was. But why should they be exempt from the moral law? If he had not the style to refute them in argument, then he ought to steer clear of them. But then there was something rather charming, quicksilvery, original about them too. What were they on about now?

'The mortgage is go for next week, man.'

'The Trust wants six names now, not four,' Happy said.

'Oh, well, Andrea has a brother and *he* has a sister-in-law. No sweat.'

'The Council won't know?'

'That they're still in Jamaica ... ? Oh, no.'

'I've told the commune that if any one blows this thing, they're through – like that.' Happy gave a lazy karate chop at the air.

Gradually the project unfolded. It was quite a project; there was a bit of everything in it. There was money in it, for a start; whence and how and for whom it was not quite clear, but there was money. And there was charity, to black people from white and, it seemed, somehow back again, though perhaps not ending up with quite the same white people as it had started with. And there was idealism in it, and dancing and sex and living freely and together and holding all things in common, although again it seemed that perhaps some people might, so to speak, have more of a hold on the things that were held in common than other people.

Gunn soon got the outline of it : a mortgage granted by the local council on concessionary terms to an immigrants' housing association, half the property thus secured to be let out to witless monoglots fresh off the boat, Pakistanis perhaps, at rents sufficient to repay the entire mortgage, the other half to be occupied rent-free by a multiracial commune whose twin consuls would be Happy and Nigger, the whole beautiful experiment in living to be shielded from public scrutiny by a board of trustees composed largely of those of Nigger's connections who were still cutting the sugar cane in complete ignorance, blissful or otherwise, of the scheme.

'How does that grab you?' Happy asked him.

105

'It's against the law. You'll get caught,' Gunn said stonily. Happy stretched himself like a cat in front of the fire.

'Man, yes . . . and. . . ?'

'And what?'

'What happens after we get caught?'

'Oh, I don't know . . . jail? Depends whether it's your first offence. Jail, I should think, though. It's fraud.'

'No, no, *no*. What happens is, we fill the house with real live spades and get the media on to it. Sure, the house is a little over-crowded, sure the people don't exactly match the names on the list. But, man, look, the house is full of immigrants and white folks *living together*. Messy, untidy – all that. Against regulations. But it's integrationville, Philadelphia W.10. You want to smash all that to please the bureaucrats? No, man. What you want to do is show your humanity, go down and see for yourself, shake hands with the project leaders. Well goddamit, if there aren't two project leaders with precisely the same name – and one is black and one is white. Ain't that just a purty multiracial parable – camera . . . action! If the Minister would please stand between the two Mistah Browns.' Happy leapt off the divan and darted round the room, mimicking the crouch and freeze of a press photographer.

These alien waters roared in Gunn's ears, stung his eyes. All this swapping and swindling. He didn't know where he was. Was it a joke? Worse, was it an old joke between the lot of them? Should he mention it to Lil, or would she laugh at him for taking it seriously? Laugh at it himself then? She might be appalled by his callousness. He didn't mention it at all and took care not to be left alone with Poppy, though he still thought of her hoisting herself over the wall and running down the long lane.

The strain was telling on him. He could not keep up. They were too quick for him. But nothing else felt quite the same after them. He took out a secretary from the office. He found himself listening out for clichés in her talk. He could not stop watching the way she made up her face, with little curved gestures of lipstick and eye-pencil. She wore green eye-shadow and bright red lipstick like his mother. He could not look at her and shut his eyes as he kissed her. He did not take her out again. He realised too that he would not dare to bring any girl back to Brondesbury. It would be easier in fact to take a girl down to meet his parents if he wanted to. He did not want to.

He took relief in solitary pleasures, eating mostly : steaming bowls of minestrone, great breastworks of *tagliatelle*, mountainous sticky puddings. He became I Scacchi's lucky mascot. When he entered, the Red Bishop took to making a low bow and calling down to the kitchen : 'Ees a good day. The *Professore* is here.' Then Gunn began to fancy that he was becoming a sort of mascot in Brondesbury too.

'You eat too much. You're getting *fat*, Gunn,' the Clique said, looking at him with sad eyes.

'There is nothing wrong with gluttony,' said Antic Hay. 'Gluttony is the holy evasion, the saint's escape route from sexual responsibility. Eat and stay pure, unsoiled by the world. Think of Kierkegaard, or Gogol, or G. K. Chesterton, or St Thomas Aquinas.'

'Thomas Aquinas?'

'Very fat.'

'Fatty Arbuckle was not pure,' said Happy, 'Nor was W. C. Fields.'

'They had an inner purity.'

'I am not fat,' Gunn said.

Not fat exactly perhaps. Yet there was increasingly something heavy about him. He was cake that had failed to rise. He had always looked tough, even as a child. His flesh was never plump, had no bloom on it. What he looked now was solid – an aspect which deterred affection though it might exact respect.

A rainy July evening. The rain was swollen with the dust and pollen of summer. The smell of the rain crowded in upon him. He had not been walking hard, but he was out of breath. He stood in the porch, shaking the rain off his mac. The thought came to him of other prematurely solid men standing in porches, shaking the rain off them. There must be a hundred such men within shouting distance. They were probably all thinking the same thought as his. Perhaps he should shout to them. They could compare notes, form a club.

He hardly noticed that the front door had opened. Xanthe stood there.

'You look like a bat,' she said, 'shaking your cloak like that.'

107

'It's not a cloak. It's a mac.'

'I know that. I am six, you know.'

'Do you know about Batman? In your father's old comics.'

'Comics are silly. *By the way,*' she said looking at her feet with casual menace, 'Lil is not here.'

'Isn't she?'

'She has *gone out* with Happy. To the cinema, I believe. I don't know what film, though.'

He must shout to the hundred other prematurely solid men and tell them the news. She's gone, walked out with King Rat. Oh no, they would shout back, she's just gone to the cinema, she was bored; she'll be back.

But she would not. She was definite in her decisions. There would be no ends left loose. What should he say, what would the hundred other solid men say? Perhaps they were facing similar predicaments, peering at notes pinned to doors or held down on kitchen tables by empty milk bottles.

He stood dumb in the porch. Xanthe looked up at him waiting for action.

'I'm going upstairs.'

'Poppy's in the sitting-room but everyone else is out,' she said.

'Well, why don't you go and – ' He could not complete the sentence.

'Go and what?' She pursued him up the stairs. As he passed the sitting-room, Poppy came out to see who it was.

'Oh, it's you. Come and have a coffee.'

'I don't want a coffee.'

'Come in anyway.'

He went in.

'You know where Lil is?'

'Yes,' he said. 'Gone out to the movies with Happy.'

'Ah,' she said. 'Then you *know.*'

'Know what?'

'Well, you know the crazy things Happy's been saying. His *plan.*'

'He always has crazy plans.'

'Don't be so uptight. I mean the plan about us. Come on, you know what I mean.'

'All right. I know what you mean.'

'Well, this is it,' she said. He hoped that she would look away

108

from him, stare at the floor, out of the window, anywhere. But she looked at him straight and steady.

'Don't be silly. Anyway, it takes two.'

'To be accurate, it would take four. But you mean: would Lil? Well, in the however long you've known her, has she ever gone anywhere with anyone else?'

'No,' he said.

'Well then.' She continued to look at him so steadily that every blink was a miniature surprise.

'It's a fantasy,' Gunn said.

'No, it isn't. This was what he said he was going to do. And he always does what he says he's going to do. That's what makes him so creepy.'

'Have you and he finally split up?'

'Oh *finally*, I don't know about that. He likes to keep an eye on the discard pile. But for the time being or whatever, yes, we have.'

'Happy is incorrigible,' said Antic padding in and flopping down in an armchair like a tired dog. 'You know the bus shelter in the Brondesbury Road?'

'In Brondesbury Park Road, you mean?' Poppy said.

'There is a bus shelter in Brondesbury Road too. Near the corner.'

'There isn't.'

'There is but let it pass. Assume the shelter in question to be in Brondesbury Park Road for the sake of argument or rather of no argument. Well, passing this shelter, I saw Happy necking passionately with a girl. Quite extraordinary he is, a genuine man of action. Only last night he was saying how much he longed for a proper old-fashioned evening – take a girl to the pictures, eat popcorn till you're nearly sick, heavy petting in the back stalls and then more petting in the bus shelter. And now here he is hard at it, before the programme's even started. I shouldn't think anyone's necked in that bus shelter for twenty years. Like Don Quixote trying to revive the customs of mediaeval chivalry.'

'Happy seems to score more often than Don Quixote,' Poppy said.

'Ah, my dear, it is the pursuit not the goal that matters. I often think. . . .' Antic stopped and looked at them intently.

109

Gunn suddenly became aware that towards the end of his talk with Poppy, he had sat down next to her on the sofa.

'It would not, on the other hand, I suppose be conceivable,' surmised Antic with an air of elephantine roguery, 'that Happy might for some reason stand in need of consolation just now. I wonder whether this splendid replay of the romantic scenes of his youth might in reality be a cover for a certain . . . disappointment in other quarters.'

'Wonder away,' said Poppy crossly. Gunn got up from the sofa.

'Ah,' Dick Inskip put his head round the door, 'Is Lilian here?'

'No, she's gone out,' Gunn said.

'That was what the child downstairs said. I should not have doubted her word. Yet it was reasonable for me to do so because it was Lilian who asked me to come here, or rather to come and see her here. It was not a social invitation, at least I did not take it as such. I assumed she was in some kind of distress. Her manner was certainly distressed. I almost thought that she was phoning me not as a brother but as a parson. In fact I thought she was asking for counsel.' Having secured his audience, he lunged forward into the room, like a footballer striving to get his head to a cross.

'Did she say anything about being in *trouble*?' Poppy said.

'In *trouble*?' Dick continued lunging right up to her. 'You mean, was she pregnant? I assumed she knew how to look after herself better than that, though of course I took it for granted that she was not a virgin.' He used the plain words with the relish of one accustomed to strip the euphemisms of people who could not face reality.

'No, I didn't mean that. I meant any sort of trouble.'

'Not exactly, no. She just said she wanted to see me. The hard fact is that we parsons so seldom get requests for pastoral counsel these days that we rather jump at the chance when it does come, and I'm afraid we sometimes jump at chances which aren't there. But perhaps that is better than failing to help when we might have. It may be better to risk rejection and embarrassment than to pass by on the other side, if you will pardon the shop.'

'She's gone to the cinema.'

'Gone to the cinema?' Dick flinched. He looked at his watch. 'This makes matters very difficult. I have a fellowship meeting at seven.'

'Well, there you are.'

'I shall wait,' Dick said. He sat down. 'You must be Poppy,' he said. 'You're Lil's friend. You were at school with her. You're a teacher. And you like dancing.'

'The memory man.'

'I'm interested in people. And I train myself to remember things about them. It helps me to fix them in my mind.'

'You find it hard to fix people in your mind?'

'I say that because otherwise you might think I remembered something about you because you are an attractive young woman. But if I may take an example in complete contrast, we have a dosser down at our place. Tony. Insignificant little chap, suffers from psoriasis and chronic emphysema, father a merchant seaman who beat his mother, torpedoed when Tony was two and a half, mother took to the bottle, Tony brought up by an aunt, and so on and so on. I have dozens of these potted biographies in my mind. It's amazing what the human mind can be trained to take in. Not that my intellectual powers are anything out of the ordinary, very much the reverse, in fact.'

'Mm,' said Poppy.

'And of course these little tricks of memory are no substitute for forming human relationships. I look on them more as levers.'

'Levers?'

'Levers or jemmies for prising open the shell in which most of us live most of the time – a way of getting through to the real person. If we are serious about forming one-to-one relationships, we must scrap our defence mechanisms. We must put away childish things and meet each other face to face. After all, that's what we're all here for, isn't it?' He looked round the company.

'Have a drink, padre,' said Antic Hay.

'A drink? It's kind of you but I have this fellowship meeting.'

'And do you find that when people really have come to you for help, that you can find something . . . helpful to say to them?' Gunn asked.

'I can't speak for the results. I can only speak for the effort that we put into it,' said Dick. 'When you came to see us you may perhaps have got the wrong impression.'

'Probably did,' Gunn said.

'No, please, I don't want to imply that you missed some kind of point. But you may have thought that we were just running an old-style soup-kitchen, you saw only the nuts and bolts of the operation. Not that that isn't very important – you can't fill minds when bellies are empty.'

'Grub first, morals later in the words of the great Beebee and I don't mean Berenson,' said Antic Hay, filling a tankard from a fresh vat of swallow-wine.

'Yes, quite,' said Dick with the nervousness of a spectator who has lent his watch to a conjuror with a hammer. 'But what we are after is to get through to people. Basically we want to relate.'

Gunn lost interest. He could think only of the couple relating in the bus shelter.

He looked back at the wasted months, the unspilt seed. He began to understand the reality of regret. He should have had her. He might have had her. Now he would never have her.

Her round face, her trudging gait, her way of talking – these individuals were now the fossils of memory. And the rules permitted only nostalgia, not revival.

This was the first article of Brondesbury faith. Each moment was to be savoured separately, time was an infinite series of such separate moments, nothing continuous or connected about them. To be loyal to the past was as foolish as to be concerned about the future. The past was just the litter on the cutting-room floor. There was no sense to it. Over Happy at least the past had no hold. Happy was born yesterday. He had no heritage. What was gone was dead. If he did ever come back to Poppy, it would be just another trip down memory lane. Poppy would be a clip from an old movie. Was it the same for Antic too? Antic had his vulnerable side. And to be vulnerable was to remember, to acknowledge the hold of the past.

'You look wonderful, Poppy,' said Antic Hay. 'I'm so glad for you.'

'What the fuck do you mean?'

'Happy was draining you. He's a vampire, that man, he'd suck every drop out of you if you let him. You'll be much better off without him.'

'I didn't ask for your opinion.'

'Well, you know, living in the same house, you can't help noticing how people change when they're together.'

'*You* may not be able to help noticing.'

'I wonder if I can help in any way,' said Dick Inskip.

112

'No,' Poppy said.

'It's very kind of you, but. . . .' Antic spoke a fraction sharply, as a specialist rebuking the intrusion of a colleague from a neighbouring discipline.

'When long-standing relationships come to an end, one is often left with a feeling of emptiness. I know that in my own case when, shortly before I was ordained, I had to sever a close friendship which had meant a good deal to me at the time. . . .'

'You speak in abstract terms, padre,' Antic said.

'Dick.'

'Dick. This friendship, was it with a man or a woman?'

'A man. But it doesn't matter much, my point was a general one.'

'It matters enormously. We must know the nature of the sexuality involved and whether it was overt or suppressed.'

Dick laughed. 'Christ,' he said. 'If you'd seen old Alan, you wouldn't have asked that question. Even Freud would have found it hard to make a sex object out of Alan.'

'A common misunderstanding of Freud,' Antic said. 'As it happens, Dick, Freud did not regard the human race as obsessively randy. Basically his theory was that matter tries to get by with as little trouble as possible. Inertia is really its preferred state. Human beings, being rather more complex associations of matter, tend to get a little agitated now and then but ultimately we are like the rest of the universe – all in favour of a quiet not to say slothful life. A theory I find not only comforting but considerably more in accordance with my experience than most theories I have come across.'

'You know, I find that kind of materialism rather old hat,' Dick said.

'It's not a question of the age of the hat. I'm talking about what Freud happened to think. And it seems that your affair with Alan – with its low, unconscious sexual voltage – would fit in rather well. If the hat fits, wear it.'

'It was not an affair.'

'Well, if it wasn't an affair, why did you have to break it off?'

'I didn't break it off. He went to New Zealand.'

'Then why did you talk about severing a relationship? It would surely have been more natural to say that you lost touch with him because he went to New Zealand.'

113

'I find it sometimes helps in counselling sessions if I put things in a rather vivid way.'

'This is not a counselling session,' said Poppy, suddenly roused.

Sitting opposite the open door to the landing and the stairs, Gunn saw the two heads come up into view. They stopped when they were cut off at chest level, then bent together in consultation; Lil, on the higher step, had to incline her head a little to whisper into Happy's ear. He nodded. They separated. She ran on up the stairs to the attic without looking into the sitting-room. Happy sauntered in.

'Hallo, folks, you all having a dandy tahm?' He cranked out a southern drawl. 'Say, Reverend, mah friend Lilyanne would much appreciate a word in your ear.'

'Upstairs?'

'If you please, Reverend.' Dick stood up, straightened his jersey and followed Happy up the stairs.

Poppy began to cry.

The three of them sat in silence.

Then Antic said :

'What can she want him for?'

It was not long before Dick came down the stairs. He was about to carry on down the next flight then decided to put his head round the door again, keeping his feet safely anchored outside as before.

'Goodbye for now,' he said, rather nervously.

'What did she want you for?'

'I'm afraid I can't tell you.'

'Didn't she explain it properly?'

'No, they asked me not to say.'

'*They?*' said Poppy.

'It's my house they're living in,' Antic said.

'I appreciate that,' Dick said. 'But all the same. . . .'

'Well, don't you think it's just wunnerful news?' Happy burst in, waltzing round Dick with his hands clasped behind his back like a formation dancer.

'What news?'

'You mean the old hoss-thief hasn't told you? Well, *you* certainly don't believe in breaking the seal of the confessional, I'll say that for you.' He slapped Dick on the back. 'I see I shall have to be the one to let you good people in on our secret then. Well,

114

the truth is that Dick's little sister and I are going to be married and Dick here is going to marry us. Isn't that the sweetest, happiest ending you ever heard?'

Gunn stood up, nodded at the rest of them, and walked out of the room. He went upstairs and began packing. As he was folding the trousers of his spare suit, he stopped and looked round the cold white attic. Then he took the long-stalked string instrument down from its nail and swung it with all his strength at the corner of the bookcase. It twanged. He put it down on the floor and jumped on it. As he picked his feet out of the limp wires and fragments of polished wood, he wondered whether it was called a mandolin. Then he finished packing.

# IO

'Would you care for a small glass of cider?'

Gunn's father brought out from the back of the cupboard the dwarfish glasses that he reserved for alcoholic drinks. Above the cupboard hung framed views of Attica photographed while on holiday: a blurred tuft of thyme or asphodel in the foreground, one or two pillars (usually fallen), sea and sky. He scorned those of his colleagues who displayed reproductions of Van Gogh or Gauguin on their walls. The furnishing of the house was equally Attic in its severity.

'You seem to have brought all your suitcases with you. Do you plan to stay here long?' Gunn had not been in the house twenty minutes. He knew, however, that unless the precise date of his departure was established immediately, his father would fidget.

People who had come to tea were liable to be assaulted when still wriggling out of their coats by questions requiring the answer yes ('*nonne*-questions' as Gunn's father called them, '*num*-questions' being those which required a No) such as: 'Can I take it that you will have to leave at a quarter to six?' Those who had come by train were an easy mark, as they had to be taken back to the station. Visitors who had come by car, a more alarmingly flexible method, were subjected to a sequence of rhetorical hypotheses: 'I assume you will be returning home for supper. It is a distance of, I suppose, twenty-five miles. Your motor car, if that modest saloon outside is yours, I take to be capable of an average speed of thirty miles per hour over country roads. We may therefore reasonably allow an hour for the journey. You will thus be in ample time if you leave at, let us say, a quarter past six.'

Gunn hastened to explain that he had two days' leave and named the date of his return to London.

'After breakfast on that day? Good.' Pause. 'It will be pleasant to have you with us for so long,' he added, after some thought.

116

'Yes,' Gunn said.

'And the suitcases?'

'I moved out of the place where I was staying.'

'London rents are, I believe, exorbitant.'

'It was not the rent.'

'Not the rent? You paid the rent with equanimity? I take it that you are absurdly overpaid. . . .'

'Well. . . .'

'I do not wish to know the precise figure. I have no wish to pry.'

'I don't mind telling you at all. In fact. . . .'

'No, no. It would only stir envy in my country schoolmaster's breast. In comparison with my own salary, a dustman earns a prince's ransom. Even the parsons have overtaken us now that the Church's investments in houses of ill-repute have paid off so handsomely. Truly, they have sown their seed upon fruitful ground. Aubrey Wood now has a new Ford Anglia. He nearly pitched me off my bicycle yesterday.' The school Gunn's father taught at was a Church of England foundation. He affected a mild anti-clericalism to keep his spirits up. It also annoyed his wife.

'I saw Margaret Wood in London. And her husband.'

'Another parson, I understand. It runs in the family. A melancholy heritage.'

'Yes.'

'You seem to be rather fat. The expression "fleshpots" springs unbidden to my lips.'

'I have put on a bit of weight.'

'It is not advisable for a man of your age to be fat. "Mauve Mabel", as you will remember the boys called him, was only thirty-six when he died. Obesity. Though disagreeable in many if not most ways, he will be hard to replace in the mathematics department. He was not on the establishment and the headmaster is making difficulties.'

'Poor Mauve Mabel. I think I'll go out for a walk.'

'You will find us very short of rain. It has been a dry summer so far.'

The mouthful of cider still glowed faintly in his throat; sweet, musty memory of the austere treats of his childhood. The splinters from the rough bench used to prick the back of his bare legs, the cider tickled his nose; after the fizz had died away he had a sensation of apples rotting under an ancient sun. There was something hidden away behind the sweetness of the cider, something old and dry and hollow.

Gunn walked swiftly along the asphalt path to reach the pub before it shut for the afternoon. The council had made the path after a child walking along the road had been knocked down by a car coming too fast round the corner. The path had looked slick when new; its single tubular guard-rail threading the concrete stanchions gave a townee look to the road. 'We shall be in the suburbs before we know it,' his father said. Gunn liked the sound of the suburbs, imagining them to be a raffish district of amusement arcades and roller-skating rinks, but the suburbs never came; instead the cow-parsley shrouded the rail, and the seasons cracked and nibbled at the asphalt.

He looked at the cracks in the path. He wished Lil's boots were there, plodding through the craters of dust and dandelions beside him. It was a hot and silent afternoon. The great helmet of sky pressed down on his head. He did not really want to go to the pub. He wanted to sit by the muddy stream and watch the cows. His mood was bovine. The cow-parsley gently swished across his cheek. He thought of the Indian bead curtain which chush-shushed in the hall at Brondesbury, trembling guardian of Antic's seraglio. How stale they had made everything seem. They knew so much or pretended to. They did not really see the sprays of elderberries winking through the dry leaves or hear the telephone wires singing softly above the casual rustle of the alders. They could not sniff the chalky dust of the road or feel how hot and quiet it was.

The midday bus roared past like a tank bringing shoppers back from the town where the school was, along that flat road still traversed twice daily by his father's stately bicycle. The bus made a request stop a few hundred yards ahead, then went on to the main stop at the far end of the straggling village.

Through the deader silence the bus left behind came the clip-clop of high heels. The noise slapped him. It was so thin and sharp, and yet it made him tremble with thoughts of fullness. Clip-clop, clop-stumble-clop in the cracks of the asphalt, clip-clop on through the blank afternoon.

Gunn knew what she would be like, the wearer of the high

heels : in a two-piece suit too heavy for the weather, hair freshly set, cheeks reddened by the sun, a farmer's wife.

Framed by the meandering high walls of cow-parsley she took shape : the square somehow flouncing shoulders, the droopy neck. No farmer's wife. Margaret. She greeted him without surprise, was surprised indeed that he should affect to be startled by seeing her back in the village where they had both grown up.

'Why shouldn't I be here? Just came down to see my poor old dada, as it happens,' she said.

'I didn't expect it would be you wearing high heels, that's all,' he said.

'Well, on a Sunday. . . .'

'I had forgotten it was Sunday.'

'In the country people are fussy about that kind of thing. Particularly with a vicar's daughter.'

'And a vicar's wife as well.'

'You say that as if I was a kind of freak . . . because of inbreeding or something.'

She grinned at him awkwardly, throwing her head to one side. She looked tired but her awkwardness, that disjointed way of going about things, not so much going about them perhaps as charging at them, gave her a jumpy sort of freshness. Though there were lines round her eyes and down the flanks of her nose, she was somehow untouched.

'Let's sit down,' he said.

The path broadened out. They sat on a mown bank.

'Wearing scent too?'

'Do you think they'll think I've gone to the dogs in London? I always wear scent with high-heeled shoes ever since a girl at college said high heels make your feet smell. I don't know whether they do or not but I've worn scent ever since.'

'Ah.'

'Was it – were you surprised to hear about Lil getting married?'

'Yes.'

'Dick said you seemed a bit . . . taken aback. Of course I say getting married but I don't know whether they actually. . . .'

'Nor do I.'

'I mean, they seem to have just disappeared off the face of the earth. Dick was very disappointed, not just because Lil won't be coming to Down But Not Out but because he was looking

119

forward to doing the ceremony. He doesn't, as you know, make a practice of marrying people, but he is very fond of Lil. . . .'

'Well, they have disappeared.'

'He seemed a strange man, Happy. Lil brought him to the centre once. He took a lot of photographs of the tea-urn.' She became aware of his moroseness and looked at him, uncertain which way to go next.

'Are you still living at that place?' she asked, finally.

'No, I've just moved out.'

'I suppose there was not much point now that Lil isn't there. It sounded a funny sort of household, but interesting.'

'Yes, it was. Is. But you could have too much of it.'

'You were very gone on Lil, weren't you?'

'Yes.'

'You were quite different with her.'

'Quite different from what?'

'Oh more . . . cultivated. In fact you're quite different after her even now. Softer.'

'Soft, cultivated. . . .' He mimicked a camp flip of the wrist.

'Well, before her you would have denied you were gone on her. And you would have jumped down my throat for talking about it.'

'Where does all this brilliant intuition come from suddenly?'

'Just because I'm a vicar's wife, doesn't mean I don't notice that kind of thing. Dick's very observant too.'

'Dick.'

'I think you've got Dick wrong. A lot of people do.'

'How do you know where I've got him?'

'No, I can see what kind of impression he's making.'

'Mm.' He lay back and looked up out of the clearing in the cow-parsley to the biro-blue sky. Sitting up again to take off his jacket, he noticed the stray curls along the back of her neck.

'Strange to be sitting here with you like this,' she said. 'When did we last meet?'

'At Down But Not Out a few weeks ago.'

'No, down here, I meant.'

'Not for years . . . and years . . . and years.' He hummed drowsily.

'A long, long time.' She stretched herself out on the bank. Her skirt was too tight for the fashion. It slid up her thighs.

120

His hand stroked her hair away from a shorn-off thistle. He watched the hand free a strand that had got caught. The hand seemed to have a life of its own. Her smile of gratitude had a life of its own, too, moving across her face like a patch of sunlight on an open field. The smile opened her mouth, showing off her sharp canine teeth. Her canines were so much whiter and larger than her other teeth that they might have been clip-on teeth from a cracker. Her mouth closed again. Her lips slid gently together over the white dog-teeth.

Her thighs were slightly raised. Their outline shimmered in the heat. Her stockings had an old-fashioned sheen. As he leant over to fish his cigarettes out of his jacket, he let his hand rest on the nearer thigh, putting no weight upon it but letting her feel the pressure of each finger.

She jumped, then started to her feet in a single move of panic. Gunn went on with the business of fumbling for his cigarette and lighting it.

She stood smoothing down her skirt, shaking the grass mowings out of it.

'I can't lie here all afternoon. I must go and meet my father. He's in the church,' she said.

'Can I come along?'

'Yes. Yes, if you want to,' she said. 'He's clearing up the flowers. He takes them on to Paddenford for evensong.'

'Making the lilies of the field earn their keep,' Gunn said.

'I don't like that kind of joke.'

'It's not exactly a joke, more, well, a turn of phrase.'

'I don't like your turn of phrase then,' she said.

'There seem to be a lot of things you don't like.'

'I don't know why you think that. What sort of things?'

'There's a disapproving face you put on. It's hard to ignore,' Gunn said.

Why had he rested his hand on her thigh? Well, yes, that was easy enough to answer. It was a hot afternoon. And it was so stupid her wearing high heels and scent. But there was something about a girl who had just got off a bus, something blown in, hazardous. Girl though, hardly. Married woman. The vicar's wife, like in a comic song, her legs lolling in the cow-parsley, crushing the thistles.

They stood at the door of the church. He glared at the rusty

121

studs in the wood while she gave the little push and twist the doorhandle demanded.

'You wouldn't know the trick, would you?' she said, mocking his non-attendance as a boy.

'There's a lot I missed,' he said, happy to be out of the argument. He was still thinking about the hand on her thigh. He had spread the fingers just a little. The leg was warm and soft to his touch, but firmer than he had expected. Was there a moment, a split second before she had jumped to her feet, an instant when she had tolerated if not accepted the hand? She was probably just drowsy and slow to notice it.

From inside the church, there came a chuckle, a prolonged chuckle which started with a whinnying hee-hee, then descended through a ha-ha-har to a dying rumble of heuh-heuh-heurrs. Margaret's father. Gunn would have recognised the chuckle anywhere. It evoked the Reverend Aubrey Wood more memorably than any words : vibrant, convivial, brimming with melancholiac warmth. His bouts of depression lent a fuller sweetness to his manner.

Light flooded down through the tall windows on to the worn pavement. Margaret's father glistened like an angel, his arms outspread as if about to enfold the small elderly woman he was talking to. The woman was bent, almost crouched. His charm seemed to have physically stunned her. She trembled under a burden of pleasure almost too intense to bear. Seeing Gunn and Margaret, she began to make her escape, limping towards the exit, anxious to get home for a cup of tea over which she could review the miraculous conversation. He pursued her with praise down the aisle.

'A wonderful woman, Mrs Small, a smashing lady. I don't know where we would all be without her.'

At each fresh encomium, she put on speed as though in terror that she might be dragged back into contact with the paralysing force of his personality.

'Gunby Hallam Goater,' Aubrey Wood chuckled, boomed, whistled, intoned his full name, as he always did on seeing Gunn, partly for euphony, partly because he regarded Tennyson's verse as slush. In childhood, this calling of his name had been a moment to be dreaded, an intimation of the calling of the roll at the Last Trump. Gunn had even ducked down the lane at the back of the church, the long way round, in order to avoid the vicar. But with the passing of years, the name-calling had taken on a comfortable quality. It was a reassurance of personal identity, a token of the continuity of things.

'How are you, Mr Wood?'

'Blossoming, dear boy. In full bloom. And you, are you on the trail of the licentious Lincolnshire clergy? Got any good scoops yet? I can tell you the Anglo-Catholics are the ones to go for. Father Lancaster at Bowby is said to sleep in a coffin. And Father Van Cleef is peculiarly attached to his goat.'

The noise of his talk bounced back from the rafters and rolled around the empty nave, spending itself upon the musty air. Each spasm of bonhomie was a kind of defiance.

While the vicar was talking to his daughter, Gunn looked round the church. He stared up at the Elizabethan memorial on the north side of the choir. Its miniature brown marble pillars framed the head and shoulders of a bearded dignitary and his wife, the two of them ruffed and frilled, all dignity and composure. Beneath this panel, there was another, smaller panel, less finely carved. It showed a man and woman lying side by side, naked. They were easily to be recognised as the same couple as above. The man still had his pointed beard. The sculptor had taken care too to reproduce the woman's beaky nose on a smaller scale. The man's nearer hand rested as if by accident on his wife's thigh.

The body, Gunn suddenly remembered, was to be resurrected as it had been in life; in this case, middle-aged, wrinkled at the neck and elbow. The man had a hint of a pot-belly; the woman's shoulders seemed to droop. Thus in such imperfect guise had they broken open their tombs and blasted off into the leaden sky above Aubrey Wood's church.

Yet, looking closer, he realised that in fact they had not risen – they were still in their conjugal coffin. The flesh had not decomposed. They were just dead.

He read the inscription beneath the lower panel:

Behowlde youresleves by us sutche once were we as you
And you in thyme shal be even duste as we are now.

He felt sick. This smug reminder of mortality disgusted him. To live with one eye on the clock was a kind of escapism, a mean-spirited excuse for not dealing with life properly. You could hear the same sort of glib fatalism any evening in the pub : when you've got to go you've got to go, you can't take it with you, it'll all be the same in a hundred years.

Aubrey Wood's holy gusto was no better. In fact his joviality was ultimately more depressing. Life seemed to need so much jollying up when he was around. Why couldn't he leave other people alone to mess up their lives in peace? Gunn felt an over-powering desire to get away from these retired people, to plunge back into the swim and splash through the scum one more time. He muttered surly goodbyes and clattered off down the aisle, his steel-rimmed heels ringing like the spurs of a mediaeval knight who had rejected God. He could feel their blinkered eyes patting his back and their holy minds thinking 'he'll be back.' Well, he wouldn't.

'Going so soon?' His father said with glee.

'I've been called back to London.'

'Called? There has been no telephone call in this house.'

'I rang from the call-box. I suddenly remembered something I hadn't finished.'

'What a hectic trade yours must be. Will you have another small glass of cider before you go? Your mother will be sorry to miss you. You know how she looks forward to your rare visits. I say nothing of the effort she makes to prepare your room for your arrival. I believe clean sheets were mentioned. Flowers freshly picked too. From the garden,' he added, as though that made it worse.

'Tell mum I'm sorry. I'll call her when I get back to London.'

'She will look forward to that. If ever your plans should change again at such short notice, perhaps you will make up for her disappointment on this occasion and drop in on us.' There was a reckless courage in this claim that the house was open to being dropped in on.

Gunn went back to London. He worked. He lived a solitary life, returning each evening to his new flat, a cheerless burrow in Baron's Court, to gulp down a firkin can of Watney's and plop out a tin of goulash on to a plate while staring vacantly at the television. He began to dislike the idea of love or friendship. He only wondered why he had not felt like that as soon as Lil had gone off with Happy. The hand on the thigh crept into his now disordered dreams. One night, the hand became a woman's hand

and there were bristly hairs on the leg. He began to worry whether there was something odd about him.

In a way, he had been proud of his recent chastity, involuntary though it was as a badge of resistance to the prevailing orthodoxy, a token of genuine feeling. All the same, he did begin to wonder if abstinence carried to excess might not have undesirable side-effects. His romance with Josie, so unremarkable at the time, began to shimmer in restrospect. He liked the quiet evenings they had spent with her widowed father, a district surveyor, who retired to bed early.

Now and then he rang up Brondesbury. Happy and Lil had vanished, none knew where. He usually spoke to Poppy who seemed to be at home more often than the others. At the end of one such call, after the noise from the Australians pouring out of the pub opposite had subsided, he found he had asked her out that evening. She wanted to go to the Café Lautrec.

This dubious caravanserai occupied a large basement not far from his. At the top of the area steps, there was an old French street-lamp, or at any rate a street lamp that looked old and quite French. Down below, customers entered, one at a time, through the green metal screens of a *pissoir*. The fittings had been removed, but the aroma of its former life still clung to it. On the other side, customers, still filing singly because the passage was narrow, paid ten shillings each to an unshaven Greek, who then stamped the back of one hand with an indelible luminous mauve stamp in the design of a woman dancing the can-can. This served as proof of entry which could be checked even in the darkness of the interior. Its eerie violet glowed in the rickety booths and now and then flickered amid the huddled masses on the dance floor. The morning after, a faint smudge still remained as a reminder of the night before.

They sat in a booth. He had a coke, she had a beer. Listening to Poppy talking about teacher training and the problems of the polytechnics, Gunn began to wish he had not asked her out. He had not realised how didactic she was. At Brondesbury she did not talk much. It was strange, though, to hear the Clique voice caress these unyielding topics.

The flimsy wooden partition at his back shook at the cramped grapplings of the people in the next booth. They made a loud sucking sound which Gunn could not immediately identify. Once or twice, he had to ask Poppy to repeat herself. When they got on to the dance floor, she immediately clung to him and kissed him fiercely. When they returned to the booth, she began to talk about the polytechnics again.

Then they began to neck in the booth. Gunn soon realised that they were making the sucking noise too. It was caused by rubbing against the synthetic material covering the seats.

He became aware that he was not concentrating on Poppy and began to kiss her feverishly just below the ear. She sprang away from him, as far as the booth allowed any springing.

'No. We mustn't.'

'Why not?'

'Because of Lil, and Happy. We mustn't make the other half of his plan come true.'

'Perhaps you shouldn't have come out with me then.'

'Perhaps I shouldn't. Perhaps I shouldn't.' She seemed interested by the possibility of drama.

'I'm not complaining,' he said. 'But you did ask to come to this crummy place.'

'Mm, yes. I suppose I just wanted a night out,' she said with poignance.

'Do you want to go home now?'

'I suppose we ought to.'

'It's your decision.'

'We could stay a bit longer, I suppose.'

They stayed another ten minutes, until Poppy had finished talking.

Then they went back to his flat. Poppy trembled, not with pleasure, when he had her. She cried most of the night. He did not think of the skinny girl hoisting herself over the wall.

Gunn ate so much that autumn that he had to drink more to wash the food down. He felt dry the whole time. He needed at least a bottle of Valpolicella for lunch at I Scacchi, after which the Red Bishop would pour him a large Grappa on the house. He would have a couple of drinks in the pub on the way back to the office. When he lost his temper, his whole face now flushed a dirty pink.

It was when he was coming back from such a lunch one December day, having sworn at the Red Bishop, that he found the

126

message on his desk. 'Ring Lil' it said, in her handwriting. He rang the Brondesbury number, knowing no other.

'I came to your office just now. They said you were still at *lunch*.'

'I was. What do you want?'

'Come and see me. Here.'

'When?'

'Now.'

'I can't get off work.'

'Can't you . . . please?'

In the taxi he rehearsed anger, forgiveness, indifference. As it turned out, though, there was only curiosity in his voice as they walked side by side up the stairs with her arm round his neck, as though she needed helping home.

'What are you on about? Why did you call me?'

She just grinned. He looked at her carefully, found her thinner, somehow more loose-limbed. She was paler too.

'Where's Happy then?'

'*I* don't know. Don't ask me all these questions.'

In his arms she went soft in a way she never had before. He let her hang back at arm's length, admiring his catch. Her hand strolled down the buttons of his shirt and then more firmly strode down his zip.

'I would never have believed it.'

'You had better believe it,' she said.

Gunn let her drift down on to the white bed, the scene of so many unfinished beginnings. And then he laid her. He started gently with all the thoughtfulness he had so often imagined would win her in the end. But then the accumulated rage and humiliation of their months together no less than their weeks apart took hold of him. He was scarcely conscious of release. Pleasure no object. Then the drill again, forcing her to cry out for breath as much as ecstasy. Eventually exhaustion. Silence. Even a trickle of sweetness.

'That was what you wanted, wasn't it?' she asked.

'Yes. . . . You?'

'Oh, thank you for having me. Such a lot of fuss about . . . well. . . .'

Her smile was so smart and winning that it sent his mind scurrying to reconstruct each moment of this meeting, to scan every instant since he had come into the house. How had she looked at him strangely perhaps, nervously, with affection or only nostalgia, or fear even? Had she expected him to be angry or cold or what?

He was surprised how little there was to say now. It was not that there were subjects he could not refer to because of the recent past; there was just nothing much that he wanted to say or thought she would want to hear. He felt sorry that the chase was over. In a way he had enjoyed Poppy more. Now he had had both of them; or rather neither.

'Do I . . . see you again?'

'Again?' There was surprise in her voice as if he had asked her to repeat a trivial formality.

'Yes,' Gunn said.

'Oh I don't know. Hadn't we better . . . think first?'

'I remember you asking me once what I wanted to think for.'

'Well, now I want to think,' she said.

'And after. . . .'

'Oh, Gunn, please don't go on.' She pulled the sheet over him and rolled herself off the end of the bed.

He watched her pink body straighten, watched in a haze as she pulled on her jeans in the same brisk way he had noticed the first night he had spent in this room. The heavy denim looked harsh against the softness of her skin.

'I'm doing the late shift at Dick's.'

'Can I come with you?'

'No, it would muddle things.'

'Well, I'll wait for you here then.'

'No, you won't. I'm not really meant to be here. I had quite a hassle getting the key from Antic.' He noticed for the first time that the bed was now the only furniture in the bare room. The floorboards were dusty and there were dampstains at the corners of the skylight.

'Where can I call you then?'

'You can't. I'll call you some time perhaps. Now will you leave here soon, please.'

'You can't go like that.'

'That's the way I'm going.' As she pulled on her donkey jacket with LAING on the back, she seemed to gain in confidence. She

128

bent down and kissed him like a matron and skipped out of the room. He lay there, testing the languor in his legs. Then he began to dress.

There was something brothelish about Antic's attic stairs: the stair carpet worn at the treads, kicked upstairs from some grander part of the house, the old corset ads carefully clipped and perspexed like works of art and the overhead light glowing with the dull red and blue of the London Transport insignia.

'I want to give the feel of an escalator on the Piccadilly Line in the late 'forties, something from the early Rattigan period – Leicester Square, say, or Covent Garden,' Antic said.

'There are no escalators at Covent Garden and the ones at Leicester Square are much longer,' Clara said. As it happened, this decoration had been growing up the stairs, item by item, over the period that Gunn had stayed in the attic. For this reason, it was imbued with a special romance for him. The memorable moments in its creation—the installation of the London Transport light, the laying of the carpet – were interwoven with moments of stillness and desire with Lil. He could not precisely relate one to the other, say whether the early Slenderella poster had been in position the night he saw Lil's arm rise from the sleeve of her nightshirt to switch off the light, or whether it post-dated even the later night they had shared with Noone, but these objects and these memories were all jumbled together in what he now thought of as his life at that time, a life that was over. Like the attic it led to, the decor on the stairs was scenery for a fantasy and that fantasy was now acted out. He wished now he had had the courage to ask her straight out about Happy.

On his way downstairs, Gunn met Antic leaning against a door-post on the lower landing. Seen from above the grubby robe made him look more matronly than Moorish.

'Well, you *are* a stranger,' said Antic in the tones of a skittish madame. 'I must say I never expected to see the old homestead used as a house of assignation. You could have knocked me down with a feather when Lil came and asked me for a key. I hadn't seen her for months. Don't even know where she lives.'

'Shove off.'

'And rough trade too.'

Gunn walked on past him down the stairs.

'I'm afraid I can't come out for a jar.'

'I wasn't asking you,' Gunn said.

'Anyway, I can't. I've got to stay in and guard the Piddingtons.'

'Where's Clara?'

'It's her night out. Your night in, her night out.' He giggled. He seemed to have had more to drink than usual by that time of the evening.

'Where does she go?'

'She just goes. How should I know? I just look out of the window and watch her pad, pad, padding along the street. She looks so beautiful with her duffle bag over her shoulder. All trim and neat. Toothbrush, hairbrush, pill. Pill, pill, pill.' He flicked imaginary pills, like a boy flicking cherry stones.

'You seem rather down,' Gunn said, looking back up the stairs at his bedraggled ex-landlord. A sudden rush of sympathy, even affection. He climbed the stairs again.

'I am. Down, down, down.'

'Do you have to keep talking in threes?'

'Three is a magic number. I like three.'

'How are Elfin and Xanthe?'

'Joan and Ann, you mean. They have spurned the names they were given at their baptism – or would have been given had they been baptised. They have chosen new names for themselves. And who am I, who indeed are you, to stop them?'

'I didn't say I wanted to stop them.'

'Of course you don't want to stop them,' Antic said firmly. 'You understand children, you have the heart of a child. You would not wish to thwart that impulse of solidarity, that reaching out for a simple, ordinary destiny which has led my darling Piddingtons to call themselves Joan and Ann.'

'It might have been worse. It might have been Maureen and Doris.'

'It may come to that yet.' Antic looked moodily out of the darkening window on the landing. He breathed on the glass and with his finger drew a snake in the mist. He gave the snake a huge forked tongue.

'God, here she is again.' Hurriedly he wiped away the snake with his sleeve and pressed his face against the window-pane. 'I wonder what she's forgotten now. Handbag. Or scarf, or. . . .' He darted into the bedroom next door, and began to burrow in

130

the litter of clothes, toys and books that Gunn could see through the half-open door. He could not tell whether Antic was searching for the hypothetically missing article in order to give it to Clara, or to hide it from her, or simply to deduce some incriminating intelligence from it.

When she came up the stairs, Antic was standing on the landing facing her with his legs apart and his arms clasped behind his back. He looked both inquisitorial and self-conscious. Gunn wished he had got out while the going was good. He wondered if he would ever see Lil again.

In contrast to Antic's figure, Clara was all movement and flowing. Her beaky, naturally reposeful features were disturbed, full-blown. There was a kind of anxious exuberance about her, a quality which hovered on the edge of ill-temper. She was wearing a long skirt which she had to hold with one hand to avoid tripping.

'I forgot – '

'The pill?'

'Yes. You hid it, I suppose.'

'Of course not. I have, if not better things, at least other things to do. Besides – '

'Where is it then?'

'On the top shelf behind the kaolin-and-morphine.'

'You seem to have been nosing about,' she said, as she walked past him into the room.

'Not particularly. I merely wished to confirm my suspicions.'

'Suspicions? You'd better not talk like – '

'Not suspicions in the sense you mean. I just wanted to confirm my reading of your character.'

'What do you mean?' The voice came hollowed, presumably from within a cupboard.

'You wish to avoid the central issue by leaving behind the one item indispensable to its success.'

'*Central issue,*' she shouted as she returned with the long, thin flat packet. Its unusual shape and the strange diagrams rather like the keyboard of a piano together recalled some prescription of far more ancient date, an alchemist's love-philtre or even tablets of the Hittite sort. 'Central issue – you can't ever say anything out straight. Why can't you say sex?'

This abrupt challenge appeared to crack Antic's self-confidence.

He seemed to cave in physically. 'You can't talk about sex all the time,' he mumbled.

'It's not a question of all the time,' she said. 'You can't talk about it ever, not when it's to do with us.'

Having shouldered past Antic, who cowered by the window on the landing, she was now facing Gunn as she talked, like a counsel putting the prosecution case.

'Gunn just dropped in, ducky,' Antic said.

'You don't have to explain him,' Clara said. 'Are you all right then? Have you been seeing Lil?' The two questions were elided, nasally drawled in her more familiar tone which had temporarily been amplified, enriched, distorted by her emotional state, as though filtered through a complex hi-fi system. Taken together, the questions were both motherly and prurient, concern for Gunn's welfare being mixed with a yen to learn the precise state of affairs.

'Yes,' Gunn said.

'Well, well, just like old times,' Clara crooned, stuffing the packet into her bag. 'Oh I *am* late,' she added archly, catching sight of her watch. Antic seemed too sunk in gloom to make any outward sign at her going. It was only when she was weaving her way through the bric-à-brac at the foot of the stairs that he stirred himself enough to say:

'What shall I give the Piddingtons for their supper?'

As she opened the door, she turned, looked half-upwards and then stretched out an arm in a balletic gesture, turning the wrist and spreading the fingers.

Something about this nonchalant gesture jolted Antic back into his old groove. As she slammed the door behind her, he said in his high manner:

'What would you say that gesture represented, in the language of the dance, I mean? Welsh rarebit? Crisps and ice cream? Or simply go take a running jump and see if I care?'

'The running jump.'

'I wonder do you ever get a feeling round about this time of evening that your life is cracking up, coming apart, something like that? She'll be back, of course. That is not the point. The trouble is that you reach a stage when your marital arrangements become so complicated that you can't remember them all at once. I don't just mean as far as the central issue goes, though that is, of course, central, but you can't remember the detailed clauses of the agreement you made after matters came to a head the last time – about money and days at home and days out and who's looking after the children and when and how and in what circumstances it is right to refer to "we". Yet failure to remember all these things is the most disastrous error of all, leading to such upheavals that one may well have to start negotiations all over again. I speak darkly. It is hard to explain until you have been through it yourself.'

He led Gunn down to the kitchen where he began ferreting in cupboards for materials for the children's supper.

'These crisps are a bit soggy. Still. . . .' He shook them out on a plate and went out to the foot of the stairs and called 'Piddingtons.' There was no answer. 'Elfin. Oh hell – Joan, Ann.'

The two girls came downstairs in a stately fashion and, paying no attention to the mound of crisps, went straight to the fridge and took out a block of strawberry ice cream and a large bottle of coke. They sat down and ate in silence, brushing aside Antic's hesitant questions about how they had got on at school.

They had grown taller since Gunn had last seen them. Clara's decisive profile was beginning to break through in both their faces. They wore green skirts and green blazers with the motto 'A Green Thought in a Green Shade' emblazoned on the breast pocket.

'I apologise for their uniforms,' said Antic. 'The school is quite progressive in some ways. Why don't you take your blazers off and relax like other kids do at home?'

'Miss Pinning says concern for the school's good name should not end at the school gates,' said the taller girl.

'I think parents ought to wear uniform too,' her sister said. 'They'd look much tidier if they did.'

'I wouldn't like to go around wearing the same as parents do.'

'They could have their own uniform.'

'It would take a mile of material to make a uniform for Hay.'

'Hay would have to lose weight first.'

'You remember Gunn, don't you?' Antic broke in.

They looked at Gunn as though they had only just noticed that he was in the room.

'Of course we do. He used to live with Lil.'

'Now then Piddingtons, what do you fancy? There's Top of

the Pops on the box among other things. Or we could all play Monopoly. Gunn would enjoy that.'

'I think,' said the elder girl, 'that we had better go up to our rooms. We have rather a lot of work to do.'

They got up and shook hands with Gunn.

'Little fascist prigs,' Antic muttered as the two girls went upstairs. After several minutes, Gunn heard the faint sound of laughter from an upper floor. He wished he could see them giggling.

Antic and Gunn sat drinking in the kitchen until a couple of hours later the elder sister came downstairs. She was in her dressing-gown with the belt tied into a careful bow. Her well-brushed hair shone under the overhead light of the kitchen.

'You may come up and say goodnight to us now.'

They went upstairs. The younger girl was already asleep. She lay on her back, her soft moon-skinned face drained of all intention, the lines of mouth and nostril and eyebrow as delicate as calligraphy, released into the equality of sleep.

'I love them when they're like this, like sweet vegetables,' Antic said, bending down to kiss his elder daughter. 'They look so nice and empty.'

'I am not a vegetable,' the girl said, 'and your breath smells funny.'

# II

'She's not here.'

'She doesn't live here. You ought to know that.'

'She only came for the afternoon.'

'Hay doesn't know where she lives. We asked him.'

The two girls spoke alternately. They sat on opposite ledges of the porch, kicking their legs to and fro at each other. The rain drumming on the tiles almost blotted out their flat voices.

'Why the hell aren't you at school?' Gunn asked.

'It's the first day of the holidays.'

It was the astrologer whom, in the dim light of The Shed, Gunn imagined to be sitting at his desk when he came into type out his copy that evening. But as the figure put down the telephone with a thump, he saw that it was Rory Noone. In the half-gloom thickened by cigarette smoke and steam lingering from a recently brewed kettle he seemed more eerily puckish than ever. The way he was sitting unnaturally upright in Gunn's chair gave him the look of a changeling, substituted for Gunn by some extra-terrestrial power as part of a fairies' pointless joke.

'Afraid they had to let you go, young feller,' he said. 'They were looking for an older man.'

'I'll just clear my desk then,' Gunn said.

'The sober truth is I was having a quiet one with the war veteran here,' he indicated the Last Man Out Of Dien Bien Phu, who had his feet on the desk and was lying right back in his chair like a dentist's patient waiting for the drill.

'I have been handling your calls, young man,' Rory said.

'Thanks for covering for me.'

'It's nothing at all. I'm just the switchboard girl,' said Rory.

The telephone by his hand, entering into the spirit of the skit,

135

rang with the erratic muffled jangle common to all telephones in The Shed.

'Hullo and who is *this*?' said Rory in the tones of a pantomime dame.

'Hi,' said the voice at the other end, unruffled. 'Is Gunn there?'

'For you, sugar,' Rory passed him the telephone.

'Gunn, this is Happy.'

'Yes, Happy.'

'Ah, don't go all stiff and British on me.' Gunn could not immediately identify the original of this parody. Was it the heroine of some Hollywood drama of the war years or the star of a more recent television series – Barbara Stanwyck, say, or Mary Tyler Moore?

'Gunn baby,' Happy went on, 'I just wanted to say how very glad I was that you and Lil were able to have such a good, good time yesterday.'

Gunn was silent.

'My, you did enjoy yourselves. Why, Miss Lil's sheets afterwards looked just like an early Jackson Pollock. What them laundry folks will say don't bear thinking of. But you know what Miss Lil is like at this tahm of the month, she will – '

Gunn put the receiver down.

'Funny bloke that Happy,' said Rory anxiously, 'Bit of a sod really. Do you see much of him?'

'No.'

'No, nor do I. Not since I pulled out of that place. Didn't suit me really. I liked your girl, though. Lil. She's a good girl.'

'Shut up will you.'

'I am not offended. I am not one to take umbrage. I have already sampled the thick end of your temper, young man. Besides, I have appointments to keep. There's nothing like being between offices for keeping you busy.' He blew a kiss at the Last Man Out Of Dien Bien Phu who was now fast asleep, maintaining perfect balance in his tilted chair.

Enjoying this phenomenon of equilibrium, Rory tiptoed round behind the chair and spread his arms wide in the gesture of a talent show compère demanding applause for a performer.

'Takes years of practice, does that. Would anyone care for a hand of poker at the Press Club?'

Silence. He placed a green felt hat of leprechaunish aspect on

136

his head, carefully, with both hands. Then with his right thumb he knocked the hat to the back of his head, at the same time wrenching at his tie with his left hand. He then thrust both hands deep into his pockets and sauntered out, completing with a dry wink this mime of a Chicago newsman of the old school.

The removal of this civilised personage unleashed Gunn's rage. Foaming, pumping, blood-red, scum-laden, hot as peppers, viscous, the fury leapt out of the depths and surged up against his ribs. The telephone rang. His fury swept up its crippled ringing like a ping-pong ball on a whale-spout.

'Yes.' It was a bark, hiss, bellow, all in one.

'Gunn. It's Margaret.'

'Yuh.' A grunt, fortissimo.

'Gunn, have you seen Dick today?'

'No, I have not seen Dick today.' Each word was spaced out, howled, a dressing-down for a deaf child. 'It's not my job to look after cracked parsons. I don't give a damn where Dick is.'

'You see, I'm worried about him.' Margaret continued, seemingly oblivious in her agitation of Gunn's fury. 'He went out this morning and hasn't come back.'

'Don't you trust him by himself?'

'No, no. He went to the doctor. He hasn't been well. I wondered whether the doctor might have said something.'

'Presumably he did, unless he fainted at the sight of blood.'

'Pains. In his chest. Shooting. . . .'

'Heartburn.'

'And down his arm. And coughing, too. Terrible coughing.'

'Hypochondria.'

'Oh, Gunn.'

'Oh, for Christ's sake. You. Cow.' He smashed the receiver back into its cradle with such force that the whole instrument skidded off the desk and crashed on to the floor.

'Steady on, old boy,' The Last Man Out Of Dien Bien Phu jack-knifed, neatly swung his legs off his blotter and jumped to his feet. Standing erect, he stretched his arms to his side and raised them slowly till they met above his head. He gave to this conventional gesture of waking up the precision demanded in competitive gymnastics.

'Trouble at home?' he enquired, revealing that a monitoring

service had been in operation even though his eyes had been serenely closed.

'Not at my home,' Gunn said.

'That's something.'

'Not much,' said Gunn, feeling the rage drain out of him.

'You'd better say sorry. It's best, in the end. At least, that's what I've always found. But then my track-record is not so hot. In that department anyway.'

As Gunn left the office, early newspaper vans were bouncing through the streets in the mild evening. Scraps of last night's papers danced in the now empty space at the back of the vans. Through the open sliding-doors the drivers' mates cocked their legs on the mudguard, cavalier, flicking ash from the cigarette nestling in the palm. A damp-scented darkness closed in over the few people still walking the pavements.

The night air was a relief. Dick was not the only martyr to chest pains, he reflected, as the increasingly familiar iron bands began to squeeze his ribs.

Walking off his anger, he kept up such a pace that the city skyscrapers soon fell behind him and he came into a strange, battered area. Long rows of old workmen's cottages, condemned and boarded up, tailed away into wasteland, piles of rubble and weeds, guarded by rusty wire fencing, occasionally dignified by a notice board into OPEN SPACE or PLAY AREA. On corners, a few tumble-down shops still kept going – a tobacconist with curling mock-ups of a giant box of Cadbury's chocolates or a barber's window with a fly-blown series of photographs of the backs of men's heads, each coiffed in a style already long out of date. Beyond blackened railway bridges and builders' yards piled high with planks, reared the new tower blocks, at this distance their premature weather-stains not to be discerned. Only the used-car lots ,with their phosphorescent price-cards on gleaming bonnets, had an air of optimism and possibility about them.

In a place so emptied of community, so desolate of speech, street signs were the only language. Gunn half-muttered them to himself as he strode along : *Vote Mikardo – Sir Robert Fossett's Amazing Circus – Secrets of a Sex Stripper – We give them away, You drive them away – Law Not War – Spurs Wankers – We give them away, You drive. . . .*

In the alley, the signs died away suddenly like noise behind a

138

closed door. The alley was too narrow or too damp to be worth the bill-posters' while. Like many of the side-streets here, it was still cobbled. Feet slipping on the rounded cobblestones struck up thoughts of Dickens : Fagan's rookery, Nancy's steps, the whole panoply of uncomplicated evil. The alley twisted past the end of a street, at the bottom of which a main road could be seen with another squad of used cars arrayed under floodlights on the far side. On the right of the alley, the blank walls, backs of warehouses and depot yards changed to a row of housefronts. Everything except their front walls had been demolished. The windows had been knocked out so that Gunn looked through a series of openings into the cleared ground behind. The front walls themselves were still comparatively intact, some of the doors and doorknockers had been recently painted as had the names arching over the semicircular fanlights. The names reflected the glory of empire : *Tel-el-Kebir, Balmoral, Inkerman Villa,* the pretensions of these enscrolled titles short-circuited by the crudely daubed LEB OFF beside the door.

In the far corner of the space behind these theatrical façades, there was a bonfire, a spluttering, sporadic blaze on one shoulder of a big heap of crags of lino and broken wooden beams with chunks of plaster and masonry still sticking to them. Gunn could see the children who must have started the fire standing beside it and making excited gestures. As he walked past, his eye caught a flicker of flame through each window-opening, neat and tiny like a pier peep show. Only when he stopped to look did he appreciate the scale. The cleared ground was at least two hundred yards deep, both the pile of rubbish and its blazing escarpment bigger and further away than he had first thought. And the gesturing children were not children but winos waving their arms.

He hopped up on to the crumbling sill of the next window-opening and squeezed through. The plaster dusted his head and shoulders. It began to rain. His shoes, sharp-cut city-slickers, slid on the wet clay and rubble pounded flat by the bulldozer. As he stumbled towards the bonfire, a white figure threaded its way in and out of the winos warming themselves at the blaze. He noticed that this figure too was sliding on the mushy ground, white coat flying, hands outstretched to recover balance, halfway between flight and dancing. As he got closer, he saw that it was Margaret. She stopped to talk to the winos, bending slightly to do up the bottom buttons on her long white mac. Seeing the rain in her hair and on her flushed cheeks, he ran the last ten yards.

'Have you seen him?' She turned to Gunn and asked the question without greeting, but he had already started on his prepared sentence :

'I've come to say sorry.'

'Have you seen him?' She repeated patiently.

'No, I haven't. Sorry I was so rude on the phone.'

'Oh that. . . .' she said.

'You've asked them?' He pointed to the tramps who had shambled into an untidy ring around the two of them. He recognised Dusty and also the broken-down old man who had sat on his bed in the hostel and stared down between his knees, saying 'fuck it' over and over again.

In the dark and the rain, the tramps looked wilder. The water glistened on their firelit faces and ran down into their beards. The incoherent shouts and chuckles sounded more like a language of its own. Although there seemed little sense to be got out of them, they appeared to have grasped Margaret's distress. One of them, a man Gunn had not seen before, put an arm on her shoulder, rather more firmly perhaps than he had meant to because the gesture made her jump, which threw him off balance so that he staggered half a step backwards, grinning meekly at her to show no harm was meant. Gunn had not seen them like this before, on their own ground. Their black silhouettes stumbling around the flames alarmed him.

'Wouldn't you like to go indoors?'

'Yes, perhaps . . . perhaps you would all like to come back to the centre.' Margaret issued the invitation raising her arms from her side with a limp graciousness.

The winos mumbled and shuffled away from her. It was early yet and the bonfire was still crackling. The rain had eased.

'All right then, we'll see you later,' she said.

Down But Not Out was a few yards round the bend at the bottom of the street. They climbed the stairs in silence. The wet creaking of his shoes sounded loud. As they came to the last flight, he could hear her breathing grow heavy and jerky. She opened the door and half-turned to switch on the light, and he saw that she was crying.

'You wouldn't believe how much weight I've lost.'

140

'Weight?' He could not think why she was talking about her weight. He was still watching how the tears ran together from opposite ends of her eyes into the single deep line which stretched from the corners of her mouth down to her jaw.

'I am much thinner.' She unbuttoned her mac and opened it, pulling the lapels right back to show her jersey and tweed skirt, both thick but not too thick to hide how much flesh her wide bony frame had lost. Her cheeks had been flushed with panic and running. As she got her breath back, he noticed for the first time how flat the sides of her face had become. The dark brown mole where her cheek had been fullest, which had been a beauty spot when she was a child and prompted jokes casting her as Margaret Lockwood, now stuck out of a sallow plain.

He advanced into the room, shaking off his coat as he moved. She stood still in the bare attic. Not wanting to seem eager to pass close to her, he sidled along the wall and banged his hip on the the corner of the bookcase. Surprised by the blow, he stumbled a step forward. The ornamental gourds in the bookcase rattled.

'Coffee?' she asked in a sharp, rising voice, as though the word meant 'get back'.

'He could be anywhere, I suppose,' he said, just for something to say.

'Oh, not anywhere, do you think so? *Oh, no.*'

She ran forward with arms held high in front of her, crying with the fury of a child who has lost a game, and threw herself at his chest. Her legs gave under her as her head flopped against him. He had to put his arms round her to hold her up.

They stood in the pose of exhausted lovers for what seemed a long time to Gunn. The room was quiet and still. To relieve the stillness and because he thought he felt her slipping out of his arms, he pulled her upright, bringing her closer to him. She let her head loll back, so that her hair fell down away from her face. He bent his lips towards hers, blank, uncertain of purpose and gave her a kiss which hovered between charity and passion. He felt her mole hop along his cheek. Her breath had a faint staleness about it which he associated with her unhappiness, but she opened her mouth and twisted her tongue round his without misgiving. He forgot her unhappiness and began to take pleasure in the thought of her drooping shoulders curled against him. He liked the warmth of their bodies in the cold white room, hers soft,

141

giving, his warmth solid and unyielding. The wet strands of her hair dampened the heat of her cheek against his.

He was seized by a vengeful rage. The memory of Happy over the telephone exploded within him. That odious confidence with which Happy stepped up the mockery by switching casually from one funny voice to another . . . not even bothering to describe the details of the trick . . . leaving Gunn to work out for himself exactly what Lil's instructions had been . . . stirring suspicion that even greater humiliations might have been intended. And the humiliation for Lil too, in her infatuation for Happy, dutifully pretending to be a willing partner in the business while still innerly revolted by it – or perhaps not revolted, perhaps so spellbound that she thought no more of it than if he had asked her to go out for cigarettes.

He ground his body hard against Margaret, until he could feel her bones. Leaning slightly to one side, he reached down with his right hand and pulled up her skirt.

Her response was immediate. She rammed her elbow in his ribs, and levered enough space to drill her knee into his stomach with all her strength. His grip slackened and as she pulled away from him he staggered forward, gasping and coughing, heedless of the steps on the stairs and the flinging open wide of the door behind him.

'Oh, Gunn. Looking for something?' Dick said, seeing the doubled-up figure stumbling across the floor. 'Things are always rolling under that chair.' He sank on all fours beside Gunn and slowly moved his head from side to side in a searching gaze.

'What exactly is it we're looking for?' As Dick turned towards him, Gunn realised that he was drunk.

'Button,' Gunn said.

'What sort of button?'

'It doesn't matter what sort of button,' Margaret said. 'Get up off the floor and stop looking so ridiculous.'

'There's nothing ridiculous about looking for a button.'

As Gunn clambered to his feet, he stared with foreboding at her flaming face. She was miserable, her face now screwed up with disgust or shame. The high tension which had made her seem calm, almost serene in her anxiety had now snapped. She was shuddering so violently that even Dick noticed.

'What's the matter?'

142

'Where, where have you . . . I've been so . . . I thought. . . .'
She could not go through with any of the sentences she tried.
Gunn saw now that it was anger, rather than relief or guilt, which
was shaking her.

Dick stood up straight, not swaying. He put up a hand to call
for silence. For several seconds he said nothing.

'I have been praying for guidance,' he said at length.

'You have been drinking,' said Margaret, suddenly catching on.

'I *have* been drinking,' Dick said. 'With Tosh. In the Commercial. Then I prayed for guidance. Afterwards,' he added, waving
a hand to indicate the passage of time.

'Where?' Gunn asked without quite knowing why he asked.

'Holy Trinity. I am not, as you may know, High Church by
inclination, though, of course, I regard all these fine distinctions
of high and low as fatal to the true spirit of the gospel. In any
case, in moments like these . . . besides, Holy Trinity is close to
the Commercial. And in a sense, my talk with Tosh was a kind of
spiritual preparation. Even, I might say. . . .'

'But what did the doctor say?'

'It was a comforting talk. A very good talk. People who live
on the margin of our world, people like Tosh, look at these problems in a different way. They give you a new perspective which
transcends the concept of counselling as we know it. Tosh is really
a wonderful man, in his fashion a holy man.'

'What did he say?' Margaret screamed.

'What he said is beside the point or rather it is secondary to
what he is, just as merely doing good is secondary to the grace
which permits us to do good. It is the relationship with Tosh as
a person, the one-to-one relating that. . . .'

'Not what Tosh said, what the doctor said.'

'I don't think,' Dick said with a modest smile, 'That our friend
here wants to hear what the doctor said. He doesn't want to be
burdened with our petty problems.'

'Go on, then, Gunn, get out,' Margaret spoke the words in a
matter-of-fact way which Gunn prepared to obey.

'No, Gunby. I would not like you to leave us in that spirit,'
Dick broke in warmly. Standing under the bare light-bulb he
shone with a flickering refulgence. He was swaying a little now,
from exhaustion or strength of feeling or both. 'While I do not
believe in burdening others with troubles when we are fortunate

143

enough to have the strength to bear them ourselves, I do not believe in secrets, particularly where purely material matters are concerned. My case is a straightforward one. I have what is called a heart murmur, the result of some fractional displacement of the heart. It is very slight indeed. A course of pills will even out the rhythm. The doctor says that if I behave sensibly I could have years of useful work ahead of me as far as that is concerned.'

'Thank God,' Margaret said. She sat down.

Gunn began to frame words of tempered congratulation.

'Unfortunately,' Dick said 'that is not all. I had to wait for these to be developed.'

He slowly unbuttoned his raincoat and pulled out of an inner pocket a large envelope, from which he drew three or four X-ray negatives.

'If you'd care to have a look at these. . . .' He spread them out on the low table. They knelt round the table, bending their heads together : family group examining holiday snaps. Margaret's hair brushed Gunn's cheek with moist caress.

'There now, you see the shadow.' In fact, Dick's pointing finger under the overhead light threw so heavy a shadow of its own that they could discern very little in the X-ray. He began coughing, a brassy, grating cough which made his finger shake.

'Get your finger out of the light.' As she spoke, Margaret pulled his hand away with hers.

'There. And there again. That is seen from the back.' Dick spread another dark transparency beside it on the scrubbed pale wood of the table.

'And what ought it to look like?'

'Ah, now, that's what I wanted to know too. They very obligingly let me have somebody else's clear plate, so I could compare. There,' he pointed. Now they could identify the precious dull-grey space which in Dick's plate had had a thick slug of darkness wiggling its way round the edge of it. Gunn imagined what exhilarating, singing relief its owner must have felt when he saw its glorious blankness. Or perhaps the owner was merely one of the staff who had had his chest photographed to provide this service of comparison for the patients.

Gunn himself felt nothing, at least nothing appropriate. He was conscious only of Margaret's jerky breathing and their shoulders pressing slightly against each other.

'They were very quick,' Margaret said. 'It's a very quick diagnosis. I thought they would make you wait for days.'

'Um, I had been before.'

'I know you've been to the doctor before,' she said angrily.

'No. To the hospital.'

'All the time you were saying you knew there was nothing wrong –'

'No, not all the time,' Dick said. 'Anyway, Gunn doesn't want to hear all our –'

'Not at all,' Gunn said. 'I mean, I am, it is kind of you, it is a sort of . . . privilege.'

'I am glad you think of it like that. Glad indeed,' Dick said. He got up and shook Gunn enthusiastically by the hand. He often shook hands with people. In fact, this was his way of establishing that he made no distinction of persons, not merely from the point of view of money or class, crass criteria long since discarded, but also from the point of view of intimacy. It betokened a positive determination to impose his own vision of fraternity. In that vision, each meeting with another human being, however apparently fleeting or casual, represented a tremendous possibility of fellowship. Yet, in the context, the handshake was bound to seem not so much a celebration as a farewell. And because it seemed so like a farewell, Gunn felt compelled to stay on in order not to turn it into one. To have said goodbye immediately after seeing the photographs would have been too much of a scuttle.

He sat on the bed while they began to consider the consequences of the news. Plans were hard to make, because the prognosis was so uncertain. The disease was in its early stages. Surgery might work. There were a few, rather shaky cases of spontaneous remission. If not, anywhere between six months and two years.

Dick began to talk about the future of Down But Not Out.

'I suppose we should start to think about alternative arrangements. We can't leave our customers to the tender mercies of the local authority. We could set up a Trust . . . Perhaps the Trust could set up centres in other cities too . . . Inskip Centres, no, no, perish the thought. Anyway, Inskip Memorial Centres they would have to be.' He gave a laugh, dry and bleak. He did not often laugh and when he did, even in less trying moments, his laugh was like this, giving a glimpse of some desolate hinterland behind the

145

rich landscape of faith and purpose. Gunn wondered whether Dick might disapprove of laughter.

'I, we, no I – I must try not to speak for others – have been happy here,' Dick said. 'I know we are not supposed in our line of work to consider what makes us happy or unhappy. But you can't do good unless you feel good. Is that true? I don't know, I've only just thought of it.' He was playing with the X-ray negatives as he spoke, shifting them backwards and forwards across the table as though practising some giant three-card trick.

'You could have a permanent headache and still discover . . . penicillin,' Gunn said.

'Or a cure for cancer,' Dick completed the theorem firmly. 'But in dealing with people – '

'Stop rabbiting on about people,' Margaret said, her voice trembling. 'You don't know anything about people.'

'I don't, of course I don't. But I have been happy here, so that disproves my theory. I have done no good at all, but I have been happy.' Dick sat down with his patient parson's smile stretching his flaky skin. He clapped his hands round his legs, looking juvenile and humble.

'Don't strike attitudes,' Margaret said. 'You know what a lot of good you have done.'

'*We* have done, my dear. But have we? Would our friends have been any worse off in the long run if we had just left them in the old doss-houses? Can you tell me the answer to that one?'

'You know they would. You're just tired.'

'I have been happy. On winter nights when there's a touch of frost and I look out of the window to draw the curtains, you can see all the way to the river from up here. It's a grand sight with the cranes, and then you look down and you see the lads begin to come round the corner, perhaps there's even a bit of singing, then I feel that we are justified, whether by faith or works, I don't know, but I am convinced of it.' He shuffled the X-rays together and put them back in the envelope, like a newscaster tidying his papers.

Gunn looked at Margaret sitting upright in the chair. Her face was expressionless.

# 12

Monday had become his day for visiting the house. He took the tube from Charing Cross. At the end of the journey he walked through dark streets, impatient and fearful. When he reached the house, he stood in the shadow of a thick plane-trunk opposite and watched the windows. There were usually lights on in the big windows of the sitting-room, sometimes in the kitchen below too, not in the attic. He never went up to the door. When he telephoned beforehand, it was Antic who answered. Gunn would hang up without speaking. Some nights he could see Antic standing at the window. The curtains were seldom drawn.

He knew no other way of looking for Lil. She had not gone to Down But Not Out for months. Dick had no idea where she was. Gunn even rang up her parents. At first they thought he was the police. They knew no more than Dick. It seemed strange now to Gunn that he had no friends in common with her outside Brondesbury.

He waited for about ten minutes before going off to the cinema or to have a drink with one of the other reporters on the paper. One Monday evening, as he moved off out of the tree-shadow into the light of the street-lamp, he heard the rasp of a window being thrown up across the road.

'Gunn. Come on in.'

Reluctantly, he crossed the road. Antic opened the front door as he reached it.

'Come down to the kitchen. It's warmer there. You must be the heavy-breather who keeps on phoning.'

'Clara here?'

'She's left me, you know.'

'Oh,' Gunn said.

'Well, moved out would be a better way of describing it. She comes and goes, to see the Piddingtons, sleeps here sometimes

147

when I'm away. Everything's so . . . sloppy these days. But I suppose moving her suitcases does still mark a kind of break. It's all very civilised. Or confused.'

Gunn noticed on the way down to the kitchen that the Museum of the Twentieth Century had deteriorated since he had last been inside the house months earlier. Beads had come off the oriental bead curtain Several of the political berets on the antler hat-rack were missing. Perhaps they had been commandeered on rainy days. The Great Memorial Exhibition was little more than a memory. The White Cliffs of Dover had never recovered from Poppy's nose-dive at the Happening. The bundles of herbs hanging from the kitchen ceiling, once full and fluffy, were now withered stalks.

'That'll be Clara,' Antic said the moment the telephone rang. 'She pesters me.'

He tucked the telephone in between shoulder and chin and fiddled with the cord like a violinist fingering. 'Oh. No. He's in the States. I'm sorry. Goodbye." He put the receiver down. 'Some sod wanting to speak to Happy which is more than I do. He unsettled this house, you know. Things were never quite the same after he came.'

'You asked him to stay.'

'I did. I was intrigued by him. He made us all hum. Didn't you feel that?'

'No, he just made me feel uneasy,' Gunn said, 'as if my zip was undone.'

'Exactly,' Antic replied. 'I rather like that. I'm a glutton for embarrassment. I think Lil likes it too.'

'Shut up.'

'I only meant – '

'Shut up,' Gunn said again.

'All right.'

'I suppose if Happy's in America, I might see her there.'

'Big place America. Going there, are you?' Antic asked.

'Yuh.'

'Journalists always want to go. They're a gang of con artists, if you ask me.'

'Who, journalists or Americans?'

'Both.'

Gunn was angry that he had shown interest in Lil. He had

148

meant to radiate a kindly indifference. Part of his reason for going to America was to leave all that behind him. He continued to haunt Brondesbury only to tell her that he was going and to say goodbye. It was irritating to hear that she might have beaten him to the New World. The news made his departure seem so much less like a heroic gesture than a lovelorn pursuit. All the same, he had had enough of London. He had to get out. The thought of Margaret made him ashamed, the thought of Lil was humiliating, the thought of Poppy an embarrassment. For a shortish, stout young man with small eyes he had wrought enough emotional havoc for a lifetime. If he stayed in town any longer, whole streets would erupt in laughter at the sight of him, Goater the Destroyer.

The editor had liked the impudence of his request for a foreign assignment. Gunn was young for it, but young men ought to be assertive, intrusive. Doors were there to be kicked open. Besides, Gunn had come on and might now be responsible enough to man an overseas post. He was given the number two spot in New York.

'New York, is it?' Rory Noone said. 'New York's a great town for a reporter. They treat you right. There's none of this door-stepping. The mayor asks you right into his parlour. The cops take you along with them when they make the big arrest. The fillum stars . . . it's an open town.'

'I didn't know you had been in the States, Rory.'

'I was never there myself. They don't give old legmen the over-seas plums. You ought to know that by now, young fellow.'

'I've got a stack of mates in New York,' the Last Man Out Of Dien Bien Phu did his jack-knife trick, taking his usual split-second to travel from apparent deep sleep to full alert. 'A stack of them, old man. Can't remember all their names now. But you just drop my name in the bar at Twenty-One. The bar not the restaurant.'

'I will,' Gunn said.

'You might meet up with Keithie in New York.'

'He's there, is he?'

'He was. They put him back on the story about the missing bastard.'

'They're round the twist. That caper must have cost them five grand already.'

'This time he has a hard lead. Documentary proof.'

'Proof of what?'

'That would be telling,' Rory said, 'And I can't tell because they never tell me anything.'

'How you getting there then?'

'I don't know, fly I suppose,' Gunn said.

The Last Man Out Of Dien Bien Phu pursed his lips. 'I wouldn't. Not your first time. Go by boat. Get a sense of the distance. Unwind.' He followed his own advice and stretched out his neat body again. The toecaps of his small shoes glinted on the desk like paperweights.

'But would the company pay?'

'Pay.' He snorted. 'That's not the way it works, old man. The thing to remember is that when you get to New York you'll need a cash float. That's what the company ticket is for. You sell it back to the airline on arrival, gaining the odd few dollars on the exchange rate.'

'But how do I get there then?'

'You work your passage.'

'Work my passage?' Gunn was startled. The suggestion seemed a blatant infringement of the freeloading ethic.

'Manner of speaking, old man. You get yourself fixed up with a facility trip on one of these cruise ships. Free passage, free booze, take your pick of the deck-chairs and all they ask is a couple of grovelling paragraphs in your next travel supplement. You needn't even let them have that much if you're not satisfied with the service. But I find a little gratitude greases the wheels for the next time. It helps to get a name in the trade for saying thank you nicely. I could fix you up if you like. I have one or two contacts in that line.'

'Well –'

'There's nothing like the sea voyage. If you don't grab it some other sod will.'

Gunn agreed. A few days later, a letter arrived inviting Mr G. Boater to take part in 'an entirely new concept in cruise travel.' A first-class ticket to New York was enclosed. Gunn took the Last Man Out Of Dien Bien Phu out to lunch.

There had to be a leaving party. Gunn decided to hold it on the eve of his sailing in the upstairs room at the Thirsty Seadog instead of in the office pub. This return to the scene of his first Fleet Street triumph was not universally welcomed. It was a bit off the beaten track, according to Rory who regarded all residential areas with suspicion. Still, it was against his principles to refuse a night's free drinking.

All the Last Men came. The astrologer arrived at the party in a fur coat of the proportions assumed by pre-war impresarios and heavily larded with after-shave – 'dressed in rabbit-skin and soaked in stoat's piss, like a bloody nature ramble,' Rory said. The nameless young women who held cigarettes at birdlike angles were brought along too. Gunn had come to know their faces from other Fleet Street send-offs. He knew one of them was called Blossom but he could not remember which.

It was much like Gunn's first night at the Thirsty Seadog, except that this time the editor came too. He stayed precisely fifteen minutes and shook hands a lot. In taking his leave of Gunn, both his thanks and his encouragement were guarded. There was none of the reckless joviality with which he said goodbye to people he was getting rid of permanently.

Ted began to play the piano. He played the same tunes as he had played the night the Last Great Englishman lay dying: 'Who's Sorry Now', 'Goodnight Kathleen', 'We'll Keep a Welcome in the Valleys', 'I'm for ever blowing bubbles', 'Oh you beautiful doll'.

A rasping melancholy took hold of Gunn. Evenings like this stretched before him to the brink of the grave, evenings spent in the company of people whom he was not allowed really to know however many years he might have spent with them, who permitted only surface good fellowship, evenings trying to remember old jokes or think up new ones, evenings when the only thing that mattered was to keep his end up. He could not talk to anyone here, not really talk.

'Do you know "He's the stuff to give the troops", Ted?'

'New one on me, old man. Something to do with the war, is it?'

'Ted wouldn't know about the war. He's the only man they paid to be a conscientious objector.'

Time and again, it was the quickness of the joke that deceived the ear. They weren't funny, really, but they were so quick. That was what stopped them really talking, for it was impossible to talk

151

seriously without hesitating for the right shade of meaning, the exact judgement.

'Ted reminds me of my mother,' he said.

He let the sentence hang. The others waited patiently for the follow-up, the expected reference to unpunctuality or ignorance. But he was silent. The silence made it dreadfully clear that he was serious. He had mentioned his mother in a matter-of-fact way as if she was a car or a wine or some other acceptable topic that could be discussed quite straightforwardly. Awkward.

'How – '

'The way his head tilts back as he plays. Against the light there. It's how my mother looked when she played.'

'She's not – she hasn't passed on, has she, old man?'

'No. She just doesn't play the piano any more.'

Not quite true. She did still play sometimes when Gunn's father was out of the house; his criticism froze her fingers. Gunn, though, preferred the more dramatic story of total renunciation.

'She ought to give Ted a few lessons,' said Noone breezily, trying to clear the air of this unfitting seriousness.

'She doesn't play very well.'

'Oh.'

'Must be great to have a mother who plays the piano to you,' said the astrologer suddenly. 'My mother was tone-deaf. In fact, she wasn't an educated woman at all. The only thing she was educated at was opening her legs.'

'I didn't say she played the piano to me. She just played, that's all.' Gunn vainly tried to recapture the initiative.

'At least you knew who your mother was. I never knew who my mother was. Never knew at all,' said Rory.

'I thought you said she was a dancer,' said the astrologer.

'That was auntie. She had been a dancer. We called her auntie. She brought me up. Bloody hell, I didn't know if she was my aunt or not. She wasn't my mother anyway. She was old enough to be my grandmother. Her daughter now, she was old enough to be my mother.'

'Perhaps she was your mother,' said the astrologer.

'No, she was straitlaced. A secretary she was. In the Civil Service.'

'All the more reason. They often do it. A respectable girl slips up. Doesn't want to lose her job or her chance of a man, so she gives the baby to her mother. Mother brings the baby up as her own or her niece, or something.'

'Nephew.'

'What?'

'Bloody nephew, not niece.'

'That's how it was then, was it?'

'Knock it off. That woman was never my mother. Anyway, don't you try to tell me who my mother was. I tell you I don't bloody know who my mother was.'

They crumpled into uneasy laughter. Gunn felt like a bather who had found a sheltered pool and begun to swim idly across its cool depths, watching his white body refracted through the dark green water only for the quiet and solitude to be broken by the splashes of local boys jumping in beside him. Yet that first true, tentative plunge into memory was still sending its ripples through him. Looking at the winking bottles on the mauve bar which had been brought out from the wall for the occasion, he was carried on back to the wet evenings of his ordered youth.

Like many places in the east of England, the village had been slow to catch on to electricity, because gas was said to be so cheap for what it was. The soft light of the gas-lamps let the fire dominate the room. The simper and crackle of the logs broke into his mother's reading to him, supplying the sounds of gunfire, horses' hooves and sickening thuds. And the firelight – that flickering, fading glow – jumped and trembled across the photographs of classical sites framed in their black tape. The fire was sometimes so bright that its reflection hovered like an olympic flame on the grass-fringed flagstones and fallen pillars in the photographs.

Whenever the door in the upstairs room at the Thirsty Seadog was opened, the draught rocked the two overhead bulbs, splashing light up and down the rows of bottles and across the illuminated address above the boarded-in fireplace.

'Strange how the light in here – ' Gunn began.

'Auntie kept an off-licence – I apologise, you shoot first, young feller.'

Gunn waived his rights. The reminiscent effect of the light could not compete.

'You see, she kept this off-licence. It was in a decent area but a bit adjacent to the rough-and-tumble. So there was a wino come in one day – '

'Mr Noone.'

'Who takes my name in vain?'

'There is this matter.' The barman from downstairs. The lugubrious character in shirt-sleeves who had attempted to deny knowledge of Rory on Gunn's first visit to the Seadog.

'It may matter to you,' said Rory, his rapier blunted by the unmistakable aspect of the paper.

'Your . . . account. From last time.'

'Last time?' Rory's tone – brisk, even impatient – suggested that his visits to public houses in general, let alone this one, were well known to be rare.

'You had a party up here. A hell of a party.'

Rory was not softened by this flattery.

'I do recall having a few beers up here one night. A long time ago,' he added severely.

'Thirty-six pounds ten exactly.'

'I don't believe it. That is a large sum of money.'

'We still have your passport to prove it.'

'I fail to see how my passport could confirm your arithmetic. In any case,' he waved his finger with forensic relish, 'what exactly are you doing with my passport?'

'It fell out of your pockets when we carried you down the stairs.'

'I don't care how it came into your possession. What I want to know is why the hell didn't you send it back to me. There is such a thing as the postal service.'

'We were keeping it for you until you came back to pay your bill.'

'That passport is not my property, you know. It is the property of Her Britannic Majesty's Principal Secretary of State for Foreign Affairs who requests and requires all whom it may concern, if my memory serves, to let the bearer pass without let or hindrance. I have had to turn down several important assignments as a result of your obstructive behaviour. Noone, they say, can you pack your bags in half-an-hour and catch the next flight to Mexico City. No, I say, and for why? Because I haven't got a bloody passport.'

'Thirty-six pound ten,' said the barman, placing the paper firmly in Rory's hand.

'I will look into the matter,' Rory said.

154

'The boss has got the passport in the safe. He'll get it out for you any time during opening hours, after you've paid.'

'That's what comes of frequenting hostelries off the beaten track. You can't say I didn't warn you,' said Rory, turning to Gunn.

He stuffed the long tally into his breast pocket so that the end of it curled forward over his lapel like the plume of a white feather sported by a defiant non-combatant.

'Are we going to stay in this dump all night, or what?' He asked.

'Or what,' said a sleepy voice hidden at the back of the bar by the music stands.

'It's my party,' Gunn said.

'*Party*. Bloody debtor's prison, if you ask me,' Rory said.

'You could move your party, old man,' said one of the Last Men.

'I'm not going to pay for the drinks all night.'

'We could go to the Mucky. Or the Armpit.'

'The last time I was here, I danced with a beautiful girl,' said Rory Noone. 'Inge. You remember Inge? She is married now. To a ponce with a picture box. She has gone to live at the end of the world.'

'Where's that, old boy? The end of the world, I mean.'

The phrase spoke plangently of old cuttings fluttering in newspaper libraries, dog-eared stories of epic journeys through trackless wastes and untrodden snows.

'Frigging Petts Wood, that's where.'

'There's nothing wrong with Petts Wood.'

'There is everything wrong with Petts Wood.'

'I tell you it's a very pleasant place, Rory. I ought to know, I live on the edge of it.'

'Then you live at the end of the world, too.'

'To be strictly accurate, I suppose we're really more in Bromley.'

'We must rescue her, take her away from that accursed place.'

'Hey, now then.'

'There are things that a man has to do even if he has to go to hell and back.'

'Where are you going, Rory?'

'Speak not of *you*, laddie. We are going to the abode of desolation. Dateline Petts Wood.'

The guests with homes to go to began to trickle away, flinging back idiosyncratic goodbyes as they clattered down the narrow stairs.

'*Ciao.*'

'Keep the faith, baby.'

'If you can't be good, be careful.'

The Blossoms primped their hair and took a firm grip on the arms of the men with whom, by luck or management, they had ended up. Only the desperate spirits were left for the excursion to the end of the world. The astrologer had a new Jaguar.

'This is a fine heap of metal,' said Rory, patting the dashboard as he settled himself in the front seat.

'Plenty of poke,' said the astrologer.

'That must be the Crystal Balls', Rory said, turning round to the back seat for approval.

'It's a three-point-four with automatic transmission,' the astrologer said.

They drove past silent government buildings and black parks. The amber glow from the street lights flicked on and off the round tip of Rory's nose and the ball of his cheek. Sitting in the back behind the driver, Gunn watched these twin belisha beacons bob up and down as Rory chattered away. There were four of them in the back, the Last Man Out Of Dien Bien Phu and a man Gunn didn't know with the last of the Blossoms seated across his knee. There was no room to move. The astrologer drove like a statue. He was so still that the steering-wheel seemed to be pulling at his hands. He wore gloves which glistened like sealskin under each street-light.

Only Rory, in the passenger seat, was all action. He fingered every control on the facia, wound the window down to gulp in the night air, then wound it up again. Even the silent avenues of the suburbs trembled with adventures past and yet to come.

'Mottingham, you wouldn't believe what goes on at Mottingham. There used to be these birds. You got off the train from London Bridge and there they were, leaning up against the estate agents' posters, talking like whores in a film – like a nice time dearie – and all the rest of it. Fish-net stockings, the whole Irma La Douce routine. In the middle of a residential area. Trouble was, where did you take them? No hotels, doss-houses in a residential area. So they used to have it off in the left-luggage

156

office. It was closed but you could get in round the back. And there was this great wall of suitcases, jig-jigging like crazy.'

Gunn felt the weight of the Blossom girl pressing against his thigh. Her heavy scent filled his nostrils. The face of the man she was sitting on was hidden by her body. Now and then Gunn could hear him talking softly to her in short sentences. The only word he caught was 'collateral'. On the other side of him the Last Man Out Of Dien Bien Phu appeared to be asleep.

As they climbed over the North Downs, a crescent moon slid out of a black bank of cloud. The moon was pale and thin.

'Bloody moon's flat on her back. What's that mean, maestro?'

'New moon, old boy.' The astrologer reached over to take a hip-flask out of the glove compartment. He took a gulp and passed the flask to the passengers in the back. 'Moon's in the second house now,' he murmured.

'I'm a Cancer,' said the woman.

'I'm Taurus,' said the man she was sitting on.

'I'm a Cancer,' the woman said again.

'I have quite a good Saturn,' the man said. 'They tell me that's pretty rare.'

'It is,' the astrologer said.

'How would you rate my business prospects, as of now?'

'I can't say without knowing your exact time and place of birth. I do most of my horoscoping by computer now.'

'Just a rough idea would do. I'm in public relations.'

'Well, if you have Jupiter ruling the second house, your financial career may prosper more than you expect. But the opposition of Mercury to Mars could introduce an element of risk. It would be irresponsible if I were to say any more than that, at this stage.'

'Thank you,' said the man.

'What about marriage prospects?' the woman said.

'Depends whether Venus is afflicted,' the astrologer said.

'You're telling me,' the woman said.

It was a long way to the end of the world. They had to ask the way several times. The people they stopped were frightened by the flushed faces hanging out of the car windows. The instructions given were confused and contradictory. Once they drove up a cul-de-sac which ended in a timber yard. As the astrologer backed down again, wheels spinning in the mud, they

157

could hear dogs barking inside the yard. Eventually they turned into a crescent lined with leafless trees where the astrologer stopped the car. They got out.

The street was empty. The night was damp, but it was not raining.

'This would be a great night for growing mushrooms,' Rory said.

'I think that must be the house.' The astrologer sounded as if his enthusiasm was on the wane. Rory passed round the hip-flask and the party moved across the road like a deputation with bad news.

'Go on then,' said the man Gunn didn't know.

Rory Noone cleared his throat and gave a kind of yodel. Silence. Even from this distance Gunn could still hear the dumb roar of the city.

'They'll be fast asleep.'

Another yodel. Silence. Rory swung open the wicket gate, advanced down the concrete path and knocked firmly on the door.

The scented woman's face had gone dead white under the glare of the street lights. She stood quite still. The unfamiliar man put his hands on her shoulders, as though about to leapfrog her.

Noone lost patience. He bellowed, 'Wake up there you dozy peasants. You better be quicker than that when the gestapo come for you. Sharpen up, you suburban sods, bring out your bloody dead.'

At last came the heavy creak of feet descending stairs. The light in the hall came on. A shadow grew behind the stained-glass panels of the front door.

'We know you're in there. Come on out with your hands up or it'll be the worse for you.'

'Who is that?'

'Swingers from town, that's who.'

'Go away.'

'You'll have to do better than that. We got enough firepower out here to reduce your rabbit-hutch to rubble.'

'What do you want?'

'You know what we want. Inge. The beautiful, fantastic Inge. Give us the girl and we'll call the dogs off.'

'There's no-one called Inge here.'

158

'Stop fooling and hand her over or – '

The door was violently thrown open and a small angry man in a chinese dressing-gown burst out of it. He held a large blunt object resembling a baseball bat. The dressing-grown had scarlet dragons romping all over it. It was a little too big for him.

'Get the hell out of here.'

'It's not him,' Rory said. 'It's not that poncing photographer. It must be the wrong house.'

'This is the address you said.'

'This is Number 45, isn't it?'

'Get the hell out of here.'

They retreated, keeping their faces to the householder like loyal subjects.

The moon had abandoned them. Wind began to saw through the tops of the plane trees. The trees made a thin, tinny sound. It was a hard cold black night. The inside of the car was cold too now, cold and stale. It smelled of cigarette-smoke and scent and sour, sour sweat.

'Where do – '

'Don't ask me, young feller. It's your party. You're the boss.'

'I've got a boat to catch in the morning.'

'There you are then. Problem solved. We see young Gunby off, we weep into our hankies as the boat pulls away from the quay. We wave till the floating city is no more than a dot on the horizon. To the south, maestro, and don't stop till you reach the sea.'

'I've always wanted to go to sea,' said the woman.

Out of the city and into the country dark. A hedgehog blinked in their headlights at the side of the road. They stopped to urinate. Gunn stared into the patch of blackness in front of him. A fir plantation. The slender dark trunks, regularly spaced, were like bars in a cage. Deeper in the wood, he could hear small animal noises : rustle in the brambles, little feet padding across the carpet of needles. The streaming arcs of the four men pissing, faintly lit by the headlamps, hissed in the bracken like dozy snakes. He could just see his breath turn to short, steamy puffs in the gathering cold.

The car horn sounded. The woman must have got bored of waiting. The bark of the horn cut sharply through the mumblings of the night. It reminded Gunn of the fox if it was a fox baying

159

at the Brondesbury sky. He longed for the purity of Lil's white attic : the three erotic postcards propped in a row on the book-case, the broken sofa and Lil's face peering down at him, framed by the patchwork quilt clutched around her shoulders, and the pink heels going away to her bed, hardly brushing the ground, to avoid splinters in the wooden floor.

The horn again. All lost, lost utterly. He would not pass that way again. As they drove on, he thought of each house, each filling station : 'I shall never see that again,' as though the lozenge glass in the front door or the line-up of the pumps had piercing signi-ficance for him. A girl's bare arm raised to pull the string to put out the light like the huntsman's arm raised to put the horn to his lips. On darkening Lincolnshire afternoons, the harriers would draw the cover outside the village and the horn would sound 'Gone away' as the hare raced along the hedgerow that sloped down towards the stream and the sewage farm.

The car swooped over the crest of a long, bare hill.

'The Hogs Back,' said the astrologer.

'Didn't know he'd been away,' Rory said and applauded the ancient word-play, clapping his small hands vigorously.

The light began to thin over a vast grey panorama; the trees soft wisps of sponge, the road ahead a pale string.

'It's the bloody dawn,' Rory said, yawning.

'I love dawn,' the woman said.

'How would you even know what it looks like?' said the man she was sitting on.

'Can it,' the woman said.

The astrologer pressed a button underneath the facia and a locker Gunn had not previously noticed opened to reveal three bottles snugly fitted into satin-lined compartments.

'Built-in tantalus. Woodman-Barnes. Special conversion job.'

'Well, thank my lucky stars the planet Bacchus isn't afflicted,' Rory said.

It was clear day by the time they found the right dock. A couple of dockers were humping crates up a single gangway.

'Passengers can't board until nine,' one of them said.

'I have an important message for the captain,' Gunn said.

They clattered up the slippery gangway, drowning with their

steps the suck and slap of the salt waves against the quay. The astrologer bore the tantalus in front of him like a chalice.

The ship smelled of fresh paint. Gleaming new signs were nailed up everywhere : *Dining Saloon, Purser, Gymnasium, Library.* Down below, redecorating was still going on, carpets being laid, brass burnished, cabin doors numbered. They stumbled along past unshaven workmen slapping more paint on rusty metal. At the end of a long passage they came to a door marked *Cruise Director.*

As Gunn raised his hand to knock, the door opened and a girl with large round eyes and a greenish-tawny skin slipped out and closed the door behind her with a soft, insulating clumph.

'He's still asleep,' she said, patting her perky little stewardess's hat down on her raven-black hair.

'In that case, could you tell me where my cabin is?' He showed his papers.

'Certainly. Are these other gentlemen sailing?'

'No, they've come to see me off.'

She looked at them, narrowing her wide eyes somewhat. 'I regret,' she said, 'that our entertainment unit is not open yet.'

'That's all right darling,' Rory said, 'we'll make our own.'

They sat in Gunn's cabin drinking up the contents of the astrologer's tantalus. The ship seemed to be rocking a lot considering that it was still at anchor. Gunn began to feel his grip on reality slackening.

'I'm going up on deck to do a bit of navigating,' said the Last Man Out Of Dien Bien Phu, stumbling through the suitcases Gunn had had sent on in advance.

'Well, thanks for everything,' Gunn said.

'Don't thank me. Thank Jimmy Brown. He. . . .' The rest was lost as Gunn's mind swam off on its bumpy trip down Lethe's rapids.

He woke to find a steward bending over him.

'The Cruise Director would like to see you now, sir.'

'We're at sea,' Gunn said, recognising the thrum of the engine and the churning motion in his stomach.

'Yes, sir. At last.'

'At last?'

'We were delayed six hours by the tragic incident.'

'What?'

161

'A gentleman stepped overboard. There was a section of taff-rail being replaced. He must have banged his head as he fell. It took the police diver two hours to find his body. He wasn't even a passenger. Come to see somebody off he had. Gone up on deck for a breath of air. A newspaperman, apparently. Little fellow. The police found his glasses on the deck. They wanted to hold the ship. But Mr Brown persuaded them that with so many sick people aboard, they could dispense with some of the formalities.'

'Brown . . . Brown?'

Gunn hurriedly spruced himself and scurried along to the Cruise Director's office.

'Come.'

A young black man was standing beside a polished desk. His slender body was draped in a dark double-breasted boating jacket. He was as smart and sober as a sidesman.

'Nigger.'

'Gunby. Nice to see you. Are you – '

'This accident.'

'It was a piteous business. His friends were so distressed, especially Rory. I was sad to meet him again under such circumstances. He told me that it was your cabin they had all been visiting.'

'Why the hell didn't you wake me?'

'How would that have helped? You could have added nothing to their story. The police might have wanted to hold you for questioning. I didn't want to spoil your cruise.'

'Or delay the boat.'

'That too. This boat is carrying 435 passengers. Many of them are sick or elderly. Some of them have invested their life-savings in this project. I cannot disappoint them.'

'I could have got off the boat. He was my friend.'

'I fear that charges may be laid against the friends of the deceased. Charges of drunkenness in a public place. Gunby, I regard you as my friend too. I had to act quickly. It was not for me to go telling tales to the fuzz. Please forgive me if I have offended you.'

'He was . . . was a great reporter.'

'I understand he was the Last Man Out of Dien Bien Phu.'

'You knew that too? He was a legend.'

'Rory told me. Several times.'

162

To his chagrin, Gunn felt tears escaping from his eyes. He felt weak. Nigger Brown bowed his head out of respect for this display of grief.

Gunn tried in vain to stop crying. The more freely the tears flowed, the more clearly Gunn saw that he had not particularly liked the dead man. Perhaps nobody had liked him much. Perhaps nobody liked anybody. That was an even more terrifying thought than Antic's proclamation of the end of love.

'Would you like something to eat?' Nigger asked in his gentle voice. 'Or I could show you around the boat.'

'What are you doing here anyway?' Gunn croaked. 'I thought you were mixed up in that housing scheme with Happy.'

'There was some premature publicity,' Nigger said. 'The media arrived before we were quite ready for them. We had to adopt a low profile for a while, so we moved into the charity area.'

'It's a charity, this cruise is it?'

'Yes, registered in the Bahamas. The company, not the boat. The boat's registered in Panama.'

They climbed up on deck. It was late afternoon; damp, chilly sunshine, clouds crawling across the sky, the wind flicking the open sea. Gunn shivered. He was hungry, hollowed out by his careering across country.

'And Happy?'

'Happy is a non-executive consultant to the project.'

'Is he still in the States?'

'Yes.'

'Lil with him?'

'Could be. You two went through with that proposal you were discussing then?'

'What proposal? Oh, that. No.'

'I thought – '

'Well, you can stop thinking.'

'I am sorry. I must not be overly curious. Let me make amends by placing you next to the most fantastic chick on the boat.'

She was a pale girl with frizzy hair. She had come on the voyage to recuperate from a serious illness. She did not really feel strong enough for the trip, but she had not wished to disappoint her father. It had been a sacrifice to raise the fare. She was too bony to be counted beautiful on land, but her youth glowed a little in the sad senile company of the captain's table.

163

Even the ill-starred waiters relented their surly mien when attending to her.

'I saw you talking to the Cruise Director,' she said.

'Yes, I knew him before,' Gunn said.

'He's a fine-looking man, I think. I wouldn't have thought they would have had a black man running a cruise like this. I'm not prejudiced but I should have thought a lot of passengers would be.'

'I quite agree,' said the man sitting on her other side, 'I think it's a disgrace. It's not a question of prejudice, but surely they could have found one of our own people.'

'I don't see anything wrong at all,' said the girl firmly. 'I think it's rather original.'

'Nigger's quite an operator,' Gunn said.

'What do you mean, an operator? He's not a doctor, is he? And it's not very polite to call him a nigger.'

'It's a nickname.'

'I know it's a nickname.'

'I mean a friendly nickname.'

'Oh. . . .' she didn't sound convinced. Gunn admired her directness. All the same, he felt they were unlikely to become close friends. He guessed they would irritate each other.

After dinner the passengers processed into the lounge. Gunn escorted the girl with frizzy hair. She still walked with the hesitancy of an invalid.

They moved at minimal cruising speed, behind a dignified grey-haired couple who looked married.

'What are we going to do now?' The wife asked.

'Play bingo,' the husband said.

'We used to play housey-housey on the Mary. In the old days.'

'It's the same thing.'

'I thought bingo was a common game.'

'I tell you, it's the same thing.'

'I don't like the sound of it.'

The captain drew the chunky counters from out of a worn canvas bag. He called out the numbers rather lifelessly. The waiters, by now truculent and whisky-breathed, stood behind the passengers' chairs to relay the numbers to those who could not hear them and to point out the corresponding numbers on the card to those who could not see them.

164

'Two little girls from Pompey, forty-four, four and four . . .
Betty Grable's legs, all the ones, number ee-leven. Sweet sixteen,
never been kissed . . . on the boat deck.'

At intervals, the man who had thought Nigger's appointment
a disgrace bellowed : 'Shake the bag.' The captain shook the bag,
before continuing :

'By itself, all alone, number one. . . . Number ten, Harold's
den.'

Later, Gunn strolled up to the promenade deck and gazed out
over the dark wallowing sea. The mild rumble of wheelchairs
on the deck heralded the less mobile of the passengers taking a
breath of night air. The bingo must have broken up. He felt tired
and queasy.

He watched the chairs coming towards him like a miniature
artillery column : heads poking out of shawls and rugs, cocked
towards the sea, the chair-pushers leaning forward, a little to one
side in order to talk to their charges.

Nigger joined him.

'Marvellous evening, Gunby. And good evening to *you*, Mrs
Carnegie. Mrs Johnson.' He made a tidy half-bow and smiled as
the wheelchairs passed. The wheelchairs smiled back. He was
already popular. Nigger had grown in self-assurance since their
first meeting in Brondesbury. His diffidence had melted into an
equally attractive quiet confidence. The shimmering, inconstant
way he had of speaking lent a charm to everything he said.

'I like a warm night at sea so much. It's exciting. Makes you
feel so good. You feel anything could happen. The air is soft, like
being brushed with feathers. There's nothing more relaxing than
a long sea voyage. Just one big high.'

It was like listening to a brightly coloured bird darting in and
out of the bushes.

'That girl you were sitting next to, Gunby, that lovely girl.
As soon as I saw that girl, I said to myself, "Hey James, you got
lucky again", but then I remembered what my mammy taught
me, you must always *share*, James, and I have my dooty to do
too, I have to entertain the gentleman of the press, so Gunn baby
if you. . . .'

'What are you talking about?'

'The girl you were sitting next to. You can't have forgotten
her already. She's a *lovely* piece of ass.'

165

'But she's been very ill.'

'Well, we want to make her better, don't we? We're at sea, baby. You never heard of shipboard romance?'

'Christ, you're just like Happy.'

'Happy? He's my soul-brother. My brother bore me in the southern wild, and I am black, but O! my soul is white.'

'Why can't you leave her alone?' Gunn said.

'You think she wants to be left alone, at this time?'

'How do you know she doesn't?'

'We can only enquire.' He paused, rippling his fingers along the railing. 'You know something, Gunby, I don't think you like me very much. I just have that feeling.'

'I wonder why.'

'Don't put me down, man. I want to analyse these hostile feelings you have.'

'You're a prick, Nigger. A great big prick.'

'No, really? That bad? Cool it now, will you, baby, or those wheelchairs will come and get us.'

'Piss off. I'm going to bed.'

'So early, on a night like this? Well, you have had a long day. Pleasant dreams. Mrs Carnegie again. Mrs Johnson, a fabulous evening, isn't it?' He turned to greet the wheelchairs creaking into their second lap, heads now tucked back into shawls, the warmth fading from the air.

Gunn walked away down the deck. As he turned to go indoors, he was seized with nausea. He reached the rail in time to fire a plume of sick over the side. He clung to the railing, watching the pale skein spiral down into the sea. He shuddered with disgust and exhaustion and gripped the cold metal harder as if trying to prevent himself from being washed overboard. Why the hell was he on this nightmarish ship? As he took his hands off the rail, he saw that they were covered with orange rust.

He did what he could to keep out of Nigger's way. But passing along the games deck two days later, he was accosted by a lazy 'Hi, how about a work-out?'

Nigger had a ping-pong bat in each hand and was idly flicking a ball from one bat to the other. Several passengers were already sitting in wicker chairs alongside the table, shading their eyes from the afternoon sun burning through the glass. Gunn could not refuse this public challenge. He was a steady player, usually a

166

hard man to beat. Nigger was the other sort, all touch and under-cut and top spin. He had the kind of service that seemed barely to clear the net and dribble along the table. Somehow the pitch and roll of the boat always made Gunn's drive sit up and beg to be smashed while Nigger's drop-shot clung to the table like a ferret running down a hill.

Nigger took on the role of a sporting English gentleman, crying 'bad luck' and even 'hard lines' whenever Gunn ballooned a ball off the table. This made him even more popular with the passengers, particularly in contrast to Gunn who always found it hard to control his temper when playing ball games. When Gunn angrily banged the table with his bat, Nigger put on an expression of stifled pain. Gunn was also inclined to sweat while Nigger looked cool in white shirt and bow tie. His boating jacket was hung round the back of the wicker chair which contained the frizzy-haired girl. The next day Gunn saw them together coming out of the first sitting in the ship's cinema, arm in arm.

The evening before they reached New York was fancy dress night. For the past few meals Gunn had heard other passengers talking about the prospect in sceptical, nervous tones. He did not believe in their apprehension, imagining that in their cabins they were secretly busy sewing sequins on to nightdresses and making hats out of cardboard. He expected them to surprise him with their inventive energy.

But as soon as the dining-room began to fill up, he realised that he – and the cruise directorate – had miscalculated. He was prepared for the passengers to look a trifle grotesque, had braced himself to congratulate an emaciated shepherdess or a shrivelled Hercules in leopard skin. He had not realised that they would look pathetic. They were nearly all too decrepit for masquerade. The best most of them had managed was a borrowed sailor's hat or a crude bonnet made out of crepe paper. The two or three wearing high-quality costume – a pierrot, a Henry VIII and a houri of sorts – seemed by contrast immeasurably fitter. The pierrot explained to Gunn that he always took fancy dress with him on a cruise : 'I like to know where I am.'

Nigger was wearing a short royal-blue tail-coat, a yellow waist-coat and red trousers. He had brushed his hair into a skimpy black halo.

'You look familiar. But I can't think what. . . .'

'Aw, come on Gunby. The golliwog on the Robertson's jam label. Didn't they bring you up right? Mrs Carnegie here guessed straight off.'

'How could you know about Robertson's jam?'

'Happy wired me the idea. Cute, no?'

'Yes and no.' The truth was that Nigger, though accurately costumed, did not look quite right. He lacked the outgoing air of the golliwog who, whether skating, holding a tennis racquet or just striding across the marmalade label, always maintained a kind of awkward innocence.

Gunn himself had assembled a Father Neptune rig: cotton wool beard, cardboard trident, green surgeon's gown from the surgery. He had been asked to judge the fancy dress along with Nigger and the captain. The captain delayed his entrance until the last moment. He too was dressed as Father Neptune. His crown glittered with aquamarines. His golden trident frothed seaweed. His gown shimmered with all the rainbow hues of the deep. His beard was his own. He was magnificent.

Gunn sat crossly beside him, as the entrants filed slowly past. The prizes were awarded to Henry VIII, the houri and the pierrot, in that order. They accepted with the nonchalance of trophy-hunters. Gunn went straight to bed after the prize-giving.

Pale early morning. He stood shivering on the deck. He looked up into the birdless silence. The white mist veiled even the orange of the funnels. The thick wires were as faint as cobwebs. The little knockings and creakings of the boat seemed to come from far away, the sounds of a ghost ship shadowing them. Only the water below was black and choppy, coal-hard. The fog crept down into his throat, crawling over him, surprising him with its sharp cold tang. No birds sing, he thought, not for the first time, teased by this symbol of oceanic isolation. From the deckcabins behind him, he heard coughing like the noise the sheep made in the fenny mists of his home terrain. Sounds of life, yet not breaking the feeling of being alone on a drifting hulk.

Then the birds came. Two or three gulls cawing like rooks as they settled into the rigging. And quite soon, sooner than he had thought, the land-birds, brown and perky and warm-looking. They fluttered and chirruped, pleased to have found a perch. He felt a thump of pleasure at the sight of them. The birds hopped along the deck, poking their beaks from side to side.

168

Pressing his eyeballs against the mist, he began to see, or fancy he saw, a pale line drawn along the pallor, very thin and faint. The line disappeared, then came back again, broken this time by patches of drifting fog. His eye travelled along the line and saw how it stretched immensely. At last it began to thicken, take shape into a headland, a bay. Then trees. Finally houses along the shore as neat and tiny as a row of bathing-huts. A new world.

From the far end of the deck a couple of human figures sharpened out of the mist. They walked with a luxurious swaying slowness, almost like dancing. The man had his arm round the woman. She leant her head on his shoulders.

The girl with the frizzy hair had her face tilted upwards, bathing in the tang of the morning. Her eyes were closed. Nigger talked quietly to her, like a man soothing a horse.

As they passed Gunn, Nigger smiled and gently waved at Gunn. There was no triumph in the gesture, only a recognition of their shared fortune in being on deck to greet America.

Later, at breakfast, Nigger said to him :

'I surely do appreciate your courtesy.'

'What courtesy?'

'If you don't want to talk about it. I won't either. Anyway, I hope you've enjoyed your time with us.'

Gunn said nothing. They went up on deck.

'I'm jumping ship here, you know. They're taking the regular Cruise Director on board to go on down to the islands. I shall be sorry to leave this boat.'

'I shan't,' Gunn said.

'But this is a fantastic town. You are so right to come. Look at that now.'

The great suspension bridge stole forwards out of the sunny haze, stretching itself on the water, long and low like a cat on a dewy terrace, so low that the orange funnels and the radio mast looked certain to smash into it.

The liner glided under the bridge with only a few feet to spare.

'The first immigration test,' Gunn said.

'My folks had no trouble with immigration,' Nigger said. He leant on the rail and stared impassively at the towers glinting grey, ethereal human dovecots. 'VIP lounge. Straight through boy. Clank, clank.' He mimicked the walk of a man hobbled by chains. 'I must go wrap up the show now. See you around, Gunby.'

169

'Goodbye,' Gunn said.

Gunn waited a few moments on the quayside to get his breath back after the tremendous experience of treading American soil. He counted his pieces of luggage several times, calming himself.

He stood watching a tramp stumble and fall into the roadway on the far side of the arrival shed. Cars snaked round the fallen man and accelerated up the ramp leading to the street. The tramp got up and staggered out of the road, then had to dive back sideways to avoid a luggage trolley pushed at great speed by a man in a rod anorak with a cigar clamped between his teeth. The tramp sat by the side of the road, his head drooping to one side. This must be an authentic Bowery bum. Gunn wondered what the Bowery was.

There was a small bar a little further along. Men in soft hats and overcoats peered out of the window down the quayside. Gunn was surprised how untidy and rumpled people were. Even the officials looked as if they had slept in their uniforms. It was like the morning after some city-wide party. Behind him he heard men and women quarrelling :

'For Chrissake, I told you to keep it in the cabin.'

'But the cabin wasn't. . . .'

'I *told* ya. In the cabin, for Chrissake.'

Then Gunn saw the dune-buggy zigzagging through the crowd like a hot-rod porter's trolley. The buggy was electric purple, freckled with psychedelic stickers – dragons, slogans, Mickey Mouses, cute pre-packed graffiti. Riding on the rear off-shoulder was an elegant young black man in a boating jacket, his arm twined along the roll-bar. He was talking to the white girl in the passenger seat, heavily muffled in a scarf and pre-war motoring goggles. Gunn had no trouble recognising her. There was a panache about her get-up which seemed new to him, but she looked as warm and dogged as ever. Beside her Happy was crouched over the wheel, snaking the buggy through the piles of luggage.

Gunn shouted 'Lil', and ran after her, but the buggy slewed into the line of cars, accelerated round the bum, who had wandered back into the middle of the road, and roared up the ramp out into the noisy air.

170

# 13

It was the spring of the match scare. Gunn must have heard the story half a dozen times in his first week. Nobody quite knew how or where the trick started. Names and places were hard to come by. It wasn't even the kind of thing that happened to the cousin of a friend. It was just there, lurking dark and immense down every unlit street.

Everyone knew how it worked, though. It was like an initiation ceremony, vaguely tribal. The young black – lacking employment, status, self-respect – had to prove himself. So, when the moon was absent, he sauntered out downtown and asked for a light. Just like that, politely: 'Excuse me, have you got a light?' Whitey fumbles for lighter, matches. Left them in his other coat, non-smoker maybe, or just fresh out of matches. Swish, a sliver of silver in the dark, knife in the heart, honour satisfied. The assailant's courtesy was the most sinister detail of all. Nobody knew whence came this chivalric code which demanded that the victim give technical offence by failing to provide the light. But you sure better keep yourself supplied with matches. Gunn, not quite believing it, refilled his lighter all the same.

If you did have a light, though, you were in the clear. Darkie leant forward, lit his cigarette, cupping his pale palms, nodded pleasantly and strolled off. The tiny beacon was a lifesaver, like the flicker of light that saved Tinker Bell. All over the city chalkies were lighting up to keep away the darkies. The little tadpoles of light trembled on street corners and in the parks.

'Folklore, pure folklore, baby,' said Nigger when quizzed. 'I haven't called to listen to that kind of crap. I want to have you come to our neighbourhood ball.'

'Ball?'

'It's a multiracial love-in. Every Uncle Tom on the block will be there.'

171

'All right,' said Gunn ungraciously. 'And how's the cruising business?'

'I understand there was a liquidity problem,' Nigger said. 'The crew jumped ship in Miami.'

'And what happened to the passengers?'

'Happy handled the details. I'm into a totally new area now.'

The party was on the lower slopes of Washington Heights near the Columbia Medical Centre. Gunn was tense with excitement as the taxi rattled up St Nicholas Avenue through Harlem. He did not know quite what to expect, but the decrepit brownstones and the staring, sullen figures sitting on the doorsteps fitted in with his apprehensions. He was disappointed when the cab dropped him outside a new apartment block facing on to a small well-kept park. The smartly dressed porter who took him up in a lift was a letdown too. Gunn, still in his thick English clothes, felt sweaty. The evening was warm. Summer had arrived with unnerving speed.

'Yes, it is a nice pad,' Nigger said. 'It belongs to friends of mine, Columbia types.'

'Where's the party?' Gunn asked, looking round at the empty apartment furnished in modest comfort: books, squashy armchairs, bull-fighting posters on the walls.

'Outside. On the piazza.' Nigger waved his hand at the window. Above the air-conditioning's purr, Gunn could just hear the distant thump of rhythm and blues. He wanted to ask about Lil but he feared that would mean hearing about Happy. Anyway, he was unsure of his ground wth Nigger.

'What are those photographs?' he asked at random, pointing at the grainy blown-up expensively mounted prints which were propped on every vacant sill and shelf. Most of them showed images blurred by movement: a dark blob amid a judder of paler lines barely recognisable as a man in a raincoat going down a street, the face of a woman laughing made gauzous and undulating like a sea anemone, a crowd at some kind of open-air meeting turned into a nightmare of white shifting faces.

'Oh those,' said Nigger, turning from mixing the *cuba libre* he insisted Gunn should have. 'That's Assembly Line stuff. Happy and me are getting it together for a show. You know about Assembly Line, Gunby?'

172

'No.'

'You will, man. They're just going critical. Hey, we'd better drink fast. That party's beginning to move.'

On the way back down in the elevator, Gunn looked at Nigger's trim figure, now transformed from cruise director to campus man but still dapper, denim jacket and jeans just right, hair a little more afro but only a little. There was a great gulf between him and the mumbling assistant from the supermarket who had wheeled round Gunn's groceries that morning. All the same Gunn thought they gave him the same kind of look, watchful, proud.

The springtime wind had died away in the last few days and the air had become still and humid. The apartment block was a hollow square with a large courtyard in the middle : at the near end a small swimming-pool surrounded by patio furniture; beyond, a stretch of grass with two dogwood trees, their blossom a pale blur in the gathering dark. Through the beat of the music came a ripple of conversation and an occasional splash.

The deck-chairs and lounging-chairs and li-los and swinging-seats and hammock-chairs and birds'-nest-chairs were mostly already occupied by guests whose gaudy beachwear glimmered in the dusk. Those who had not got seats sprawled and propped and braced themselves against those who had, so that, whenever one person levered himself out of the patio furniture, there was a little tourbillon of movement as the people around made way for him or got out of the flight path of the swinging empty chair or dived for their glasses.

Nigger introduced him to a string of people. The whites said how glad they were to have the opportunity to show a British journalist a truly multiracial party. The blacks said : 'Hi.' Both were friendly but edgy, taking refuge in a kind of bruising chaff :

'She's a lazy slut, you know that? She's so *lazy*. . . .'

'That man. Why, he'd piss in his pants to save going to the toilet.'

'When I left Sol, the first time, he didn't even bother to call the number I put on the Dear John note.'

'That wasn't laziness, doll, that was relief.'

'You know, Martha's just the same. She's Mrs Convenience Food.'

Gunn squatted beside Sol's lounging chair, idly chinking the

173

ice in his glass until his thighs began to ache and he sat down on the grass with his arms stretched out behind him. He watched the broad stripes of Sol's beach shirt rise and fall as his stomach twitched with laughter. Gunn's back began to ache too, so he lay down on his side supporting himself on his elbow until cramp struck his thighs and he clambered to his feet.

'You're restless tonight.'

The voice was so slow and caressing that Gunn expected to see a black girl gently laughing at him when he turned round. But he found himself looking into a serious white face.

'I'm Susanna.'

She was wearing a swimsuit in toothpaste stripes. She looked very healthy in spite of an outbreak of spots on her forehead. Drops of water still hung on her cheeks and at the end of her short nose. When she smiled, she showed rabbit teeth which lit up her sunburnt face.

'This is Winslow. He's a councilman.'

A portly black man in a business suit put a towel round Susanna's shoulders and shook hands with Gunn.

'From England? And how is England now he's gone?'

'He? Who?' The question was puzzling. Happy? Nigger?

'He must be sorely missed,' continued the large man. 'We shall not see his like again, I fear.'

Gunn realised that Winslow was talking about the Last Great Englishman.

'Do you intuit a shift in values?' Winslow peered into Gunn's face as if trying to read small print. 'Have your people begun to cast aside some of your ancient shibboleths and creeds outworn?'

'I'm afraid everything seems much the same to me.'

'Is that so?'

The record-player was playing the Woody Guthrie number, 'This Land is your Land'. The group round Sol began to join in. As they reached the great swinging chorus, Susanna joined in too, still rubbing her long fair hair with the end of the towel.

'From California to the New York Island. . . .'

Winslow too, resigning himself to a break in the conversation, added his hoarse bass. Sol's spectacles glinted as he threw back his head and sang : 'From the red-wood fo-orest to the Gulf Stream Waaters.'

Even Gunn, uncertain of words or tune, bellowed along with

174

the others. Susanna took his hand. He put his arm round her damp waist.

The sound echoed round and round the apartment walls like a cry for help, finally rising from plaintive claim of ownership to triumphant assertion of national destiny. *Made* for you and me – no other land could say as much. Gunn exulted at second hand as the victory chant soared into the smoggy square of night sky above them.

Thus baptised, he was ready, beautifully ready for a coffee at Susanna's place. Come and talk to me while I get dressed, she said, pointing to the middle floors on the far side of the block.

'Oh you're part of this . . . this co-operative too?'

'Condominium. Yes, but we're quite co-operative as well.'

She was more. She was an enthusiast. Her little hutch on the fifth floor was a glorious gymnasium. The distant music and the chuckles and the splashing from the party were an unseen accompaniment to their movements. She held nothing back. He had all of her without having to say a word.

In fact she didn't want him to say a word. They went out together several times without confiding much.

'Verbalising is mostly shit,' she said a lot later. 'Why are you so curious? I'm just a person.'

'Oh, back home we like to know something about a person. It's a kind of tradition.'

'O.K. then. Caucasian. Female, Twenty-five. Hundred and twenty-six pounds. I've been in the army most of the time since I came out of school.'

'The army? That's interesting.'

'Why interesting?'

'I've never met a girl in the army before.'

'Nobody ever has, outside of a base. It's like being a rare animal. People ask you all sorts of questions, mostly meaning are you a dyke.'

'You don't act like a dyke.'

'So then they think, is she just acting?'

'I don't. What did you do in the army?'

'Drove a truck mostly. Then I went into reception.'

'Reception?'

'I was a body greeter. No, don't ask. They unload the body bags from the transports, right? Somebody has to order the coffin

175

and the coffin-plate, fix funeral venue and pick-up point with the relatives, and escort the finished product to its destination. That was me.'

'Just you, all by yourself?'

'No, I had to have an officer with me, to do the honours at the funeral. At the start, it would be somebody from the same regiment, his company commander even. But then when casualties started getting heavy, there weren't enough combat officers to go round. So they sent anybody who could be spared, the halt and the lame mostly. I usually worked with a guy called Omar. He was unfit for combat duty. Ulcer. But he was dandy round a graveside. He had a great soulful expression when they got into 'O say you can see. . . .' He had a really neat voice too. He sang a lot as we drove across country to the funeral. Spirituals mostly.'

'What did he sing on the way back?'

'On the way back we'd screw.'

'In motels?'

'Yes. Or in the back of the Red Cross truck. There was plenty of room.'

Her face was so clear and open, they must have chosen her for that. She looked untouched by death or grief. Gunn imagined himself in the role of Omar singing 'Sweet Adeline' along desert roads, watching Susanna's pure profile jog up and down beside him. All day they would drive through a landscape of dust and wire and billboards and gas stations, preserving the formalities. Toward evening Omar's ulcer might start to play up. They would stop for a glass of milk and a jelly sandwich, still keeping their distance in deference to their silent companion. Then, the next day perhaps, the arrival in the little town. Sad, plain people squinting into the sun as Omar told the local militia how to slide the coffin out of its mounting; the wind sighing through the cottonwoods, the minister nervously sanctimonious under the weight of the congregation's grief, Omar's graveside manner and Susanna's face radiating youth and hope and sacrifice; and afterwards the wild coupling in the motel room. She sat on the edge of the bed. She had just had a bath.

'Would you like to come to Fort Clair with me?'

'Would you like me to come?'

'Yes,' Gunn said.

'You don't have to ask me.'

'I want to ask you.'

'Really want?'

'It would make all the difference if you came.'

'All right.'

And so they flew together that hot afternoon to Fort Clair, Motown on the Great Lakes, decaying metropolis of internal combustion.

'Fort Clair was my first big city. We used to ride in on the Chesapeake and Ohio once a month to buy our clothes and visit with relatives.'

'Country girl.'

'Oh, I've still got the dirt of Ohio between my toes.'

'I bet a lot of it's rubbed off by now.'

'You'd be surprised.'

In her striped man's shirt with the safety belt buckled across her stomach she looked like a homesteader's daughter.

He gazed down at the tangle of motorways spreading into the scrubby rectangles of a suburb bounded by the irregular curve of an endless sheet of water.

'But why are we here?' Susanna asked. 'I mean I just don't dig.'

Gunn tried to explain about the Assembly Line. Since seeing the grainy photographs at Nigger's apartment, this artists' co-operative had become as famous as Nigger prophesied. They were profiled everywhere.

'Ordinary people is where it's at. The only authentic art is plain folks doing their thing. And where do you find plain folks? In factories and automobiles, that's where. And how do you plug into their imaginations, really get inside their heads? Through the comics and TV ads is how. *Che!*' Nigger hoisted his glass in salute and grinned at Gunn from the squashy bowels of the sofa.

'But do plain folks like being plugged in?'

'It's free publicity.'

The Assembly Line's sallies with microphone and camera did not always go as smoothly as Nigger implied. Plain folks, it seemed, preferred the artist to concentrate on mountains and sunsets. When he started horsing around at the Fort Clair Automobile Plant shooting millions of feet of film of a melancholy Pole bolting a starter motor one-and-a-half times a minute then plain folks began to get suspicious.

177

At first, the local union leaders did not object to the Assembly Line project because they thought the film was designed to demonstrate the soul-destroying nature of such repetitive work and they remembered films like that from the thirties when they themselves had been working on the line. Besides, the name of the art group had a nice thirtyish ring to it – and the group leader, the one they called the Foreman, a bullet-headed dwarfish youth of Central European appearance, claimed to be a local boy, although nobody seemed to know his name. But suspicions were aroused when the local UAW president suggested that the Assembly Line turn its attentions to another man who was doing even more repetitive work because the Pole was flustered by this unremitting limelight, and the Foreman demurred, saying : 'Oh no, we can't *possibly* leave Frank now. He has such a homely little twitch when he screws home that nut. It would be disasterville if we missed a single second of it. And we've all gotten so very fond of him.'

Later that day, the Foreman tried to track Frank into the washroom with a hand-held camera.

The never wholly distant suspicion that Assembly Line might be an undercover time-and-motion study operation sponsored by the management burst into the open. The autoworkers' president accused the Foreman of provocation. The Foreman burst into tears and filed an injunction against UAW. The foundations threatened to withdraw Assembly Line's grants 'for exploration into the social interface between art and automation'. The workers walked out. The Foreman kept on filming, wailing, 'Frank, how could you do this to me?' with tears streaming down his face. The workers smashed any camera they could see, but there always seemed to be another camera photographing the first camera being smashed.

The rushes of Frank bolting his starter motors were whizzed to New York where they enraptured an influential audience already made captive by the blurred photographs Gunn had seen. Other Assembly Line films were also screened. The unblinking sequence 'Washroom No. 3, Gear and Axle plant' was particularly highly praised for 'its crystalline serenity, at once austere and reposeful, inescapably redolent of Piero della Francesca'. Unlike Frank's washroom, Washroom No. 3, lying isolated on the far side of a windy parking lot, was not much patronised, so that

178

for most of its five hours the film showed only three urinals with a long skylight above them accompanied by a gentle flushing noise. Now and again, a dark blur entered left and moved towards the urinal. Exactly when this would happen, which stall the blur would choose and how long it would stay there were recurring nodes of suspense.

In the taxi from the airport Gunn read out to Susanna the article explaining why the Assembly Line had chosen to descend from its fashionable New York loft into the noise and dirt and conflict of an auto plant. Partly, it seemed, they were trying to discover their real roots, not the phoney Williamsburg of clapboard churches and town meetings but the real 'Amerika' of mass production and riots and lock-outs and the violence done to men's souls. Partly also they were saying: this is life, this moment in space-time, the blur in the washroom, the flustered Polack bolting his starter motor, look, he is beautiful, he is Saint Sebastian.

'I still don't get it,' Susanna said, 'either it's good or it's bad. And it's bad. Everyone we knew in Fort Clair was trying like hell to make enough to get out of the place.'

Gunn sighed. He unzipped his bag and stuffed the newspaper back inside it.

The taxi rattled along a six-lane highway between towering embankments. Monster green signs gave an instant's warning of turn-offs to places designated only by numbers, initials and abbreviations – 14th and JFK Expwy, US20, 3rd Ave, Conn. Blvd. – as though the eye had no time for old-style language. The grass grew thinly on the red earth of the embankments. It was like travelling along the edge of a scar. Along the top of the embankments the end of toytown streets were to be seen, chopped in half by the thruway, the house-ends patched and buttressed against tumbling over the edge. High above, perched on the rim, there were people pottering in their back yards. The people were mostly black. None of them looked down at the freeway.

Gunn and Susanna had arranged to meet Nigger at the auto plant, but here they struck a hitch. The vice-president in charge of Public Affairs was delighted to show them around. He was courteous, personable, knew England well, gave them drinks but regretted he had to inform them that there had been, well, a personality problem, communication difficulties with regard to an ongoing relationship between the Company and Assembly Line

179

whom he personally found a very, very interesting bunch of creative people. In fact, he had had to throw them out. Unfortunately, as of then he was unable to identify the exact location of Assembly Line's executive headquarters. He didn't know where they hung out, but, to be perfectly frank, the security guards had orders not to let them in again.

Gunn and Susanna stood on the gleaming shop floor wondering what to do next. Luckily, an old black maintenance man who had been monitoring the conversation while slowly wiping the machinery, keeping a couple of paces behind them as they walked down the line, lifted his woolly head and said, 'You lookin' for them crazy time-and-motion men, the ones with all the cameras? They livin' on McNally, two blocks from my place. Man, are they permanently bombed, out of their skull.'

Gunn took the address.

'Uhh, you know McNally at all?' asked the vice-president in charge of Public Affairs.

'Never been in Fort Clair before, let alone McNally,' Gunn said.

'Well, McNally is a – an urban renewal area.'

'Nice place?' Gunn said.

'In a way, yes. It used to be a very pleasant neighbourhood. I was raised there.'

'Lucky McNally.'

'But in recent years. . . .' The vice-president in charge of Public Affairs looked nervously at the maintenance man.

'Ain't no place for white folks now.' The maintenance man said.

'You don't want to listen to old Ed,' the vice-president said, implying that this was just what you did want to do. 'But you know how it is. A few bad guys move in, give the neighbourhood a bad name. . . .'

They knew how it was.

It was hard to say whether McNally was the wrong side of the tracks. The tracks were everywhere, most of them long rusted up and leading only to deserted marshalling yards and sheds with broken windows. But McNally Avenue itself and one or two of the streets leading off it had a pleasant seedy spaciousness: little white frame houses with a patch of lawn and a couple of old men sitting on the porch as still as in a photograph at the turn of the

180

century. Gunn and Susanna were the only white people on the streets, but they did not feel threatened. There was too much space for a menacing atmosphere; it was not like Harlem where Gunn felt every teenager sitting on the doorsteps of the high houses drilling him with cold black eyes. It was quiet here.

The Assembly Line house was a little larger than most, set back from the road, with one or two leggy bushes in front of it. It had stone steps faced with multi-coloured crazy-paving leading up to the front door. There was a small urn made out of some rough-cast material beside the door with a geranium in it. The geranium was leggy like the bushes. The house looked like any rooming-house.

'Yuh?' A small man in overalls opened the door. In the dark of the hallway it took Gunn a minute or two to recognise Happy.

They greeted each other as old friends.

'This is the Happening Man,' said Gunn.

'Hullo,' Susanna said, giving her typical greeting with its note of surprise that the world should contain such a delightful new person.

Adjusting his eyes to the light, Gunn noticed that Happy had tied his hair back with a hairband and sported a pencil behind his ear and a spanner in the breast pocket of his overalls.

'Mending something?' Gunn asked.

'Just setting up a project,' Happy replied vaguely. 'Come and meet the gang.'

There was a big room at the back with a large window on to the yard taking up most of the rear wall. The window was latticed in a somewhat oriental fashion with long panes of amber and violet glass. The evening sun had drained the colour out of the glass and splashed it all round the room. The glass door to the back yard below was open, letting in the heat and dust.

Gunn and Susanna paused just inside the room, blinking as their eyes readjusted to the returning light after the dark hallway.

The room was dirty, cluttered : piles of old newspapers, beer-cans, snippets of film, a couple of rickety sofas, sleeping-bags, blankets. On a heavy wooden table, stood an array of film and tape equipment, battered but still gleaming black and silver.

On the sofa nearer the window, there lay a short young man, rather tubby, in a sweat-shirt and jeans sawn off at the calf; he was fast asleep, his plump chin tucked into his neck. The chin was covered with reddish fuzz. The fuzz was nearly as long as the unfashionable crew-cut stubble that covered the rest of his head. His dirty sneakers too belonged to an earlier era.

Susanna peered down at him, her hands clasped behind her back, like a museum visitor inspecting an exhibit.

'Now *he* looks familiar, too,' she said.

'Meet the Foreman,' said Happy admiringly. 'Don't you think his gear's just great? Soda fountain jerk, early fifties, Norman Rockwell reject.'

'Yes, I'm sure it is,' Susanna continued, not listening. 'Olly Zeiss. We were in grade school together. Quincy High. I didn't really know him too well. He was kind of a creep. But I liked him.'

'Olly Zeiss. It's beautiful,' Happy slapped his temple in mock astonishment, delighted by this revelation. 'Real small-town kraut *schlemiel*. I didn't realise. *He's playing himself.* Tell me more.'

'Well,' said Susanna, puzzled but willing, 'he was sort of an over-achiever. Straight As, but anxious. Oh, and he was too short to make the football team.'

'Perfect,' Happy said.

A clinking noise from outside. Through the open door Gunn could just see the empty beer-can roll to a halt in a pile of rubble at the end of the yard below. From the middle of the room, he could also see the backs of the heads of two persons sitting on the lowest of the steps leading down to the yard.

He went out to the doorway and called 'Hi' down to them. The two heads slowly turned round. He was not surprised to see Nigger and Lil.

'You see, Meester Goater, ve are all old friends here,' said Happy in the tones of a movie villain presenting the trapped hero with his adored one in a piranha-tank.

'Hullo Gunn,' Lil said.

'Hi,' Nigger said. The two of them smiled and came up the steps and enfolded Gunn in a double hug.

'Peace,' said Lil, stepping back and giving him a thorough smiling once-over. She had cut her long hair to scrubbing-brush length.

Unsure how to reply, Gunn just nodded and smiled back, as though Peace was his given name and she had done well to remember it. He had not expected this.

182

They both seemed unfamiliar to him. He felt as though he had not seen Lil for years instead of a few months. Her face was pink and sweaty. Her eyes were screwed up against the sun. Something – the heat or the beer or the Foreman – seemed to have broken her down. Her almost dour reserving of herself had been crumbled into a casual off-hand shamble.

Nigger too seemed to have changed, even in the few weeks since Gunn had last seen him. The elegant cool was gone. He was not so much nervous as gone slack. In crimson tee-shirt and dark jeans he looked more like the young men lounging on McNally. When Gunn asked him how the photographic show had gone, Nigger mumbled only a couple of sentences. Almost overnight he seemed to have lost his power of graceful phrasing.

By contrast Happy, beneath his repairman's outfit, was unchanged, as brisk and knowing as ever. And it was he who led the stumbling talk through the humid evening.

Nigger merely assented slack-mouthed, with an occasional 'Right on' or 'Tell it, man' as Happy described Assembly Line's heroic struggle with the Fort Clair auto people. Lil spoke even less, but smiled a lot, sometimes when there was nothing funny being said. She listened with especial intensity during the silences, as though there was some more delicate conversation going on behind the audible talk.

As the night came down, the midges wandered in through the open door. From off the Little Snake River two blocks away, Happy said. More of a sewer than a river, it was where the Mob used to dump their bodies in the old days. By the time they floated out into the Lake, the corpses were hard to identify and the people who had dumped them were over the state line. Gunn moved on from beer to a flagon of fiery red wine Nigger brought out from under the table. It was still very hot. There was no air-conditioning.

More Assembly Liners began to drift in with the midges. They all had a scrubbed-out look and long hair, mostly tied back with a band like Happy's. They were gentle and elegant. They talked quietly. The only sign of animation was a repeated low giggle, a secretive, nocturnal sound like the call of a small furry animal. Four of them gathered in a dark corner of the room heating a teaspoon over a candle stuck in a saucer. Gunn observed the now familiar ritual with lazy indifference as he drank. It was only a provincial obstinacy in him that even in America had kept him to the old drugs. But for once caving in to the custom of the country, he took the shrivelled cigarette Nigger passed him, their momentarily enlaced fingers casting dainty shadows on the wall from the light of the single candle.

On the sofa opposite Gunn, the Foreman began to stir. His short body uncoiled and he cautiously swung himself into a sitting position, rubbing his ferret-red eyes.

'Shit. I feel terrific. Let's go shoot some film.'

'Hey, Foreman, give us a break, willya? It's sniff'n' snort time.'

'Okay kids, relax. Hi.' The ferret's eyes homed in on Gunn and Susanna. Happy explained them.

'You look like wonderful people. Don't I know you from some place?' He put his hand on Gunn's hip and wrapped his arm round him in a jovial caress.

'You know *me*,' Susanna said.

'Oh I am glad. That's charming.' His effusive words came out oddly, being delivered not in some theatrical sing-song but in a flat mid-west executive's voice.

'You're Olly Zeiss, aren't you? Remember Susie Williams from Quincy High?'

'Hey, what is this supposed to be? This Is Your Life local time or something? We ought to have the cameras rolling. Let's have a grade-school kiss, Susie honey.' There was more than a hint of irritation beneath his comradely greeting. Susanna sensed his annoyance and babbled nervously: 'I remember you used to be crazy about the Green Bay Packers, just crazy.'

The Foreman smothered these attempted reminiscences by sweeping Susanna into a clinch, muttering, 'I love you, I really love you,' when she leant back for air. His robot qualities – flat voice, dead eyes, a certain stiffness in his movements – gave him a sinister authority.

All the same, Gunn didn't feel the Foreman to be impregnable. Even these first few minutes of meeting suggested that he might lack Happy's stamina. Nigger for his part seemed to be wilting under the pace, unable to maintain so many varieties of cool in such quick succession. Antic had already blown a string of fuses. Of this quartet of moderns – Foreman, Nigger, Antic, Happy – only the Happening Man, now perched cross-legged on the sagging arm of a sofa, survived with his style undented.

184

'You come down here to expose us, have you?' Happy said.

'Yes,' said Gunn.

'Great. I like being exposed. Gives me a high. Like free, you know, no more dirty little secrets.'

'What is there to expose?' Lil asked.

'C'mon baby, give him time. Hit him again.'

The heat in the room was thickening with the night. Gunn felt, no, heard a throbbing somewhere at the back of his head. The candle threw huge shadows; great humps of darkness swooped across the walls. The Foreman rolled Susanna down on to the sofa he had been sleeping on. They merged into one dark mass, shifting uneasily with the occasional chuckle and snort of a single dozy badger.

Gunn felt too slack to be angry. His head seemed to float away from his body on a sickly-sweet tide. He glided – it felt like gliding – towards the open door and out into the black, plush-lined night. His feet stumbling in the rubble sounded miles away.

'Are you all right?' Lil sounded miles away too, a voice homing in from another frequency. Perhaps she was on a ship. Ship-to-shore or shore-to-ship. Which of them was the shore?

'All right. *All right.* All right.' His voice came and went as though the power was fading. He laughed a noble, rolling laugh. All right: strong, beautiful words, the words of a madman, a genius. All right Nijinsky. All right Einstein. Clever, that was the word for him, clever. He had left them all at the post. Nobody knew where he was. Even his newspaper did not know where he was. Why? Because he hadn't told them. He had just slipped off to the end of the world without a word. This was the end of the world because this was where the rainbow ended, ended in a shower of colours, gold and sea-blue and orange and far-off subterranean green. And the colours were his and nobody else's because nobody else could catch up with him. He was all right and they were all left. All left was brilliant, the joke of the century. If only he could put it into words, express the brilliance of it.

'All left,' he said.

From a long way off somebody put an arm round his neck and managed to kiss his cheek. How could she make a kiss carry so far? With lips on stilts? He must ask her, send her a cable. Ship-to-shore. He must celebrate the kiss with some glorious action. What, though? What could it be? Then it came to him, the

185

glorious action. If he flexed his knees and ankles and carefully let his bottom go into a controlled descent, keeping his trunk tensed forward, he might just do it. He felt the clench of muscle, the dizzy plummet through space, the thud as his buttocks bit into the bumpy ground. He had made it. At his side he heard another crunch.

'We have sat down,' he said.

'Great,' she said.

Into his hands she passed him a cold hard object. It was wonderfully cold and hard to the touch. And rounded too, beautifully rounded. A bottle. How clever he had been to have thought of such a beautifully round and cold and hard word for this thing. Bottle. Bo–t'l. What a sharp, short clinking 'o'. He raised it to his lips and drank from it.

How quick he was, how wide awake. He could find out the colours in the dark, the shimmering oranges and greens, the deep, deep sea-blue and the savage yellow. And he could hear too. Listen, he would say, holding up his hand for attention, and they would say, but there is nothing there, it is quiet. Only he could hear the noises behind the silence, strange noises : discordant at first, those rattles, coughs, bangs, mumbles, shouts. At first there seemed no point to them. But there were wonderful tunes hidden in there, tunes that only he could hear, just the other side of the bushes or was it the other side of the house? Yes, in front of the house, that was where they were playing the tune. Quick now, follow. Down the passage beside the house. The wall of the house bulged and slapped them as they passed. The bushes on the other side of the path swished at them to stop them from hearing the tune.

But Gunn was going to hear it. As he and Lil came round the corner of the house the crowd was already coming up the avenue. Leading the parade were two swaying gaudy monsters, bigger than a man, square-bodied with small metal heads and full brightly coloured skirts like grotesque giants in a carnival. As the monsters rattled nearer, he could see that they were dress-racks. Their small wheels rumbled and jerked along the road, the coat-hangers jangling and swinging. Each monster was pushed at speed by three or four black youths, very young, perhaps fourteen or fifteen years old, their eyes hot. Some way behind came a bickering, laughing, stumbling crowd of blacks. At the back was a small boy staggering under a huge TV set pursued by a middle-aged woman hitting him round the shoulders with her handbag.

Looking down the avenue he saw flames flickering through the leaves of the trees and plumes of smoke rising gaudily in the half-light of the approaching dawn. And far off, the sound of gunfire, bunched, erratic.

As the dress-racks rattled on up the avenue, Gunn looked all round him and saw more tongues of distant flame through gaps between the houses. The bitter smell of the smoke began to tingle in his nostrils.

'Wow,' said Happy at his side, 'it's like the burning of Atlanta.'

A chorus of police sirens.

'Scram, it's the cops.'

Gunn found himself following them up the front steps. He seemed to be on all fours. How solidly the flat of his hands smacked the cold stone as he crawled into the house and down the hallway. He felt he was crawling at a terrifying speed; he was capable of vaulting through a window like a big cat through a paper hoop. As he padded into the room at the back he wondered whether he would be able to stop.

Everyone in the room seemed to be either lying down or on all fours like him. Even the Foreman was kneeling. The Foreman was thrusting his body backwards and forwards in a motion which seemed strange to Gunn. Was it a dance, West Indian perhaps, like the limbo, or something to do with yoga? And why was somebody, Susanna was it? – crouched on all fours in front of him? The room was full of strange noises. The gunfire outside, not so distant now, rattled the latticed windows; and the smell of stale smoke began to creep in through the open door. Gunn began to feel cold and heavy. He wanted to get away from the noise, the clanging, banging, wailing, horrible noise. He wanted to be tucked up and warm. He crawled under the table and curled up into a ball. Then he closed his eyes to keep out the noise.

When he opened his eyes again, the noise had gone. He looked around him from under the table, cautiously and slowly like a tortoise coming out of hibernation. His head hurt. His neck was stiff. His mouth was dry. Bodies were sprawled about the room, inert sacks of flesh thrown across each other. He could see the middle of the Foreman's body: rucked up shirt, fuzz-covered flesh, a ruff of white underpants, the belt dangling loose from

187

wrinkled jeans, his arm thrown across Susanna's long bare back. The Foreman snored lightly, like a man uncertainly humming a tune. In the far corner of the room, a couple of Assembly Liners were sitting in the lotus position, swaying gently from side to side and crooning some Eastern threnody. From where Gunn lay their heads were cut off by the edge of the table. The room was emptier than it had been. Some of the Assembly Liners must have gone out. It was still only a grey half-light that filtered through the amber and violet panes, but it was already weirdly hot and stuffy. The rest of those who remained were asleep. Happy and Nigger and Lil lay together in a sticky bundle, like sardines just prised from the tin.

Gunn's stunned senses began to take in the suffocating smell of the room, the smell of sweat and last night's smoke and sour wine and beer and sickly tobacco and sweet-sickly marijuana and piss and vomit, stinging his eyes and scraping his throat and the roof of his mouth. He crawled to his feet, banging the back of his head on the underside of the table. He found he was trembling, from head to toe, shaking on and on and on, uncontrollably.

Then the trembling went away and a single imperative surged up inside him as quick and strong as an uppercut. He grasped one of the empty bottles and threw it hard at the window. Crash. One amber pane gone. He took another. Smash. A violet pane this time, quite shattered.

'Hey! Wha. . . ?'

Crash. Crash. *Smash.*

'For Chrissaa. . . .'

Smash. Splinter. Thump. No more bottles to hand. He took a cine-camera in both hands and threw it. The cine-camera sailed through the breached window and exploded on the rubble outside. He took a few cans of film. They inflicted only minor damage. Annoyed by this, he lugged the big projector across the room and battered it against all the glass that was left in the window, before sending it whirling through the air on to the rubble. He was dimly conscious of rumpled figures around him starting to their feet.

'That stuff's worth thousands you dirty. . . .'

'This is the asshole of the universe,' Gunn said in a dignified way. 'And I am cleaning it out.'

188

'Gunn baby. . . .' Happy had unglued himself, and came towards him with the reassuring smile of a male nurse.

'Stand aside, this is a Happening.' Happy ducked as a film splicer flew past him through the splintered stumps and fragments of amber and violet glass out into the twilight. As Gunn watched it, he realised that it was the twilight of evening not dawn. He had spent nearly twenty-four hours with these creeps.

The removal of the film splicer revealed more bottles and right at the back of the table an ornate pottery hookah. The sight of this hubble-bubble, richly glazed with vine leaves and small birds, churned up Gunn's fury. He began throwing the bottles as fast as he could in order to get at this magnificent breakable.

Midway through the rapid-fire sequence, they rushed him. The Foreman butted him in the stomach. Assembly Liners seized his ankles and just as he got his hands on the hookah, Happy gripped him from behind. Even so the violence of his movements was enough to carry him to the window where with one last desperate wrench he managed to lob the hookah over the sill. It crashed on to a paving-stone below and broke into shards.

Mission fulfilled, Gunn went limp and suffered himself to be dragged down the hallway and thrown down the front steps out into the humid evening.

He lay in the dust for some minutes, feeling the gravel prick his palms, aching with satisfaction. He suddenly thought of the stringed instrument he had smashed in Lil's attic. Perhaps he was turning into an idol-smasher. There were worse trades. Inside, he could still hear voices arguing. The streets, though, were silent, the air still and heavy. The clatter of clearing up at the back of the house reached through the silence. The satisfaction ebbed. He began to feel sore and tired. He got up and started walking down the avenue.

In five minutes he came to a dusty roundabout, labelled Jefferson Circle by signposts almost as tall as the scrubby trees lining it. Between the trees and the signposts, at intervals of ten yards, stood men in khaki denims. It took a second or two for Gunn to notice that they were carrying rifles. They looked pale and nervous in the light of the street-lamps.

He passed three of them before one waved his rifle at him. The rifle had a bayonet fixed on to it.

'Hey you.'

189

'Yes.' He could not be more than eighteen, Gunn thought. Where had they come from, this strange army of the night?

'Whadda hell you think you're doing?'

'Walking.'

'Nobody tell you about the curfew, wise guy?'

'No. Nobody tells me anything.'

'Okay, that does it. You come with me. Cover for me, fellas, will ya?'

He led Gunn off down the main avenue. The soldier walked in front, holding his rifle awkwardly. Gunn wondered whether the order ought not to be reversed so that the soldier could cover him, even goad him with the bayonet, but he felt no inclination to suggest the change. The soldier walked with a curious high-stepping gait. When they came to a jeep parked between the trees on the sidewalk, he stopped and vaguely saluted the plump officer with spectacles who was sitting beside the driver. The officer gave a jerky little salute back. This gesture combined with the way he sat unnaturally rigid up on the jeep recalled an early comic film about motoring, Laurel and Hardy perhaps.

'We picked this guy up on Jefferson, Captain,' the soldier said modestly with only the faintest suggestion that Gunn's capture deserved a medal.

'Okay, soldier. Now what's your story, mac? You look like they hauled your ass through a briar patch.'

Gunn looked himself up and down, noticing for the first time the cuts left by flying glass and the dust and bruises he got being thrown out of the Assembly Line headquarters. Who were these stumblebums dressed up as soldiers and talking like Audie Murphy?

'I'm a British newspaperman. I must get back to my hotel to file my story.'

'Newspaperman, uh?'

'Yeah.'

'How come you look like that?'

'I got a bit too close to the action, Cap'n.' Gunn said.

The captain gave a grin of complicity to indicate that the brass-hats couldn't keep him out of the front line either. Searching for the next section in the dialogue, he hit upon the notion of asking to see Gunn's papers. After a fumble Gunn found his Diner's Club

190

card in his hip pocket. The Captain scrutinised it carefully and ordered his driver to note the number.

Then with a manly nod, he motioned Gunn to jump into the back seat, and the jeep bounded off downtown.

The streets were empty, dusty canyons. On each corner there was a pair of soldiers, sauntering in and out of the dark trees. Black families were sitting out on the peeling porches of some of the houses. Gunn could hear them calling out to the soldiers, their chuckling abuse floating in the sticky night like nuts in molasses.

'Hey man, you is *tough*.'

'Don't shoot, Sheriff, I'm innocent.'

'Look you guys, it's the Green Berets.'

'This is where the paratroopers take over from us,' said the Captain, as they came to a shopping street. The soldiers here looked harder, not so nervous. Two or three shops in each block were burnt out: dark-brown and black lava with metal struts curling up through, behind blackened trellis grills. The smoke was still rising from most of these desolate, spluttering bonfires. The neighbouring shop-fronts were intact, except for an occasional smashed window; they mostly had 'Soul Brother' painted across them in big letters.

The Swinging Sixties Boutique had 'Soul Sister' painted on its window as well. The high-kicking girl dummies in its display were unharmed, their electric green and orange mini-skirts and skinny jerseys still glowing bright in the dusk, their pale chocolate profiles thrown back in blank ecstasy.

'How'd it start?' Gunn asked.

'You tell me,' the Captain said. 'I was out bowling when they called me. Place just caught alight, I guess.'

'Anyone hurt?'

'Plenty. Say, you don't know much for a newsman. Where you been all this time?'

'Who got hurt?'

'Cops. Firemen. And a few negroes. I didn't see anything. They only called out the National Guard after the shooting was over.'

'Why did they do it?'

'The negroes? Had it too easy, I guess. Trouble is, these are mostly field niggers, from the South. They don't adjust to city life. That's it. Maladjusted.'

They passed a small man staring hopelessly at a wrecked shop-

191

front. Enough paint remained on the glass along the top of the window to spell out the anguished plea 'Soul Brother, *please.*' There was still a lick of flame twitching from the heap of rafters and cardboard boxes and detergent packets inside.

Downtown was untouched, the blank façades inviolate. The doormen flipped their toes, as if nothing ever happened in this city. The hotel lobby was full of paratroopers with neatly pressed battle dress faded at the edges. They too held their rifles awkwardly, like umbrellas or fishing-rods. The tidy business couples in the lounge huddled together, looking nervously at the soldiers as though their rifles might go off by accident.

Reception had a pile of messages for Gunn, some from his New York boss, some from the editor in London. As he reached his room, the telephone was already ringing. It was the editor in London.

'Where the hell have you been?'

'Oh, didn't I leave my number?'

'Listen, you have the luck to be in on the biggest bloody riot in American history and you choose to go chasing after a group of highbrow freaks. And you've gone missing for three bloody days. By now every other newspaper in Britain has got its eyewitness account of the Night Fort Clair Went Up in Flames and we can't even find our bloody eyewitness. You're fired. And let me tell you something else, the next time anyone tells me to hire a ponce with a university degree, I'm going to tell him to get stuffed.'

A wonderful exhilaration seized Gunn. He began to understand what Rory Noone meant about it being a tonic when they let you go.

'You still there?' Gunn asked affably.

'Yes,' the editor screamed.

'I won't keep you long, as I don't want to waste your valuable time or the company's valuable time. But before I finally sever our association, I would just like to place it on record and before I say this I must assure you that you have had formidable competition particularly over the last few days and it is therefore with some considerable experience in these matters that I unhesitatingly assert my belief that you are the biggest shit I have ever met. There now, I've said my say. Please give my regards to your wife.'

192

He replaced the receiver and stood for a moment, savouring his calm. Then something prodded him, a sense of incompletion, a feeling of business not quite finished. He picked up the receiver again.

'Get me long distance.' They got him long distance. The time nearing midnight, long distance had no difficulty in getting him through to London. He was on to the editor again inside a minute.

'I forgot to say – '

'Listen, if you think I'm going to be spoken to like that, you can – '

'I forgot to say,' Gunn repeated firmly, 'that this is not just my personal opinion. Everyone else thinks you're a shit too.'

He put down the receiver once more and took a shower.

# 14

'Did you not care for the United States?'

'No,' Gunn said.

'You disliked it?' His father pursued, anxious as was his way, to eliminate the confusion strewn by his *num* question.

'Yes.'

'Is your dislike of the continent connected with your departure from Fleet Street?'

'Yes and no,' Gunn said.

'I respect your evasion. I shall not press the point. You intend then to lodge here while considerng your next move?'

'If that's all right.'

'This is of course your home. We shall be glad of your company. Your mother will make light of the extra work.'

Lil gone, Susanna gone, job gone, bedsitter gone (repossessed by the landlord in his absence after the sub-tenant had failed to pay the rent), Gunn's situation was unpromising. He weighed twelve stone four, a considerable amount of lard for a short man. His eyes had almost disappeared under the soft ridges of flesh creeping up from his often unshaven cheek. They looked like the slits in a pillbox overgrown by brambles. There was a clammy, fleshy finish to his skin now.

'Did you see anything of Margaret's sister-in-law while you were over there? Lilian Inskip. Aubrey Wood was under the impression that you were a friend of hers.'

His father spoke with the artificially weary dispassion of an interrogation officer slipping in the crucial question.

'Yes. She used to be a girlfriend of mine.'

'Used to be? It is strange how all your life seems to be in the past tense. No doubt this is merely a breathing space in your career. *Reculer pour mieux sauter*, as the French have it.'

Once a week, Gunn took a train to London in search of employment. It was a thin autumn. Every newspaper was reducing its staff and realising its assets. One afternoon, on his regular patrol of ancient haunts, Gunn padded, already well juiced, down the long dark passage that led to the Shed and found the end of the passage sealed off by a wall of breeze-blocks. He stood staring at the big dirty-grey oblongs until he was hailed by a reporter.

'What're you doing down there, old man?'

'Who built this bloody Berlin Wall?'

'Oh, didn't you hear? They sold the next-door site. They knocked The Shed down a couple of months ago.'

Yet even from this ill wind, a warm gust blew Gunn's way. Many of those purged left London and found work back in the provinces whence they had come years earlier, their lives thus achieving an unsought pattern but one which in the event often proved surprisingly pleasant, even life-saving; they drank less and slept better. Among those caught up in this diaspora were two of the Last Men : the reporter a few years older than Gunn who had claimed to be the last man he knew who wore sock suspenders and the elderly man who had been the last journalist to join the *News Chronicle* before it folded. Both of them had obtained senior jobs, on one of the bigger provincial dailies in eastern England and they combined to lever Gunn into the last remaining vacancy on the paper – chief roving sports reporter.

'*Sports* reporter?' His father said.

'Yes.'

'And on the *Dispatch* too. We shall be able to read your offerings without added expense.' The extra cost of having to order Gunn's old paper had been a perennial tease.

'I've always liked the *Dispatch*,' Gunn said. 'It's a worthy, comfortable sort of paper.'

'Like me, you mean? You feel it is a paper suitable for a schoolmaster?'

'Or for his son,' said Gunn, declining the challenge.

He played himself in over the autumn by covering local football matches. It was these afternoons that stuck in his mind from that period of his life : the bursting out from warm pubs on to windy touchlines, the beer chilling the pit of his stomach, the sheltering under green trees while the rain billowed over the field, dictating over creaky telephones in pavilions that smelled of creosote, watching the flies crawl up the dusty pane while the copy-taker checked

195

the spelling of a name, and the sergeant-major's brew at tea and the stale white bread in the tomato sandwiches and the rush to the pub in the darkness.

He could not now imagine that he had ever wished to work anywhere else. He reflected on his loss of ambition without surprise or regret. It surprised him only perhaps that he found it so difficult to remember exactly what it was that he had intended to achieve. And then it occurred to him that he had noticed this fuzziness of recollection in older men too and not just in those with drink-sodden memories either. Only Dick, he imagined, would feel the pain of unfulfilled hopes as sharply as ever.

At first, Dick had proclaimed his intention of running Down But Not Out until he dropped. But as he grew weaker, Margaret had to take over more and more of the work, until finally he began to need constant nursing and she had no time to look after the dossers. They accepted defeat and handed Down But Not Out over to the local social services department, which immediately closed it down as a health hazard and transferred the remaining dossers to a huge new purpose-built hostel. Dick and Margaret moved down to stay with Aubrey Wood.

And it was in the middle of the village that Gunn saw them again. At first, he could not think what the creaking noise round the corner could be – too heavy for a bicycle, too light for a cart.

She pushed the wheelchair carefully over the cracked asphalt path. There was not much room to spare between the guard rail and the grass bank. As he came face to face with them, he realised that he was passing the place on the bank where they had lounged the summer before last.

Margaret stopped the chair opposite a break in the bank where a little stream ran under the road, no more than a trickle of water between feathery rushes. Behind her, outlined against the huge flatland sky, dull and autumnal, the rushes swayed in the slight breeze, making her seem very still. Her hair fell across her face and from the way her shoulders were bent down towards the wheelchair she looked as if she was still pushing it, uphill perhaps or into the wind. Dick sat up rather straight in the chair, but this posture of dignity did not conceal, perhaps even emphasised, how he had shrunk. He had the look of an upright little old man. Poised motionless together in front of the dull sky, as they waited for Gunn to reach them, there seemed an unsettling significance

196

to them, some iron moral drawn out of another time and dropped like a propaganda leaflet upon this by-road. The moral itself was hard to pin down – the necessity of suffering possibly, the imminence of death, even the permanence of marriage outlasting both suffering and death.

'Hullo, we have been looking forward to seeing you. Why have we not seen you earlier?'

Although Gunn was prepared for it or knew he should have been prepared, Dick's voice, hoarse and short-breathed, startled him.

'The village straggles a long way,' Gunn said awkwardly, pointing up the road with a limp, superfluous gesture. 'You can live here for months without seeing people.'

'We don't get out much. I catch cold so easily. But I had to see the autumn tints.' He twitched the rug covering him in the direction of a hedgerow elm with a few leaves still clinging to it.

'Dick's fallen in love with nature.' There was a touch of irony in Margaret's voice.

'The small birds outside my window mean a great deal to me. There's nothing special about them to interest the ornithologist, just sparrows and thrushes and a few cheeky little tits, but I find them infinitely absorbing.' Dick gave a tired smile which was wiped off his face by a fit of coughing that shook his whole body. His face was a boat-shaped white skeleton. The skin clung round the jaw and slackened down into dry sallow gullies. The retreating flesh threw the eyebrows into prominence, giving the face a look of mild astonishment.

This placid acceptance enraged Gunn.

'Nature's no fucking help,' he said.

'Once I would have agreed with you,' Dick said. 'But now I find that I am drawn more towards the psalmist's view. Man is like the grass – in the morning, it is green and groweth up, but in the evening etcetera, etcetera.'

'That's all slop.'

'I have to live on slops now. My plumbing can't really deal with anything solid.'

Unable to think how to reply to this, Gunn asked : 'Any news of Down But Not Out?'

'We went to see the new place last month. It's a totally inhuman environment with a lot of bureaucrats telling you to wipe your feet. I'm afraid I gave them all a piece of my mind.' Dick sank back in his chair, cheered by the recollection.

'But we did make Tosh and Dusty promise to come down and visit us here,' Margaret said brightly.

'At least they'd swell your father's congregation,' Dick said. 'You know, Gunn, I never used to be much of a churchgoer but in my present life-situation I find regular worship an enormous stimulus.'

'You must come too,' Margaret said.

'You know I don't believe in that sort of thing.' Gunn said, gruffly to stop himself from crying.

'Aha,' Dick said, with the muffled glee of a shepherd who has prised a lost sheep out of a crevasse. 'When did you last go to church?'

'Oh, four or five years ago, I think, for a wedding.'

'Good. Good. I would like to hear what you think.'

'Of what?' Gunn waited for his answer while Dick was shaken by another fit of coughing.

'Those cigarettes,' Margaret said in a fierce undertone, as if admonishing herself. Gunn thought of Dick dutifully smoking away while handing out bent cigarettes to the dossers, a strange sacrifice now accepted, it seemed.

'I'd like your views,' Dick resumed, 'On Matins as conducted by my father-in-law. It's a prehistoric relic. Not a hint of Series Three. Vatican Two might never have happened.'

'I thought that was for Catholics.'

'We just don't have time left for mediaeval hair-splitting. It's unite or perish.' He was so breathless now that the last few words were all but lost.

'You'll tire yourself, love,' Margaret said.

'What are we here for if not to tire ourselves?' The rug trembled under the electric force of Dick's body, as if it had been placed over his knees to prevent them scorching the countryside.

'Anyway, it's getting cold. We'd better go.'

Gunn resolved, though not without shame at his cowardice, to keep to his own end of the village in future. He did not quite know how to talk to Margaret. He wondered how often she thought about his behaviour, or about him at all. Little or never probably. She had enough to deal with. Yet his curiosity persisted and when she knocked on the door one dark Sunday morning, he accepted her summons to church.

Dick was already sitting, well muffled, in the front seat of the Morris Minor.

'Greetings,' he said as Gunn squeezed into the back.

Margaret pulled the starter which buzzed eagerly but without managing to make the engine catch.

'Probably flooded. We'd better wait a sec.'

They sat in the car, listening to the old springs creak. Gunn considered the back of her head. He liked the old-fashioned way she did her hair, her heavy tweed coat and her old-fashioned slang : Wait a sec, half a jiffy, toodle-oo.

'Since we have a few moments,' Dick said in an uncertain, effortful voice, 'it may be a good opportunity to clear up something else.'

Gunn looked at the back of Margaret's neck.

'I know, Gunn, how long you have known Margaret and how fond you have always been of each other.'

What was *this*?

'I am also well aware of how a person's behaviour can be totally conditioned by stress. So I just want you to know that I really do understand or think I understand what happened that night I brought back my X-ray plates. I take it in a way as an expression of concern for my own problems and I am touched by it.'

*No.* This was terrible. No confessional could untangle this. He could hardly tell Dick that if he had known that Dick was ill he would never have made a pass at Margaret, for that would deny Dick the consolation of a central role in the matter and deny Gunn the excuse of being under stress. Odd that he never thought Dick would find out or considered what his reaction might be.

'I hope this doesn't seem too far-fetched,' Dick went on. 'But I do feel we ought always to try and search out the true motives behind deviant behaviour. I can only say that I have done my best to understand in this instance and that I hope we may all of us continue in good fellowship.'

Gunn muttered : 'No, it doesn't seem far-fetched. No. It is. It's very kind of you. I don't know how to. . . .'

'Margaret of course told me all about it without delay. She mentioned also that there had been an earlier incident, too trivial to be worth mentioning.'

Why the hell had either of them mentioned it then? Oh, so he could absolve them completely. Christ.

199

'It's very kind. . . .'

Margaret tried the starter again. There was a welcome cough. But she let the engine die. When she tried again, the engine refused to catch.

'We're in good time,' Dick said. 'I know I've already given you a lot to think about, but may I plant one more grain of mustard seed in your heads? I would just like you to know that if the idea should ever occur to you, if you should ever feel that if the situation arose where a relationship, a permanent relationship, was a relevant possibility for the two of you, then in that situation I would like you to know that I would welcome that option. I would, as we used to say, be with you in spirit.'

The blessing.

'Yes. Well, the situation doesn't arise, does it?' Gunn said. He found he was almost barking, like a schoolmaster correcting the wrong use of a tense.

'You're waffling, darling,' said Margaret, bending her head as she tried the starter again, as though lowering wind resistance to their progress.

'I just wanted to get things clear,' Dick said serenely. This time the car started and shot forward as Margaret let in the gear clumsily.

All through the service, Gunn's head throbbed and whined. The Rev. Aubrey Wood was in awesome voice. The images of death and hell and resurrection chased each other down the cold aisles : 'And there shall be signs in the sun, and in the moon, and in the stars; and upon the earth distress of nations, with perplexity, the sea and the waves roaring; men's hearts failing them for fear, and for looking after those things which are coming on the earth : for the powers of heaven shall be shaken.' The Advent gospel made Gunn's ears ache.

There was no escaping the portents. Looking up and away from the action, Gunn's eye only ran into the Elizabethan memorial to the bearded dignitary and his wife. The smaller panel showing the couple naked, pot-bellied and wrinkled at neck and elbow seemed particularly unfair, snapshots, as it were, catching them at the ultimate disadvantage of death. Only the man's hand resting on the woman's thigh suggested resistance to the intrusion, some lingering life.

That was the last time he saw Dick. Gunn did not visit the

church again. Anyway, he heard in the village shop that Dick was too weak to go out. Gunn's own life began to take on a dreamy rhythm which was strange to him. He wondered if this sort of life was what people meant by a living death and, if so, why they minded it so much. It seemed to suit him tolerably well.

He met the district surveyor's daughter in the town one day. Why did he now think of her as the district surveyor's daughter? He had always thought of her as Josie before. He must have picked up the Brondesbury habit of attaching name-tags. Josie was pleased to see him. She had little to say, little to offer except herself which he took. He might never have been away. He watched himself behaving badly towards her. The spectacle did not affect him much. 'I treat you badly,' he told her one night in her smart flat, in the new city centre block. She seemed pleased by the remark or by the opportunity to disagree with it. She came with him to the matches and waited uncomplainingly while he wrote his copy. She was a good companion for the drinking in the evening. She seemed to have no wish to assert herself. It was a long time since he had met anyone so modest. He began to feel a faint itch of irritation.

The spring was wet and late. Most of the early cricket matches were rained off. It was towards the end of May that the news came that Dick was dead.

'I hear the fell sergeant's got him,' was how Antic put it when they met.

'Yes,' Gunn said. He thought of Dick on death parade : odd socks, no blanco on his belt. Still, he would probably get on all right in his own way. He would turn down promotion of course, insist on serving in the ranks, get up the subalterns' noses.

Playing with this fancy, Gunn was jolted by grief. He missed Dick more than he had expected. In truth he had not expected to miss him at all. This was nothing to do with whatever Dick had achieved at Down But Not Out. It was not to do with achievement at all. Although Dick not seem to distinguish much between people, he himself had an individual quality which, now that it had gone, had seemed to be an essential part of things. That quality was not saintliness and Gunn resolved never to let memory trick him into thinking that it was.

'The fell sergeant,' Gunn echoed, dwelling on the phrase.

'Yes,' said Antic Hay, 'I think death really must be rather like

201

an old army sergeant. Get fell in there, you dozy lot of layabouts. Why are you naked, you horrible little man, yes, you, call that a shroud looks more like a whore's drawers to me, and get your hair cut and your finger-nails are like a bleeding vampire's.'

They were standing drinking whisky mac in the Tavern at Lord's looking out over the ground. A thin drizzle was falling. The grass was very green. The ground was deserted, the bar nearly empty. Out on the pitch play was proceeding in a dour fashion, the cricketers almost outnumbering the spectators. Gunn scribbled notes as he peered through the steamed-up window.

'I didn't know you liked cricket,' he said.

'I don't much.' Antic stared glumly at the window. 'But my shrink thinks it's good for me. He sends a lot of his patients to watch. He encourages us to keep the score or, if you aren't mathematically minded, to master the finer points of the game — whether the pitch has any turn in it or if the fast bowlers are getting any movement and so on. My shrink used to be a butterfly.'

'A what?'

'It's a cricket club, like the MCC. The Butterflies. Tell me, Gunn, don't you feel we are missing something here?'

'What sort of thing?'

'Well, I suppose we shall be able to tell our grandchildren that while Paris was on fire for liberty we were watching Usborne, G., bowl his in-swingers to a defensive field in the hope of securing the first innings' bowling points. But will it be enough?'

'Oh that. You miss the barricades? What a pity, they're coming off.'

The rain was thicker now. Gunn could scarcely pick out the white figures converging on the gate in the pavilion fence, the outlying fielders breaking into a trot.

'I wish I knew some people in Paris,' Antic said, returning with the brown brimming glasses. 'I'd just like to go over and see it all for a day or two. Those debates in the Odéon particularly.' He pronounced it *Odéon* in a very French manner.

'I don't think it counts as a revolution until someone gets hurt,' Gunn said, fiercely spearing one of the pickled onions on the low formica table.

Fistfuls of rain began to gravel against the plate-glass. Antic took the glasses over to the bar for a refill while Gunn finished his notes. Antic was wearing new boots of the kind worn by men on oil rigs and a flak-jacket in camouflage colours. His general demeanour was stern.

'But doesn't it appeal to you though, to break free of your class assumptions, to take spontaneity as your only rule – be realistic – demand the impossible? Absolute bliss in that dawn.'

'You don't think you're a bit old for all that?' Gunn said. 'I mean for you it would be more like bliss in the afternoon. Oh, did you hear that?'

'What?' Antic asked, looking round wildly.

'They're going to take lunch early. I imagine they'll inspect the pitch at about three.'

'Well, no point in hanging about here then, is there?' Antic said. 'Anyway, I have something to show you. In fact, that's why I arranged to meet you. I want to take you to a film.'

'What film?'

'It'll be a surprise.'

*Come Blow Your Porn* was screened miles away in a side-street flea-pit. The cinema's crumbling plaster pillars were half hidden by flapping cardboard placards displaying murky stills beneath the title, ill-scrawled in lemon dayglo paint. As Gunn shook the rain off himself, he noticed that a nail fixing one of the placards to the plaster went right through the hand of the large nude sprawling across it. He thought he detected a hint of agony behind the supposed ecstasy in her parted lips and rolling eyes. He pointed this stigma out to Antic.

'Purely accidental. You won't find s.m. here. This is a soft-porn house. Come in quickly. If we hang about here too long they'll think we're scared to go in.'

'Why do we have to go in anyway?'

'Wait and see.'

The small auditorium was almost as empty as the cricket ground. The seats creaked as they sat down. The air was laden with dust and stale peppermint. The slumbrous peace was broken only by a cold draught under the seats and the oppressive whirr of the projector.

Behind the whirr, an asthmatic trickle of dance music made itself heard. After a seemingly endless procession of scratchy advertisements for Indian restaurants and Italian aperitifs, the film started.

203

Two young men were sitting in a jalopy outside a petrol station in the middle of a sandy, stony nowhere. Their tee-shirts were stained with sweat. They were drinking beer out of cans and complaining about the heat. A girl with crew-cut hair and a round face came out of the tin hut behind the petrol pumps, her face screwed up against the sun. She scuffed up the dust and stones as she slouched over to them. As she leant in through the car window, Gunn saw that it was Lil. She asked the young men what they wanted. The camera zoomed in for their reply. They both had big slobbery mouths and narrow, dull faces; one of them had buck teeth and spots.

'Let's get the hell out of here,' Gunn said.

'Sit down. You'll only torture yourself by imagining if you don't. It's quite harmless, mostly.'

'Come on. Move,' Gunn growled.

'Make up your minds,' said a voice from some way behind them.

'Shut the fuck up,' Gunn shouted.

'Shut the fuck up yourself,' said the voice.

On the screen the youths were trying to persuade Lil to get in the car with them. It was a slow business. The dialogue was mostly yeah, well, uh, I don't know, well, uh, come on, it's OK, whaddya-mean OK. Gunn standing, half-turned in his seat, yelling at the voice in the darkness, gradually found his attention being pulled back towards the screen. He sat down, ashamed at his curiosity.

Eventually, Lil agreed to get in the back. First, though, she filled the car with petrol. The camera lingered on the nozzle of the pump jammed into the petrol tank. The car roared off down the minor road. Ribbon of black tarmac. Dust. Desultory talk. Heat haze. Distant mountains. Desolation.

Then the youth who wasn't driving climbed into the back of the car and began kissing Lil on her face, neck and ears. She sat unresisting, her body moved only by the jolting of the car. The youth, not the buck-toothed one, tried to pull her tee-shirt off, tugging it up from the hem. She brought her forearms down hard on his hands and he stopped trying. The driver watching in his mirror grinned. Then she took off the shirt herself and folded it neatly on her lap. Her body was pale pink against the worn, dark upholstery. The youth brought his hand up to her breast.

The picture suddenly jumped to a scene of the car stopping

204

outside a bar. The interruption of the previous scene made Gunn's heart thump against his ribs.

'Two-and-a-half minute cut,' Antic whispered, 'Censor.'

Lil went into the bar with the two youths. There was a flabby bare-chested man of about fifty polishing glasses behind the bar. An unexpectedly square jaw jutted out between his sad pendulous cheeks.

Lil sat down at a table with the youth. As the barman waddled out from behind the bar to attend to them, his back view revealed that he was naked except for a gingham apron. He gave the customers an ingratiating smile.

'Welcome to the Bare, Bare Bar,' he said in a soft high voice that was somehow familiar. There was something familiar about his face too.

Lil patted the buttock nearest to her.

'Hi,' she said.

Gunn got up and walked out. Antic caught up with him in the foyer.

'Now Gunn, please.'

'Aren't you missing the best bits?'

'I've seen it twice already. It's mild stuff. Rather pretty in parts.'

'Oh for Christ's sake. . . .'

'Would you mind if it was another girl, someone you didn't know?'

'Of course I wouldn't.'

'Isn't that rather hypocritical? Other girls have lovers and husbands too. Do you consider their feelings?'

'Their feelings are for them to consider. Why do you think she. . . .'

'Assembly Line needed some cash – for the Fort Clair project among other things. In fact they made a bomb. At least the Foreman did. He's making a whole lot more pictures.'

'With Lil?'

'I don't know. Haven't heard from her for months. I don't even know whether she's still with Happy.'

'And is Happy a millionaire too?'

'I expect so. You see, we have not all come to sad ends. Lil is a film star, Happy perhaps a millionaire. Poppy now, Poppy is deputy headmistress of a primary school, in Brondesbury in fact.'

205

'I don't give a shit what's happened to Poppy,' Gunn said.

'You don't. I thought – '

'You thought wrong.'

'I thought you might like to know what has happened to our little coterie. You know Clara and I are getting one of those new quickie divorces?'

'Let's get on. It's raining.' Gunn hustled off towards the tube.

'She's expecting,' said Antic, running to keep up with him, one foot forced into the gutter by the narrowness of the pavement. 'I have written to the Family Planning Association to complain – Brick seems pleased, though.'

'Brick?'

'Yes, they're getting married. Can't say I entirely approve. He's supposed to be off heroin now, but I don't believe it.'

'Jesus. And what happened to – ?'

'Minty. She's off farming somewhere in Wales. Ecologically. I didn't know you knew them so well.'

'I didn't know them well. I just wanted to know what had happened to them.'

'Well, that's what,' Antic said irritably. 'Anyway, you're all right, my dear Gunn. The Neville Cardus of the *Dispatch*. Without the musical side of course.'

'Bullshit,' Gunn said. Yet there was a musical, or at least rhythmical side to his new life. He and the old Wolseley he had just bought soon found a comfortable place in the sodden caravan of the cricket scribes. In the high season they bumped along in convoy from one county town to the next, carrying all their belongings in the back, self-contained tortoises travelling slow and easy in their ancient shells. Each car had its own smell, its individual jumble of possessions : dirty shirts, jock-straps, frayed pads, golf-clubs, crumpled race-cards, a framed photograph of wife or child now usually deserted or at best visited only on rare and awkward occasions, usually a dinner jacket kept in polythene for the cricket club dinner or any other worthwhile invitation to free boozing, scrabble sets and fresh packs of cards and paperbacks for wet days. And beneath these smaller articles were wedged heavier sacred objects : a curious mahogany tie-and-trouser press, a collapsible rowing machine, a gadget for playing bridge with yourself, all nicely to hand, no worries.

Finding a bed was no anxiety either. If the hotel was full or had flung them out, the majority were happy to doss down among the junk in the back seats of their cars, the drink inside them assuaging any discomfort; others, more pernickety, doubled up with friends inside the hotel by creeping round the back and up the service stairs. But the car was home.

On appearing in his vehicle at Edgbaston one dewy morning in June, Gunn was congratulated by the doyen of the fraternity, a man famous for the augustan rotundity of his periods and said to be so learned that he was able, when describing a spate of bumpers from the Lancashire fast bowlers, to slip in a medium-length passage from Lucretius without looking it up. This personage circled the Wolseley warily, bending down to inspect the condition of the tyres before pronouncing:

'A most commendable conveyance. I always think a Wolseley has the reliable quality of a *cru bourgeois.*'

Gunn had found his milieu. These men had a soft, rained-upon quality which freed them from too much anger but did not blur their precise perception of pleasure. They were skilled both in the wangling and in the enjoying of treats. And in their work they strove towards a rough consensus which eliminated the stress of competition without smothering individuality. Nobody was made to feel inexpert. All views were welcomed and respected.

'Hey, Christ, I missed that one. I was in the bog. How'd they get him?'

'Got one to leave him.'

'Nah, went straight through, did that one. You see it, Gunn?'

'I thought it went with the arm.'

'I thought it left him.'

'Left him a fraction perhaps.'

'OK. Went with the arm *and* left him.'

The scribes slowed him down and soothed his nerves. He found that he could spend days at a time in his parents' house without losing his temper. He even began to appreciate the country round about. He began too to chart the seasons and in the following winter felt as he had not felt since childhood the bite of the east wind and the clang of the frosts. The first pale green streaks of the late, hard-won spring stirred forgotten disquiet in him, a feeling of lifting and opening which he did not quite know what to do with.

The narrow paths beside the ditches, the blaze of mustard in the fields, the crowfoot and cress trailing like a drowned girl's hair where the streams broadened, the clayponds and the tall poplars – the small delights of this working landscape stood out sharply from the blur of his memories, more sharply in fact than did his mother and father who after all were still there where they had always been. He began to realise how little he had cared for them, how concentrated all his thoughts had been on getting away, up, out. He began to feel that he had missed them irrevocably, like a book which could be properly seized and loved only at a particular age. What they had done to him and he to them was beyond change, dead and buried. Only the landscape could be rediscovered.

Rediscovery was a lonely business, though. Each moment of silence as the wind dropped and the tractor cut out two fields away only set him further apart. As he slipped home down the lane at the back of the church, the long way round, he had at first congratulated himself on avoiding Margaret, even reached the end of the village with relief. But as the spring opened up, the relief faded, and he turned off the main road with something near regret.

There was no identifiable moment at which he decided. Even before he knocked on the rectory door, he was already asking himself how he had come to change his mind. The sun clasped the back of his neck as Margaret unlatched the door and stood before him blinking into the bright light. She greeted him with that same unhesitating warmth he remembered from their meeting on the Embankment, a warmth which filled him with such joy that he felt like turning and running for it before the old embarrassments caught up with him.

'Yes, I'd like to come for a walk. I'll get my coat.'

'You don't need a coat. It's flaming July.' He was annoyed to find himself as gruff as ever.

'Oh, so it is. Why did I – walks always seem to mean coats here.' She too appeared annoyed with herself, for being clumsy.

'Have you been seeing people much?'

'Not much,' she said.

'I should have called round before. It's a year since.'

'I'm glad you didn't. I mean, I just wouldn't have been very good at talking to you. You can see, I'm not now either. I'm out of practice.'

208

'It's not a question of practice. After a week here, I can't cope with the boys in the box at all.'

'The boys in the box. It sounds very . . . I can't think quite what it sounds like.'

'Odd anyway. You did know I was a sports reporter now, for the *Dispatch*?'

'*Nice.*'

'Don't be sarcastic.'

'I'm not. I've always liked the idea of sports reporters.'

'But I remember you being shocked about me becoming a journalist at all.'

'Was I? I expect I was. I used to be very prim. No, not prim. Priggish, I mean. But Dick broadened my ideas a bit.'

'This was when you were married to Dick,' he said sharply.

'Was it? I seem to have lost count of time.'

They walked down the village street. They were standing half-way between the Baptist chapel and the post office when she stopped and turned to face him.

'I've lost my faith, you know.'

It was so abrupt that he was more angry than embarrassed. This confession was something that needed leading up to. It should have been confided in more solitary country, not on the narrow asphalt path in the middle of the village with an old woman he didn't know squeezing past them with her silly wicker shopping-basket on little wheels.

'Well, I'm sorry about that,' he said. 'I imagine it being very difficult even though I can't really understand what it means exactly, never myself having . . . was it because of Dick?'

'How do you mean? Oh, him dying.' She said 'dying' briskly rather as Dick himself might have done, as though to make Gunn feel ashamed of not having used the word himself.

'Yes, I suppose that's what I mean. I mean the senselessness.' He was annoyed with himself now, for using such a trite word.

'Anyway, no, it started quite a time before he died. That's why I used to get so irritated with his cheerfulness later on, his acceptance of it, which of course makes me feel all the guiltier now. Anyway, I'm sorry, I shouldn't really have mentioned it to you. It must seem such a trivial problem.'

'Not trivial. You might give me credit for a little imagination.'

'I suddenly felt I had no resistance,' she said.

'Resistance to what?' He asked.

'The world . . . growing old.'

'Growing old?'

'You hadn't thought of me minding about lines and wrinkles? That's how people think of parsons' wives, you see. We're expected to be above caring about things like that.'

'Did you want to have children?'

'I still do. The doctor said it was possible, but I would need a small op. Somehow, though, we never got around to it, and now I suppose it's too late.' The last words were thrown away in a rush.

'We? You mean Dick didn't want children. It's not a thing you don't get around to.'

'How could you know?' she asked.

'Well, did he want children?'

'He said, I can't remember, no, he said they would be an uncovenanted blessing, I think that's the phrase. He said they would be windfalls.'

'He didn't say he wanted them,' Gunn said.

'Not in those very words. I know what you think. You think Dick was milk-and-water, not quite human, sort of sexless. Well he wasn't. He was very interested in sex. He said it was a sacrament.'

'Like marriage or instead of marriage?'

'Marriage isn't a sacrament, in our church at least.'

'Oh. Anyway, is waiting for windfalls the right way to go about things? Oughtn't you to plant something?'

'Well, perhaps. Come back for tea.'

Clouds began to creep up from the horizon. A thorn bush, its leaves bright green, its cream blossoms already edged with brown, snagged her long full skirt. As she moved off the narrow path to avoid the thorns, the skirt, faded red-checked gingham, swirled like a square-dancer's. Length, style and material had all been out of fashion so long that they were just coming back again. He stopped for a moment and watched her walking away from him – her shoulders twisting and ducking now to avoid the overhanging branches. Her legs were already brown although it was still early summer. There was a scratch across the left leg, just where the calf swelled. The blood, from a bramble or a hawthorn, had hardly dried.

What an awkward life it must be to be confronted by such questions as faith, marriage, children, growing old, instead of, as Antic said, having to make the questions up for yourself. Unmodern, strange.

The damp cool of the Lincolnshire rectory sponged his face as he stood to let her pass through the open door under the heavy purple trusses of wistaria blossom. The tabby cat lying on the threshold got up and stepped down the hallway to announce them.

'Stooky, Stooky, you egregious beast!' The booming from the rector's study was like a series of small explosions.

By the time they entered the study, the cat was already arranged *passant guardant* on the rector's lap.

Aubrey Wood sat beneath the brass gasolier in a shabby armchair. The room was dark and mouldy. It was full of books. The beetling shelves threatened to flatten the dilapidated chairs and tables. Plump and purple-wattled now, he could scarcely get up from the chair to greet them, but held out the cat as a substitute.

'Have you met Stooky? Spelled Stiffkey, of course, after the Rector.'

'The one who finished up in the lion's cage?'

'The same. All our pets are named after scandalous priests. Our last cat was a ginger tom. Hewlett, after the Red Dean. Shake hands, Stooky.'

The cat suffered his paw to be ceremoniously held, then gently withdrew it and began washing it.

'That's right, Stooky. Can't be too careful these days. Sit down.'

Gunn removed from the chair a damp-spotted copy of the Selected Works of Cardinal Newman. Underneath the Newman and firmly stuck to it by the damp was a foreign paperback. The word *Désir* on the cover caught Gunn's eye.

'You are blooming, my Margaret. You should go out more often. I wish I could accompany you but I fear my phlebbers would make me too slow for you. Anyway, today I've been down to a tremendous do at Walsingham. The Visitation of the BVM. They really put on a first-class show. I'm quite fagged out.' He slumped back into his chair as though to confirm this claim, then jerked forward with a fresh spurt of energy.

211

'Gosh, it is a treat to see you, Gunby Hallam Goater. I'm afraid we don't see many young people.'

'I'm not very good with young people,' Margaret said.

'I must admit I rather hog her company,' Aubrey Wood went on. It was not his way to take note of gruff remarks. 'In fact, it is such smashing fun for me having her back here that I dread the inevitable day when she gets married again.'

'There's no question of that, dada,' Margaret said.

'Stooky doesn't want our Mags to get hitched again, do you Stooky-wooky?' Aubrey tickled the cat with his large fingers as though prompting it to give the desired answer. 'Stooky likes Mags to put out his saucer for him doesn't he? We don't want a nasty man to take our Mags away, do we?'

There was steel in this playfulness, Gunn thought. He began to be annoyed by the warning off but then thought that it was just how he himself would feel in the circumstances. Gunn too would try to hang on to what he had got. He liked stickers and sticky things. That was really what he had against his parents that they let go so easily, let go of him in particular. He wanted ferocious attachments.

And looking at her across the disused fireplace, the tattered books piled high behind the wire fender, he saw what he wanted. Aubrey Wood's dialogue with Stiffkey had had the opposite effect to that intended. Gunn now had a fixed determination to marry Margaret, not at all to spite her father but to gain access to her world. He wanted to be with people who if they changed their minds at all changed them clumsily and with pain, not rapidly and gracefully like a skater coming out of a jump-turn.

Outside the window the rain began, drumming on the roof of the small verandah. He remembered the rain on the roof of the white attic and thought of those few graceful moments, when he too had skimmed across the ice: soft arm on white sheet, tangled dark hair smeared straight by sweat and sweet trickle. He wondered if other men thought about such moments when deciding to get married.

As Aubrey Wood boomed on – 'Father van Cleef's cell is a bower of lilies' – Gunn began to see the Brondesbury crowd as an ice-panto troupe jumping, twirling, skimming across the ice, principal girl and boy frisky and elegant in fur-trimmed tunic and cap, Happy the trick-skater clearing Ali Baba's jars in one

212

glorious leap, Antic, veteran buffoon, landing expertly on his bottom – all catering neatly to each other's style, leaving the crowd gasping, but never able quite to disguise that awkward jolt as they came off the ice and clumped up the gangway to change for the next act.

'I shook them up by pronouncing the Tridentine blessing, but the Bishop took it on the chin.'

Margaret was only half-listening to her father. She had a look that was both concentrated and abstracted, like someone playing the piano. How serious she was. He had thought of himself as serious too, at least in the sense of getting on. That was all over. His was now an idler's seriousness, the kind encountered in the middle of a pub evening, a sudden half-focused obsession with some tiny point. But she was seriously serious, all of a piece, moved altogether not wavering, ironic or withholding. When she turned, her whole being turned. And he realised now that she had turned to him as she had once turned to Dick and meant him to see that she had.

'Flowerdew, the one who looks like a weasel, said if the papists can't have Latin now he didn't see why we should have to have it either.'

She wanted him, one way or another. Everything she had said that afternoon was said for a purpose, everything about religion and sex and children. She told him abruptly, partly because she was shy but partly also because she scorned artifice. Her one aim was to get it all out in the open and done with. She was not forcing her troubles upon him but stating her position, even her position about Dick too. His memory was not to be mocked but it was not an obstacle.

'The Bishop, however, likes to think of himself as a classicist and was more interested in rebuking me, wrongly as I have since discovered, for uttering a false quantity.'

She smiled at him, not her father. Accomplices. It was all over, like one of those games in which you are eliminated as soon as you blink or smile.

He was surprised how quickly their marriage was arranged. The 'decent interval' rushed by, Aubrey Wood turned out to be easy. As soon as he discovered that they intended to live at the rectory, he was enchanted with the whole project and claimed it as his own. Besides it seemed better to Gunn that Margaret

213

should have someone to live with and to care for while he was on tour with the scribes. Gunn's parents too, within their limits, appeared pleased at the prospect of continuing to see more of him, though they had reservations, his mother about Margaret's age and chances of children, his father about the clerical connection. Even so, Gunn had the sensation of for once having done something to please almost everybody.

There was penance to be done, though. Matins every Sunday. Margaret had not told her father about her loss of faith and Gunn wanted no arguments. They sat side by side on the cold pew, hands now and then enlaced, as Aubrey Wood expounded the Incarnation, a word he always pronounced with especial gusto as though referring to an obscure and wonderful wine.

'Does it upset you now to hear him pounding out all this stuff?' Gunn asked once, walking home.

'No, just surprising. I think, how strange that I could have believed that, and that, and that.'

'As complete and total as that, is it?'

'Of course not. In the night, when I'm alone. I feel riddled with uncertainty. But sitting there, in that pew, I am certain. I feel invulnerable. Almost scornful.'

'How weird. I just feel nothing at all, not even disbelief.'

'Now that I do find hard to imagine. Gunn, don't you think we ought to live together before we get married?'

'What?'

'I've shocked you. But don't you think we ought to see if we're . . . suited?'

'Uh, well, you caught me off balance. I suppose almost anything I say now is bound to sound rather feeble but, well, yes.'

'You'd better pack an overnight bag then. You've got an early start tomorrow. And don't pay any attention to dada's dirty looks. He won't dare to say anything.'

Her plain speaking reduced Gunn to a laggard schoolboy. He didn't mind that in the least.

The truth was that in the rush of arrangements the question had scarcely occured to him. Arriving home late and tired out with watching cricket and writing about it and drinking with the scribes, he had so far been contented with a bedtime kiss.

That night, a sticky August night, he did his best to catch up the wasted time. 'I'm not used to this sort of thing,' she said. But because she was so unused it was he who felt he had reason to be grateful. Her awkwardness, her strength renewed him. The whole hot, dark room seemed to hum with pleasure.

He lay with his head beached on her breast listening to the rustle of the creeper outside her low window and the ticking of his watch and the bump of her heart beneath him.

She talked slowly, for once gentle, with confidence. Even when she interrupted herself, there was a caressing ease in her voice.

'Do you mind me saying all the things that I expect women usually say? It's just that I had not expected a happy ending.'

'Don't tempt fate, my dear.'

'This is already a happy ending.'

'Ah, that's all right then.'

'I expect you want to know if it was the same with Dick.'

'I don't want to know. And I wasn't going to ask.'

'No, but you would wonder. Anyway, it was, or used to be. I think he was ill for a long time and overworked before that.'

He said nothing. He had nothing to say.

'I told you about the scholarship, didn't I? No, the letter came after you went off to the Roses match. They're founding a scholarship in Dick's memory, a post-graduate scholarship in social work.'

'That's wonderful, wonderful.'

'You don't mind marrying an old hag, do you?'

'You're not. You're not. You seem really younger than other people.'

'More childish, you mean. It's because I haven't been out much.'

Already, he reflected sleepily, Dick was being transmuted into superman : saint, demon lover, organising genius, the sort of man whose benign influence spread far beyond the grave. Perhaps he had been like that. Gunn let his hand rest on Margaret's warm, round thigh and thought of death and love and whether Underwood would get anything out of the wicket tomorrow.

He woke early for him. The scent of the morning pulled him out of bed. He had to bend right down to crane his neck and shoulders out of the window which started at floor level and finished no higher than his chest. The dew was still heavy on the lawn, although the sun was already above the hedge at the end of the garden. Where the hedge stopped, he could see the road

215

winding through the village. Some way off, at the point where the road lost itself in a belt of trees, a woman's figure appeared. She was small and seemed bent or rather bulky. Unusually for a country woman, she wore a long skirt. In fact, as she came closer he saw that she had to hold it up in front of her with one hand.

Then it became clear that she was not old at all. Her face was a clear pale blob and her back was not curved but simply inclined forward to balance the weight of what she was carrying. He craned further out of the window, catching the honey-smell of the buddleia in the border below. He shivered, having forgotten he was naked.

The bundle on her back was modern, a rucksack of some kind, no, a baby-carrier, one of those canvas things modelled on an Indian papoose-pouch. He was watching her so intently that when she turned in at the rectory gate at the far end of the railings, he had to draw back hurriedly to keep out of sight. But it was only when she shut the gate behind her and started up the path that he recognised her; first, the trudging gait and then, a split second later, the round, earnest face. And the recognition made him start forward.

She saw him and stopped.

'You. What are you doing up there?'

'And you down there?' He heard Margaret stirring in bed behind him. He smiled a sickly smile.

'I'll put some clothes on and come down.'

'Whoosaa. . . ?' mumbled Margaret's voice from behind him.

'Lil.'

'Lil?'

'Yes. She's . . . downstairs.' He was about to mention the baby but was suddenly absorbed by the sight of Lil unhooking the canvas carrier and placing it carefully on the gravel by the front door. He could just see a pink smudge wrapped in white wool.

'I'll go down and see what she's up to.'

'No, no I'll go.' Margaret said. But Gunn had already grabbed a dressing-gown and was running down the stairs.

As he yanked open the front door, she was bouncing the baby on her arm. The baby was moaning quietly.

'What's he called? Is it a he?' He pointed nervously as though the baby needed picking out of a crowd of other babies.

'Yes. Sixtus.'

'Sixtus. It can't be your sixth child already.'

'No. Happy thought of it, so we could call him Sixty, like a child of the Sixties.' She spoke more slowly than she used to. She seemed ill at ease.

'Oh, Happy.'

'Can't you see the likeness?' She pushed the baby forward, so that the fleecy blanket fell away from his head. The baby had a tangle of dark hair.

For a moment, clattering down the stairs, Gunn had nearly missed his footing at the thought that the baby might have been his own. Then he remembered that had all been years ago.

Screening his eyes a little against the morning sun, Gunn congratulated himself on his calm. He heard Margaret coming down the stairs.

'Baby. I had no – how . . . how marvellous. How *marvellous*. Congratulations.' She swept the baby into her arms.

'Congratulations,' Gunn said, embarrassed not to have thought of saying this himself.

'What's he – '

'Six – '

'No, what's he called?'

'Sixty, short for Sixtus.'

'How marvellous,' Margaret said, rocking the baby.

'How did you get here?'

'We walked,' Lil said.

'Walked? Where from?'

'Over there.' She waved in the direction she had come from. 'We were travelling with friends.'

'Oh. Where are your friends now then?' Gunn asked.

'They have travelled on.'

'You must have started early.'

'We always start at dawn, when the earth is free.'

'Where did you sleep then?'

'In the fields.'

'What about Sixty?'

'Sixty was in the van. Have you got any *food*?' She made it sound like a magical substance.

'I'm just getting the breakfast. Come in.'

'This house has good vibrations,' Lil said as they went into the kitchen. 'This is a good place for Sixty.'

'What does your mother think of Sixty? She used to be so fond of children. She was so sad that Dick and I never had any.'

'My mother,' said Lil, in a different, sharper tone, 'says she is not well enough to cope with Sixty.'

'Oh,' said Margaret.

'I think she would be well enough if I was married to Sixty's father.'

'But you aren't, no, how silly, of course you aren't,' Margaret said. She stirred the scrambled eggs fiercely.

'What are *you* doing here then?' Lil turned to Gunn. 'I mean you're just about the last person I'd have expected to see in my sister-in-law's house.'

There was no way out of it.

'We're going to be married.'

'Wow.' Lil sat down and burst into hysterical laughter.

'What a glorious baby.' Aubrey Wood always made a scene-stealer's entry: noiseless and sudden if the action was already rolling, rumbling from afar and building up to a crescendo if hush prevailed.

He bent down and looked solemnly at the baby lying in the canvas carrier, as though meditating baptism, then moved on to Lil, 'Lilian. My dear. A treat. Are you all right?'

'Yes, I was just laughing.'

'Laughing?' Behind his good humour there was a hint that she had infringed his copyright.

'This is your baby?'

'Yes, do you like him?'

'He is a joy.'

'You really mean that?' For the first time Gunn began to take in how scared she looked, scared and bedraggled like someone who had just been arrested. Her way of emphasising certain words was no longer a cute trick, a Clique badge of superiority. It was a reverberation of her unease. She had let her hair grow long again.

'An untold joy,' said Aubrey Wood.

'I want him always to hear it like it is. I want him to have an aura of truth.'

'I'm sure he will.'

'I don't want him to get fucked up by words. I want him to touch and feel, you know, reach out.'

Keeping his eye steadily upon Lil as she spoke, the Rev. Aubrey Wood groped for his coffee and his spectacles. When these were in position, he began to unfold his copy of *The Times*.

'That's all shit,' Lil said, tapping the newspaper with the spoon from the cereal, leaving a milky ring on the small ads.

'Not all,' Aubrey replied. 'I have found the clerical appointments perfectly reliable.'

'It's full of shit.'

'Anyway you mustn't hurt poor Gunn's feelings. Or do you exclude the *Dispatch* from your commination?'

'Gunn swallows shit, like the rest of them.'

'I only do the cricket reports. I am quite harmless,' Gunn said.

'Cricket is full of shit.'

'So am I,' Gunn said.

She suddenly changed mood, gave a pale smile and took Sixty out of the carrier and bounced him on her knee.

'I think he has a good karma,' she said, taking a plate of scrambled eggs from Margaret.

'Yes, they're fresh, from the butcher,' Margaret said absentmindedly, looking fondly at Sixty.

Gunn felt quite detached. Lil revived no pangs of love or lust. She was simply a person from another country.

Unusually, the ground was within easy reach of the rectory, but Gunn had to drive fast to arrive in time for the start of play. Once inside the press box, he began to feel sleepy. The sunlight through the glass bore down upon his eyelids. An opening batsman recently imported from Pakistan was taking the visiting bowlers apart. Underwood had pulled a muscle and was not playing. The batsman was a small man, beautifully made. He leant into his drives and swayed away from his cuts like a skater. The ball seemed to stop and start to suit him. Gunn began to doodle a few lyric flights in his mind. His head started to loll against the wooden partition. As he drifted off, his detachment disappeared.

Images of anxiety – people running, scared, upturned faces – began ganging up on him. Or was it only cricketers fleeing indoors from the rain? No, there was something behind the rain, some alien intimations to be glimpsed, quicksilvery, amoral movements, hinting at passion and danger. And something white too, like an umpire's coat, or a doctor's, or was it a sheet, crumpled, just a crumpled stained sheet? And that heavy clattering trying to frighten him, trying to stop him . . . stop him doing what?

'Come on, Gunby. We've just got time for a swiftie before they come back. *Solo pioggerella.*' There was a running competition among the scribes to see who could say 'It's only a shower,' in the most different languages. Another of their running jokes was to invent Wisden weather records :

'It's the second wettest June since Patsy Hendren found a frog in his box at Old Trafford.'

They were still clattering down the wooden steps leading from the press stand. It must have clouded over suddenly as it had on so many days that summer. The rain was heavy now, coming straight down from a bruised sky. The ground was empty. The rain had reduced the marks of the pitch to faint brown traces on the overwhelming green. Now and then the sun behind the slow-moving clouds made the rain glisten. As the day progressed, the clouds came to a halt. They spent the afternoon drinking in the press tent.

Play was abandoned at teatime, when the ground was water-logged beyond recall. Gunn took the Wolseley very slowly home along minor roads. Overhanging branches, heavy with rain and full summer leaf, slapped the sides of the car as if joined in boozy camaraderie with the driver.

The rain lightened and a bleary wash of sunshine sprawled across the flat horizon. Gunn's spirits lifted as he came out of the twisty woodland lanes, on to the long straight road across the fenland.

There was little traffic so that the raspberry-coloured dot in the distance caught his attention at once. He watched it grow into a raspberry-coloured Bedford van, doing about seventy and painted all over with gaudy butterflies and kabbalistic graphics : several signs of the zodiac, a couple of Chinese ideograms and the Egyptian sign of life over the bonnet. In the same instant he saw Lil sitting in the front seat. She had her eyes closed. The driver was only a blur of beard and tank-top.

Gunn thrust his head out of the window making the Wolseley swerve. There were more graphics on the back of the van

220

dominated by the scientific signs for male and female boldly painted, one on each door. The van soon dwindled back into a raspberry dot and that was the end of it.

He braked and brought the car to a halt. He was seized by regret, not regret for the loss of Lil herself, that had bitten him more sharply the other time he had seen her driving off in a painted wagon, from Pier 92 in New York City. But that time the wide open spaces lay ahead of him. Now the openings were closing up and self-pity had a free run. Seen in the light of five double Bell's between the lunch and tea intervals, the disappearing raspberry dot looked like the end of youth.

At the sound of his car, Margaret rushed out of the front door. 'She's gone.'

'I know. I saw her on the road.'

'Why didn't you bring her back then?'

'She was in the van going like hell. Anyway, she's free to go.'

'No, but she's left the baby.'

'What do you mean, left?'

'Left. What else could I mean, Gunn?'

'No, I mean for how long – a day, a week?'

'Oh. No, for ever.'

'For ever?'

'Well, for a very long time. As far as she can see ahead, I suppose. Look.' She handed him a note.

The note was written in big letters on several pieces of kitchen notepaper held down on the kitchen table by the teapot which was still warm. The biro had scratched and blurred on the grease-blotched paper. The lines wavered unevenly up towards the right-hand side, echoing the appeal contained in them :

'Please look after Sixty for me. I'm afraid I would fuck him up. Nappies and stuff are in the carrier. Peace. Lil.'

'Why didn't *you* stop her then?' Gunn asked.

'There was a vestry meeting. I asked her if she would be all right by herself and she said she would make herself some tea. When we came back, she was gone and Sixty was lying asleep in the cot in her room. She asked if she could stay here for a few days. She said she needed to rest.'

'She must have planned it – waited till you were both out of the house, then I suppose rung her friends or perhaps they were just waiting round the corner.'

221

'What are we going to do?'

'Get her back. She's probably gone to meet Happy somewhere.'

'I don't think so. She said Happy was into politics and that wasn't her scene, so they'd split up,' Margaret quoted the words with dutiful care.

'Politics? Here?' Gunn was momentarily diverted by a vision of Happy addressing an empty drill hall.

'No, out East somewhere. I didn't quite hear because I was playing with Sixty. Do you think she has gone back to him?'

'How should I know? I'll ring Antic.'

There was a noise at the other end of the line.

'I'm sorry about the noise,' Antic said, 'we're having a party. To celebrate my *secondes noces*. This time it's for keeps, baby. Oh, you didn't know? Well, in fact Poppy. You see we were the only two people left in the house and she gets on so well with Clara and the Piddingtons. Here's Clara now. She'd love to talk to you.'

'Hullo, Gunby. I'm really *much* too high to talk to you.'

'You're looking well, anyway,' Gunn said grimly.

'Oh, have you got one of those new phones then? How *nice.*'

'Listen. Have you seen Lil?'

'I'm afraid she's not here, Gunn. She hasn't been around for months. I didn't know you were still interested. How passionate you are. I'll ask Antic. Ducky,' Clara's voice rose above the party noise, 'Gunn's still in love with Lil.'

'No, really?' Antic said, returning to the telephone. 'What a drag, I should have asked her tonight. You too, Gunn. But I haven't seen either of you for so long. Anyway, I think she must be Ashrammy bound.'

'What?'

'The last time she came here, she definitely had a touch of Asian flu. You know, a lot of beads and meaningful silences and meaningless questions and giving capital letters to The Way and the The Truth. And I know for sure that she had a guru then because she was weaving a garland of flowers for him. She also took him a nearly full packet of cornflakes belonging to me.'

'Did he live on cornflakes?'

'No, I think they had some liturgical significance.'

'What was he called, the guru?'

222

'Ah now, there you have me. I think he went back to India. But there are probably only half a million holy men in India. You'll find her in the end.'

'You don't think she could have gone off with Happy somewhere, or to look for him?'

'No, no, they split up ages ago. Happy's into some kind of heavy scene.'

'Explain yourself.'

'Don't be so uptight, Gunn.'

'Don't talk like that then. I have to find Lil because she has left her baby here.'

'Baby. Yes, she looked rather plump and fulfilled when she came here. Must have been months ago.'

'The point is she's left this baby and – '

'And you want to know what to do with it. I'll ask Clara. She's great with babies.'

'Do not ask Clara anything.'

'Hey, this isn't, by any chance, it isn't *your* baby, is it? It's not like saying I have this friend who is in trouble. . . ?'

'It is not.'

'You know, it's a pity we are all so dispersed now. I have had to let the basement and the attic. Things are not what they used to be.'

'They never were.'

The Inskip parents knew less than Antic had. Gunn found it difficult to get any information out of them at all. He had not realised until he went to visit them in their neat house in the outer suburbs quite how Dick's death must have hit them. He had met them only once before at Down But Not Out. Then they had stood stiff and neat in Dick's bedsitter, bewildered by the set-up, feeling perhaps that this was an enterprise better managed through more official channels, yet proud and even excited. Their children had given them a confidence which was now utterly lost.

Mr Inskip stared at the cornice throughout the conversation. His thin grey face scarcely moved. Mrs Inskip did the talking.

'She shouldn't have left the baby. It's too much to ask, I do feel – but it's a tribute to you, I mean. She didn't tell me. Perhaps she didn't want to upset us. You know, our health has not been good but – '

'I don't want to upset you either.' Gunn said. 'It's not that we

223

don't want the child, not at all. But we can't keep him on this basis, legally or morally.'

'You want permission in writing?'

'Well, rather more than that,' Gunn said. 'Sixty's future has to be made clear. Are we just looking after him till Lil comes back from wherever she has gone? Are we to adopt him? Or are you his legal guardians or what?'

'Oh, not us, I wouldn't think us at all,' Mrs Inskip said. 'I don't think we could manage or anyway I don't think Lil would expect us to.'

'We're just his grandparents,' Mr Inskip said without changing the angle of his head.

'You see, Lilian hurt our feelings a good deal by some of the things she said. My husband had only just retired and – '

'But I thought she had spoken to you about the baby,' Gunn said.

'She did. That is quite true. And I think we both agreed that it would be too much for us, in view of the health matter you know. In fairness to the baby.'

By degrees, Mrs Inskip froze into the same state as her husband, the last drops of resentment trickling out of a mouth of stone.

Gunn had a violent longing to break up the neat little room. He wanted to smash the white china ornaments on the mantelpiece with the gleaming fire-irons. He wanted to shake the Inskips, punch them, tickle them, get them somehow to bellow out their anger and desolation.

He escaped as quickly as he could and headed for the nearest pub, a large brick roadhouse in thirties style perched above a roundabout.

He was into his second Bell's before he took in the small fat man at the far end of the bar.

'. . . and the fella said, take the bloody blanket off my head, you fool, I'm Chief Inspector Bostock.'

Rory Noone stood almost motionless after delivering his punchline, taking a swift drag on his cigarette, not even bothering to watch the man with him double up with laughter. The man had a battered, deceitful face with a turned-down mouth. He spoke with a curious chewing motion of his mouth, as though trying to shake it off the skin of his face.

Beside this knocked-about character, Rory looked rosy. He had a healthy tan and matching shirt and tie in a cheerful floral pattern. After listening to the other man for some time, Rory slid what looked like a five-pound note along the bar to him. The man finished his drink and left, glaring at Gunn who had withdrawn to a small table.

'An informant,' said Rory grandly after Gunn had greeted him. 'One of the greasy brethren who supply the raw material.'

'An exclusive, is it?'

'No, no,' said Rory, modestly flicking his ash on to the floor, 'just a matter of a little legwork. Nothing spectacular, not like – you heard about Keith, did you?'

'No. What?'

'Our lord and master had just got his hands on to the scruff of his neck, foot raised to administer the boot, when our Keithie finally cracks it.'

'Cracks what?'

'They can't print it of course but it's hard. The New York man checked it out and double-checked it.'

'Come *on*, Rory.'

'The son, the only son of the most illustrious Englishman of our time is a raging pooftah. He moves around with a crowd of blue movie-makers. He's on the production side himself. You know, deputy assistant to the assistant deputy director. But he plays bit parts too. Did you by any chance ever see a masterpiece called *Come Blow Your Porn*?'

'No,' said Gunn, unhesitatingly.

'He was the barman in that.'

Now Gunn remembered. Beneath the swollen melancholy of the naked presence behind the bar could be traced the robust features of the Last Great Englishman. Perhaps not so far beneath, either; it was wrong to think in layers. For even in the resolute mien of the father there was an aspect of melancholy, a hint of frustrated longings. Without melancholy, heroism had no resonance to it.

'That's a good story,' Gunn said.

'A *bloody* good story,' Rory said reprovingly. 'And you, young man, what have you been up to?'

'Well. You remember Margaret, we met her on the Embankment with the dossers once?'

'Yes, I remember. Old bag with a facial expression like a rabbit's arse.'

'We're going to be married.'

'Married. Christ. Well.' Rory was so taken aback that the thought of apologising for the severity of his description did not appear to occur to him.

'She's widowed.'

'They can't hang you for it then. *Married*. What'll you have . . . to celebrate?'

'Look here, Rory. Three-quarters of the human race gets married.'

'I can't help that.' Rory was genuinely distressed rather, it seemed, at the thought of marriage in general than at the prospect of Gunn marrying Margaret. The subject was so distasteful that he could not or would not give his mind to it.

'Well, we're starting fully equipped anyway,' Gunn said, 'we've already got a house and a baby.'

'A *baby*?'

'Not ours. Lil's lent him to us. Well, I say lent, but she's completely disappeared.'

'Christ, what a fuck-up. Who's the father, present company excepted?'

'Happy.'

'Happy, now there's a face I didn't think I'd see again.'

'You mean, you have seen him again?' Gunn asked.

'Yeah, well, you remember I said they'd never give an old hack like me a foreign assignment?'

'Mm.'

'Well, when I got this job on the *Mirror*, everyone on the foreign desk was on holiday so they sent me instead, to do a series on the Terror Schools. Idea was you went to all the places where the kids were being taught to hate. Jesus, what a selection of plague spots – the Falls Road, Harlem, Soweto and the bloody Lebanon. Anyway, when I was in Beirut I had a message to contact this guy. He turned up at the best hotel, very cool in a western suit, bought me a drink, very sophisticated. It took me a minute or two to realise it was him.'

'Him?'

'Happy.'

'Posing as an Arab? That is too much.'

'No, he really is. Half-Arab anyway. His father was a Scot, a pilot in the RAF. But his mother's family was Palestinian and some of them are still in the refugee camps outside Beirut. His mother had left Palestine during the war, went to work in Cairo where she met her jock. She's a fine woman. Happy, or Hassan as he now calls himself, took me to see her. She brought him up all by herself. He got a scholarship to the States. Father sugared off after the war.'

'Good God. Who's he working for exactly?'

'He's a kind of front man,' Rory said. 'Shows reporters round the camps, fends off the awkward questions, sells you the hard PLO line, but makes it sound moderate. He does it very well.'

'I bet he does.'

As Rory talked on, Gunn though of Happy in his western suit leading his party through the crowd of sullen, staring faces: the visitors all flustered by the heat and the rags and the smell and shamed by the matchstick arms thrust forward for alms and Happy so cool. Hassan, though. Gunn's father liked Flecker too and would when in relatively high spirits intone drily:

> We travel not for trafficking alone;
>   By hotter winds our fiery hearts are fanned:
> For lust of knowing what should not be known
>   We make the Golden Journey to Samarkand.

'You know,' said Rory Noone, 'it was strange seeing him like that. But he didn't seem at all surprised or really much interested. I mean, he asked after all of you, but politely, as if he'd just met you once at a cocktail party.'

'All of us?'

'Yes, even Lil. Of course, I never liked the bastard much, but I thought he might have shown a bit more interest.'

'Yes.'

'Still, he did his bit nicely. The lads all came home and wrote up-beat pieces about the new moderate face of the guerrillas. That was my intro too, but it was mostly cut to make room for pictures of starving kids with big round eyes.'

All at once Gunn didn't wish to hear any more about Hassan–Happy.

'Will you come to my wedding?' He asked. 'It will only be a small affair.'

227

'Ah, I don't know about that. I don't go much on weddings.'

'It won't be like most weddings.'

'It's kind of you to think of me, young man. But if I were you, I wouldn't rely on me. I'm a doubtful runner.'

The wedding was fixed for October. A fortnight before the modest ceremony, the Rev. Aubrey Wood had a heart attack. He survived, but for weeks was too ill to leave his bed. They feared that he would be dangerously upset if they drafted in another parson to marry them. The heart attack thus not only delayed the marriage but also made sure that when it finally took place Aubrey's wishes would come first, particularly as he had raised no audible objection to Gunn moving in ahead of the ceremony. On Boxing Day, Aubrey pronounced himself well enough to conduct the service and named New Year's Day as the date.

'We shall make a brave start to the seventies,' he whispered. 'And I think the earlier in the day, the better. I get so sleepy after lunch. Ten-thirty would be ideal.'

It was a dark New Year's morning. There was nobody on the road to see them as the small group set out for the church. Bride and groom walked side by side, Gunn pushed his father-in-law in the wheelchair that had been Dick's, while Margaret pushed Sixty in his pram. As they crossed over the road on to the narrow asphalt path, they broke into indian file, Sixty leading the way, grumbling slightly.

'I suppose we aren't exactly a conventional wedding group,' Gunn said.

'Do you think my skirt's too long?' Margaret stopped and stepped back from the pram to allow Gunn to have another look at her suit.

The suit was mustard-coloured. It was the suit in which she had gone away from her first wedding. There was no time to buy anything new and none of her other clothes seemed to match the occasion.

'No, I already told you. It's just the right length for you,' Gunn said.

'You don't mind me having worn it the first time I got married?' Margaret asked.

'I told you I didn't mind. It makes a nice connection.'

'I think I'm too fat for it.'

228

'No you aren't. It's me who's got too fat.'

'Not very fashionable to be fat, is it?'

'No, we were too fat for the sixties,' Gunn said.

'Do you think it will be fashionable to be fat in the seventies?'

'I don't think it's ever going to be fashionable to be fat again.'

'Never?'

'I don't think so.'

She bent down to rearrange Sixty's blankets. His hand had got caught in the string on which were threaded red and white plastic bobbles that rattled when he smacked them. She put the hand back under the bedclothes. He snorted mildly and was content. The wrinkles of will and character fled from his face, and Gunn, peering down at him by Margaret's side, remembered helping to put Antic's children to bed and how Antic had said as they fell asleep, 'I love them when they're like this, like sweet vegetables. They look so nice and empty.'

And yet there was something unapproachable about this vegetable solidity. The flesh was so complete, so self-sufficient, wanting nothing beyond itself. To touch and feel was only to remind you of its otherness, of how sealed away it was in its envelope of self. Gunn recalled his father's favourite story about Flecker on his deathbed pleading hoarsely to the impresario of *Hassan*, 'Can we have *real* camels for the first scene?'

The long grasses beside the path were stiff and frozen. They rustled like shaken foil in the wind. Their stems were coated with a white hoar-frost which covered the cracked asphalt too. The dead scene made the flesh seem all the more alive. Aubrey Wood's nose, gross-pored and swollen with cold, poked out of the rug like a plump red animal. Little puffs of breath from Margaret's open mouth flew white against the grey-blue light of winter. She always had difficulty breathing when she was nervous. He felt as if they were the last four people on earth, their presence was at that moment so real to him. Nothing in the dismal mummery that lay ahead of them could equal that sense of reality.

When he saw his parents standing in front of the church, they looked made of wood, Lincolnshire gothic : his father a bleak, much desecrated statue, features almost obliterated and unnaturally elongated to fill a minor niche, his mother as round as a Russian doll. It was remarkable, he thought, that of the five adults assembled for this ceremony, only one could have been said to have had his heart in it, and even Aubrey's belief was an uncertain quantity in his declining days.

Gunn's parents did not move forward to greet the bridal party. His father spoke without preamble.

'The door's locked.'

'It can't be,' Margaret said. 'The verger promised to open it at ten.'

'Nevertheless, it's locked.' His father was evidently delighted by the impasse.

Gunn squeezed past Aubrey Wood's wheelchair to test the door-handle, but Margaret elbowed him aside.

'You don't know the trick of opening it.'

She tried twisting and lifting it several times before turning angrily to her father.

'It's locked. Have you brought the key, dada?'

'Alas, no, I leave the whole business to Mr Eames. If I tried to remember the key, I should only forget it. There is a spare hanging in my study.'

Gunn could hear Margaret snatching for breath, verging on sobs.

'I'll run back and get it,' he said.

'Be quick,' his father said, 'your mother has only just got over her flu.'

Gunn put the brake on the wheelchair and set off at a heavy trot. The frosty road was slippery. He could feel the damp coming up through the thin soles of his wedding shoes. His footsteps rang out 'I'm go–ing to be mar–ried' as he sped away from the church watching his own breath now send out white puffs into the grey-blue air.

He ought to lose a few pounds. Thirteen stone was too much weight to carry for a running bridegroom of modest stature.

Printed in Great Britain
by Amazon